EAST OF THE BORDER

Johnny D Boggs

CHIVERS

British Library Cataloguing in Publication Data available

This Large Print edition published by BBC Audiobooks Ltd, Bath, 2010.
Published by arrangement with Golden West Literary Agency.

U.K. Hardcover ISBN 978 1 408 47756 4
U.K. Softcover ISBN 978 1 408 47757 1

Printed and bound in Great Britain by
CPI Antony Rowe, Chippenham and Eastbourne

For Larry Mahan and Diana McNab
'Ride the River!'

ACT I

Omohundro

Chapter One

The Theatre has not been as full for many a day as it was last night and Monday night. Buffalo Bill, Texas Jack, and Ned Buntline, the Scouts of the Prairies, have certainly drawn well since they have been in this city.

Dispatch, Richmond, Virginia
May 14, 1873

Wild Bill was in his cups—had been for the better part of a week—which explains why Ike Hoff's saloon was empty, except for my friend and one constantly twitching, wide-eyed barkeep, when Cody and I entered that groggery. Wild Bill, of course, is James B. Hickok, the famous pistol fighter and scout, and by Cody, I refer to William F. 'Buffalo Bill' Cody, the famous scout and actor. I am John B. 'Texas Jack' Omohundro, the drover, scout, and actor not as famous as either Wild Bill or Buffalo Bill.

It comes to mind that I should give you a little background on what brought Cody and me to brace Wild Bill on that muggy summer day in Springfield, Missouri in 1873. I had befriended Cody in North Platte, Nebraska in 1869, a few months after making Wild Bill's acquaintance down in Hays City, Kansas.

Making friends with them was easy since I was tending bar at both cities. Not that I'm a professional beer jerker, mind you, but being barely twenty-three at the time, an out-of-work Rebel cavalryman turned sailor turned schoolteacher turned Texas drover, I found my employment options limited, although Cody and Wild Bill later saw to it that I got work as a government scout.

Folks called us thick as thieves. Not only did we scout for the Army, we guided rich city folks—some from as far away as Europe—who came West wanting to hunt buffalo, antelope, and elk. They paid us quite handsomely, too. We drank whiskey, played poker (except Cody, who lacked the knack for paste cards), raced horses, and bet on them, wore greasy buckskins and our hair long, although mine never grew the way Cody's and Wild Bill's did, and told big windies that nobody this side of Bedlam would believe, excepting Colonel Edward Zane Carroll Judson and George Ward Nichols.

' 'Twas Nichols, who likewise brevetted himself "Colonel"' when he wrote, who made Wild Bill famous with a piece he penned for *Harper's New Monthly Magazine,* and soon afterward you could hardly walk into a mercantile in the States or Territories without seeing some DeWitt's Ten Cent Romance about Wild Bill.

Naturally you have heard all about Colonel

Judson, alias Ned Buntline. Mayhap you have even attended one of his temperance lectures. They call him the 'Destroyer of Demon Rum', and he could talk for hours—by jingo, in the play he wrote for us, *The Scouts of the Prairie; And, Red Deviltry As It Is,* after his character, Cale Durg, gets mortally stabbed in the heart with a Bowie knife, why he would spend twenty minutes lecturing his actor-killer and the audience on the evils of intoxicating liquors before he expired. Sometimes he would speak even longer, but when Cody and I saw the audience getting restless, we would run on stage and start firing our six-shooters at wild Indians in the wings, forcing Durg-Buntline-Judson to hurry up with his dying.

Anyway, Colonel Judson can give a mighty fine speech about the vice of whiskey. Fact is, when sober, he can talk about anything, and no matter if he is in his cups or as sober as a Mormon, that man can write some of the most harrowing blood-and-thunder stories that will set your teeth to chattering. Oh, yes, the play! *The Scouts of the Prairie; And, Red Deviltry As It Is* is what eventually led Cody and me to Missouri. Allow me to explain. Colonel Judson had met Cody and me, and written about us in these fanciful novels I have mentioned, and after he left us on the frontier, he returned East and even allowed a gent to pen some play about Cody based on Colonel Judson's books and Cody's life. That's when Colonel Judson

5

got this particular scheme in his head to turn Buffalo Bill the scout into Buffalo Bill the actor.

Colonel Judson was fifty or more years old, lame in one leg, had an ample belly and handful of ex-wives, would get to rambling on so—even more than I am prone to do—that nobody really knew what he was talking about, and had to be one of the ugliest rapscallions this side of the Powder River; yet he truly admired Western men, in particular Cody and me, but mostly Cody. The time I tell about was late autumn 1872, when his letters caught up with Cody at Fort McPherson, Nebraska. Cody had traveled East to visit Colonel Judson before, even saw a play at New York City's Bowery Theatre that had an actor pretending to be Buffalo Bill. What roped Cody was when the theater-goers realized the real Buffalo Bill sat with them, and they started cheering and pushing him to stage, then made him say a few words. He mumbled something, frightened as all get out, but that applause stuck with him, even months later when he went back to scouting.

I had just finished guiding the Earl of Dunraven on a mighty successful hunt when I trotted to the sutler's for my morning fortification and found Cody there, staring at a letter as if it were written in Dutch. Steeling myself for grim news, I asked him what was the matter, and ordered a whiskey.

6

He looked up at me, tears welling in his brown eyes, and said: 'Judson is jo-fired on me playin' myself on the stage in Chicago.'

I chuckled at first before realizing he was serious.

'Acting?' I said, and Cody nodded. 'In Chicago?'

Another nod. 'Chicago first. He says then we'd go all over. All the metropo . . . all them choice cities . . . Saint Louis, Cincinnati, Pittsburgh, Boston, Philadelphia, Oswego.'

'How about Norfolk? Or Richmond, maybe?'

'Reckon so.'

I motioned for another whiskey. Kansans had saddled me with the moniker 'Texas Jack' during my days as a drover, but I hailed from Virginia, and, well, it would be dandy to go home to see my brothers and kinfolk.

'What does Lulu say?'

Lulu was Louisa Frederici Cody, his pretty but hard-rock wife. A socialite from the Frenchtown district of St. Louis, a lady of class, upbringing, education, and high character, Lulu had thrown most of that away when she up and married Cody shortly after the War for Southern Independence.

'She ain't so jo-fired as Judson,' Cody told me.

'And?'

'Well, I just don't know what to do. I'd be a fizzle at actin'. I know that much.'

7

'Then tell Mister Judson no.'

'Yeah, I thought 'bout that, but he says there will be a right smart of money in it for us!'

'Us?' I was fishing.

'Judson and me. Uh . . . you want to come along, Jack?'

'Oh, nooooo.' I finished my whiskey, tossed the barkeep a coin, and headed outside, Cody tagging along like a puppy. Hell's fire, I wanted to go, not only for the money and adventure of it all, but to see my folks and siblings and aunts and uncles and cousins and pals.

Cody mounted his horse, and we rode along, all the way to North Platte, debating the merits of going and staying as we rode and camped, camped and rode, fished and hunted, camped and rode, camped and drank, drank and rode. The officers of the 5th Cavalry wanted Cody to keep on scouting, and there was money in that, too, but the odds of getting killed seemed a whole lot greater chasing real Indians than pretend ones on a stage. We talked about it some more as we washed up outside the Cody house, talked about it when we entered the Cody home, then gave it a rest as Cody fawned over his three children and bride for a spell, but resurrected the topic during supper, talked about it while we smoked cigars as Lulu put the young 'uns to bed, talked about it on the porch until Lulu

8

stormed outside, called us both fools, and muttered a few more things in French that I vaguely recalled my daddy, who spoke the language, often labeled politicians and damnyankees.

'What's a footlight, Jack Omohundro?' she yelled.

'It's a light at the foot,' I told her a moment later. Criminy, she must have thought me a dumbbell and had forgotten how I once taught school in Florida.

'And a cue?'

Her husband eagerly answered first: 'That's from billiards.'

Shaking her head angrily, she turned her wrath on Cody, who should have kept his trap closed. 'And how many plays have you seen in your life, Will?'

'There was that one Judson took me to see about me,' he began. 'Saw a couple more, too, when I was visitin' General Sheridan and Judson. And the time that fella from Liverpool showed up at Leavenworth and recited *Macbeth*. I took you, Mama, because you wanted to go. And . . . by jingo, how could I forget that one we saw in Saint Louis? The one by that Hugo fella! Why, I named Lucretia Borgia after that one.'

Lucretia Borgia was his Springfield rifle. I had never given my Sharps or Smith & Wesson any names, except when funning ink-stingers and tourists.

9

'Balderdash!' Lulu exclaimed, hands on her little hips, dark eyes turning blacker. 'Between the two of you, you've never seen more than half a dozen plays. You don't know a thing about exits, about entrances. Do you two think you could actually *memorize* lines? You'd have to study, Will! *Study!*'

She looked at me now for help, but I wanted to go East, wanted to try acting, wanted to rope more money and fame than scouting and guiding had brung me. 'I don't know, ma'am,' I said, recalling my schoolteaching days, 'if I could get a bunch of Florida waifs to recite the prologue to the Constitution, I think Will and me could learn some lines to say. Them children were lazy as gopher pitters.'

'*Prologue?* It's *Preamble,* Jack.'

I sniggered because I was funning Lulu, sort of. 'Reckon I learnt 'em children wrong.'

She shook her head like a wet coon hound, yet softened her stance, and lowered her voice. 'You'd make a fool of yourself, Will. They'd laugh at you.'

'Mama,' Will told her, 'they can laugh all they want if they're payin' me good money. I'd be doin' this for you, Lu, makin' us rich so I don't have to risk my hair chasin' Injuns. We could buy us a home back East so Kit, Arta, and li'l Orra Maude could get a real education, be smart and well-mannered, like you, Lulu.' He could warm her, Cody could. 'You'd come see us, wouldn't you, Mama?'

10

'I doubt that,' she said, but I could tell she was resigned to us joining Colonel Judson. 'Do what you will, Will. You always do.'

When she headed inside, I began to doubt Colonel Judson's wisdom. I sure didn't want to get Cody in trouble with Lulu. 'She'll come around,' he told me. 'I know her better than you do, pard. Are you game, Jack?'

My grin returned. 'What are we waiting for?' I asked.

The next day, Cody wired Colonel Judson that we would meet him in Chicago come December, and that I would be trailing along. We got a thunderous reply saying how happy the news made Colonel Judson, and we stayed pretty jolly, too, until we stepped off the train on a chilly December morning, and met Colonel Judson.

Have you ever seen Chicago, its tall buildings and scores of city folk? I would allow that the depot alone held more people than all of Nebraska. It set my stomach to roiling with fear, but even that metropolis did not scare me as much as when Colonel Judson shouted at me: 'Where are the Pawnee and Sioux chieftains you promised, Jack?' Leaning against a black cane that bent underneath his weight, Colonel Judson peered inside the smoking car, looking for Indians, I suspect.

'Huh?' said I, not knowing what the Sam Hill he meant. I had not promised to bring a thing except myself and my grip.

11

'Indians. Dear God, Jack, I've promised ten wild savages, have advertised them in the papers.' He straightened, and pointed his cane toward a hack. 'No matter,' he said, 'no matter at all. Let us retire to the hotel. No, first, let us go to Nixon's. He'll want to see my stars of *The Scouts of the Prairie.*'

Nixon's, I soon learned, was Nixon's Amphitheater, and Mr. Nixon was sure glad to shake hands with the original Buffalo Bill and Texas Jack, and pretty eager to put on a show until Colonel Judson admitted that he had not written a play, had not hired any other actors, had not done a thing but put notices in the papers, and get Jim Nixon counting premature profits.

'What?' Nixon tugged on his shiny yellow cravat as if it were a hangman's noose. 'Are you out of your mind? When are you going to have rehearsals? It's Wednesday, and you plan on putting on a play Monday, yet you haven't even written a word? Confound it, sir, it can't be done.'

'Can be and will be, sir. How much to rent your theater for one week?'

'Six hundred dollars, but . . .'

Colonel Judson was already peeling off greenbacks, licking his thumb as he counted, then slapped $300 into the astonished Nixon's hand. Astonished Cody and me, too, because, well, $600 for a week seemed more than a trifle steep to a couple of scouts who might

12

make $150 a month and think we were as rich as Jay Cooke. Not to mention a trifle steep for a theater that was nothing more than warped planks, two-by-fours, and a canvas roof 'Course, much of Chicago looked like that after the big fire of 1871. I prayed our hotel wouldn't be a burned-out shell.

'I'll take a receipt,' Colonel Judson told him, 'and shall bring you a copy of the play tomorrow morn. At which time, sir, I will pay you the balance, and you will provide me with a contract. Agreed?'

Nixon mumbled something, wrote out a receipt, and Colonel Judson led Cody and me back to the hack and on to the hotel, which wasn't burned, smoky, or being rebuilt, but was a right fancy establishment that had survived the conflagration. Colonel Judson locked himself in the suite, a big room, bigger than most houses I had seen out on the plains, and left Cody and me in the parlor with tea, mint candy, and our flasks. We did not talk much, just sat in our gloom, wondering what Lulu would tell us when we came back to North Platte like tykes in need of taking bitter medicine. The only time we ever looked up at each other was when there would come a shout from the bed chambers.

Four hours later, Colonel Judson almost knocked down the door, holding a manuscript written on just about everything—envelopes, newspapers, the Bible, and a pencil tablet.

13

'Boys,' he announced, 'we're in business. *The Scouts of the Prairie* is finished.' He raced out the door, found a bellhop, dragged him into the room, handed him a dollar, and ordered him to round up every other bellhop, clerk, anyone who could hold a pencil. In twenty minutes, our suite had filled with those boys busily copying Colonel Judson's play. When they were done, it was dawn, so I suggested to Cody that we get us some real breakfast, but Colonel Judson handed us a copy of the play, told us to learn our lines, then pulled on his hat and greatcoat, explaining that he had business to attend to, actors to hire, arrangements to make. With that, he was gone.

I looked at the scrawl. 'How long you reckon it'll take you to learn your lines, Will?' I asked.

'Near 'bout two months. And you?'

'Take me that long to learn my first line.'

Yet we learned them all, and also got an education about cues and footlights and exits and entrances, thanks to Guiseppina Morlacchi teaching me, and Colonel Judson teaching Cody. I reckon Cody drew the black bean there. I got Guiseppina while he was stuck learning the theater trade from Colonel Judson. Guiseppina, now, I know you have heard of her, the famous Italian *danseuse* and the most fetching woman I have ever laid eyes on. Not only could she dance to all sorts of tunes, but she was one fine actress, and

Colonel Judson had lured her to play the role of Dove Eye in his play. Colonel Judson had it figured that, since Guiseppina's hair was blacker than a raven's wing, she would not need a wig, and her Italian accent would make her sound like an Indian princess, too. Mostly, though, he allowed that the great Guiseppina Morlacchi would fill the seats that Texas Jack and Buffalo Bill did not. He was a savvy one, that Colonel Judson.

Well, between Guiseppina and Colonel Judson, somehow Cody and I learned our lines, learned them well and good—till opening night. Then things got a mite embarrassing for Cody. You see, mostly all I had to do was show them city folks a few tricks I head learned with my lariat, but when Cody stepped on stage that first night, his tongue got twisted like a juniper branch.

Colonel Judson, playing Cale Durg, had waddled on stage to this campfire that was not hot or smoky nor anything but orange painted wood and red bunting, and I shoved Cody out behind him. They stood there, and Durg-Buntline-Judson says: 'Where have you been, Buffalo Bill?'

Cody just stared at the audience. I have seen that man charge Cheyenne dog soldiers, seen him ride into a herd of stampeding buffalo, seen him get a horse to go down a ledge that even a rock would not dare roll down, yet I had never seen Buffalo Bill Cody

15

scared till that moment.

'I say, where have you been, Buffalo Bill?' Durg-Buntline-Judson repeated, and whispered underneath his breath Cody's real line, but Cody was so nervous, he just blinked and stared. When the line was repeated a third time, a bit louder with more irritation, Cody recognized Heath Milligan, a wealthy Chicago gent who had been on some hunts with Cody and me, in the audience.

'Why, I've . . . been . . . on a hunt . . . with Mister Milligan.'

It was the truth, now, but it was also right fortuitous, because the folks roared out a laugh at Mr. Milligan's expense.

Durg-Buntline-Judson concocted a plan right then and there, and said: 'Tell us about it, Buffalo Bill.' Cody did just that, warming up, you see, feeling a bit more secure of himself, and then I yelled—*'Injuns!'*—because I was getting bored, and a dozen supes rigged out in wigs and red face paint charged out on stage, and we 'killed' all of them, and had a rip-roaring good time. I doubt if we followed a single line in Colonel Judson's play that night, but the next night folks filled the theater again, and so things remained during our entire stay in Chicago, December 16 through 21, 1872.

It went like that all winter. Christmas week we played in St. Louis, then took the train to Cincinnati. Kentucky, Indiana, Pennsylvania, New York, Massachusetts, and those little

16

states back East that no one out West ever remembers, and finally Richmond and Norfolk, where some of my kin and friends came to see me do my roping tricks, kill these supes playing Indians, and say a bunch of flapdoodle that Colonel Judson had wrote for me to say.

Needless to say, Cody and I felt sold on acting after that, till our season ended at Albany, New York that June, and we found ourselves not nearly as rich as Colonel Judson. So, we braced that scalawag. After a grotesque belly laugh—and Colonel Judson had one grotesque belly—he told us we knew nothing about the theater, and, if we dared venture out on our own, we would come crawling back to him when we learned how difficult it is to handle the day-to-day business of play acting. I do not know how he took the notion that we wanted to do this acting alone because all we wanted was more money, but that notion took root in Cody's brain at a later date. On that day, we just parted company with Colonel Judson, and went back to Nebraska to guide rich hunters and drink their champagne instead of our forty-rod whiskey.

I had decided that fate did not want me to be a rich and famous actor until one night on the Niobrara River when Cody says: 'We can do it.'

'Do what?' asks I.

'Put on a show, better than Judson's. Jiminy

crickets, Jack, them folks didn't pay a quarter or fifty cents, even a dollar sometimes, to see Buntline. They come to see me . . . and you.'

'Well, yeah, but we can't just rent out an opera house and stand on stage like lunatics.' I paused to collect my thoughts a little better because, come to think of it, we had pretty much just stood on stage in an opera house Colonel Judson had rented and acted like lunatics. 'We'd need somebody to write a play for us.'

'You can writ it!'

I shook my head. Oh, I enjoyed writing about hunting and cowboying and stuff like that for a gentleman's sporting publication called *Spirit of the Times,* but had never really been able to make much sense of the play Colonel Judson wrote.

Before passing me a bottle of champagne, Cody snorted, and went on with his argument. 'How hard can it be to put some words together? Judson writ our play in four hours, remember? Shucks, half the time when we was on stage, I said your lines, and you said mine, or we made somethin' up. Crowds still loved us.'

I allowed that we had made a few contacts during our travels with Colonel Judson's company, so we might find us a playwright. 'I guess he could just copy some of what Mister Judson wrote, add some stuffing to it,' I said after a swallow of the fancy bubbly. 'Or we

18

could tell him some stories to put in there.'

'I'll call it the Buffalo Bill Combination.'

He would, too, and, if my head swelled as much as my pard's, I would have called him on that, but I did not mind. Cody had his faults, but I sure enjoyed his company and his get-up-and-git.

'We'd need actors . . . ,' I started.

'You think Josephine would join us, without Judson?'

Smiling, I shut my eyes. Josephine is what he and Colonel Judson called Guiseppina instead of stumbling over her Italian handle. I had fancied her from the moment Colonel Judson introduced us

'I think she would.' I hoped so. To tell the truth, acting appealed to me, almost as much as hunting, scouting, cowboying, and getting roostered with my pards. Or maybe it was Guiseppina who appealed to me. I had the hankering to ask her to marry me, but I warrant so did every gent who had seen her dance.

Well, I am rambling. Here I am supposed to be talking about our meeting with Wild Bill, yet my story is stuck in Nebraska. After finishing the champagne, we went to sleep without another word on the matter. The next morning, while the German aristocrat's chef prepared breakfast, and Cody and I fortified ourselves with a couple fingers of rye, Cody slapped his hand against his chaps, and thundered: 'Wild Bill!'

My mind remained a bit foggy, and I looked around, excited, wondering what the devil Wild Bill was doing in our camp, but saw only a bunch of Dutch royalty, needle-nose guns, horses, mules, and dead game covered with flies.

'Huh?'

'Wild Bill! We'll get our old pard to join us in our endeavor, Jack. We'll be like Dickens's *Three Musketeers!*'

'Dickens?' I rolled my eyes before downing my breakfast.

'Dickens! You know, the man who wrote about the Musketeers, Athos, Porthos, and Oliver Twist. You know, all for one and . . . and . . . shucks . . . Wild Bill! That's what matters. Buffalo Bill! Wild Bill! Texas Jack! *The Scouts of the Prairie* reborn on stage!'

The billing arrangement I found debatable, and Cody's sense of literature deplorable—have I mentioned that I taught school in Florida for a spell?—but I had to admit Cody's idea fascinated me

So, to get back to my point, that's what brought us to Ike Hoff's saloon on July 14, 1873.

Chapter Two

Everything was so wonderfully bad that it was almost good.

New York *Herald*
April 1, 1873

'Oh, God,' said the barkeep when we walked into Hoff's. 'Don't . . .'

'We are his pards,' I reassured the man. 'We are not here to do Wild Bill harm.'

Of course, with our buckskins and hardware, we resembled and smelled like rapscallions, but Wild Bill did not look overly fancy, either.

I do not imply that Wild Bill got mean once he became intimate with John Barleycorn—fact of the matter is, usually, he took to pulling one's leg or telling outlandish cuffers that ink-spillers took as gospel because Wild Bill could graft a grafter—but he had not been the same since the Abilene mayor and city council dismissed him as marshal in December of 1871. Actually he had started to pull corks like a gin barrel since September of that year, when he had accidentally killed a friend in a gun battle with some Texas ruffians. Now, I do not claim to know all the particulars about that sad affair—best leave that story to Wild Bill himself—but the newspapers agreed that the fault did not lie at his boots. Just a tragedy that comes when you mix drovers with whiskey and a marshal with hard-rock reputation. I do know enough about James B. 'Wild Bill' Hickok's character to state he is one of the finest men I have ever called a pard, and have been blessed to have him call me his pard since 1869. Cody had known Wild Bill even longer than that, although neither could agree on just when they had met.

Seeing Wild Bill alone at the table—unless you count the deck of cards, tumbler, whiskey bottle, Navy Colt, and double-barrel shotgun in plain view—made me feel at ease. We strode over quickly, excitedly, but Wild Bill never looked up from his game of solitaire, even after Cody slapped his back, pulled out a chair, and lifted Wild Bill's bottle in salute before taking a seat. 'Thunderation, it's bully good to see you!' Cody roared.

Wild Bill, still staring at his card game, greeted us with a suggestion that we go do something that would get a fellow laughed at or strung up practically everywhere but Trinity County, Texas.

Cody's mouth dropped open, and I held off on sitting down, especially with the barrels of that shotgun pointed at my midsection, not that Wild Bill had a hand on the Greener; the cards occupied all of his attention.

'Jim, on my life, I have never done anything to hurt you,' Cody said, which sounded like he was reciting one of Colonel Judson's lines, 'and it is my life that I would give for you, old chum.' *Definitely, Colonel Judson's influence,* I thought. *Or Mister Barleycorn's.* I stepped to the side, away from the Greener and into Wild Bill's line of vision. 'Your words stab me to the quick, sir. What have I done?' As Cody went on, he lifted his gauntleted right hand. 'If this hand has ever struck you, ever offended you, I will cut it off this minute with my trusty Bowie knife.'

I started looking on Cody's belt for any knife, but he must have left it back in Nebraska. Hickok looked up, pushed back his black Stetson, and gave Cody a stare. His eyes focused, and I think he recognized us only at that moment. 'Well, if it ain't Mister Booth and Mister Forrest.'

He was being funny, calling us two of the best actors around in those days, and we relaxed.

'How's that scamp you been terrorizing the East with, boys?' Wild Bill asked.

'We've gone our separate ways, Jim,' Cody said.

Wild Bill nodded. 'Good. I ain't no pal of your buddy Buntline's. Mealy-mouthed reprobate keeps killing me off with his pen, giving you credit for things I done. He's making you rich, and me irritable.' He shot me a cold glance. 'You, too, Jack.'

I just stood real still, not knowing what to

23

say. I mean, Wild Bill was right about Colonel Judson giving false credit for deeds done by him, but Colonel Judson always said that wild fiction sold better than boring history.

'Judson cheated us, Jim, much as he cheated you from your rightly deserved glory!' Cody thundered, and Wild Bill shook his head and politely asked Cody to return the bottle so he could have a drink since he had bought it, but more so since Missouri lightning made Cody talk like a gump after spending all winter and spring drinking weak city liquor. As soon as Wild Bill had taken a swallow, Cody went on to explain our new show, our chances of immense wealth, and bragged about how well we were received in the East.

After wiping his mouth with the back of his hand, Wild Bill took to grinning. 'Well received.' He leaned back in his chair. 'Let me see if I recollect this right. We do get the Eastern newspapers on the frontier. Think it was Chicago's *Evening Journal* that said, and I quote . . . "Such a combination of incongruous drama, execrable acting, renowned performers, mixed audience, intolerable stench" . . . I liked "intolerable stench" best . . . "scalping, blood and thunder, is not likely to be vouchsafed something-another for a second time." ' Next, he turned to me. 'And I enjoyed this little note in the New York *Herald* . . . "Texas Jack is not quite so good-looking, not so tall, not so straight, and not so ridiculous.' 'Back to Cody.

'The critic called you "ridiculous as an actor." '

'You remembered all that?' I asked. Criminy, I had been trying to forget that one.

Wild Bill gave me a pleasant shrug. 'My nightly amusement before I go to bed. Read it every night. Some people read the Bible. Me, I read those two reviews about my old pards.'

I figured him to be jealous of our success, but said nothing. Cody, well, he could find a positive in anything. 'You son-of-a-gun, you'll have no trouble rememberin' your lines.'

That prompted a snort from Wild Bill. 'Ain't no Thespian, boys. Ain't no paper-collar man, neither. I don't fit in in the cities. I'm a plainsman. So are you two.'

'I've bought a house in West Chester,' Cody told him. 'Yeah, I love the plains, the mountains, but I got a family to support, Jim. And if you hold truck with them papers, then you know we done business like nobody's never seen. By jingo, every performance we turned folks away. Twenty-five cents they pay, Jim. Or fifty. Even seventy-five or a whole dollar. Come to see us, they do, and they'll come to see you. A three-way split, after expenses. That's what I'm offerin'. A chance to be rich beyond your wildest dreams.'

Wild Bill pushed back his hat, and finished the whiskey. 'You really want me? That's why you really come here?'

'Absolutely!' Cody cried.

'Then you're a bigger blame fool than I ever

thunk.'

'But . .'

'Ain't interested, pard. You have your little frolic in the city. I'm comfortable where I am, being who I am.'

'Women,' Cody said in a hushed voice. 'Have you ever seen Josephine Morlacchi do the can-can, Jim?'

I cleared my throat to give Cody my best Wild Bill sneer. You did not talk about decent, God-fearing women in saloons, especially in saloons like Ike Hoff's bucket of blood, and you damned sure never talked that way about Guiseppina Morlacchi in presence of John B. Omohundro.

Cody, who was neither stupid nor blind, picked another trail. 'Women, Jim. Eastern women cotton to us scouts, old chum, from the actresses we're play actin' with to the rich society lasses who fawn over our locks and looks.' He winked, and I began suspicioning him a little because Will Cody was married to a pretty woman, not as pretty as Guiseppina, but pretty nonetheless, and, criminy, I had never even looked at another woman hardly, since I met Guiseppina, and here was Cody talking like that, him married with three fine young 'uns. 'They ain't soiled doves, pard, who'll steal your purse and leave you with nothin' but a problem in your britches and have you visitin' a doctor to ram a hot copper stick up . . .'

26

'Will!' I snapped, and he shut up.

'Boys.' Wild Bill gathered his cards, shotgun, and Navy Colt. 'I tried the East. Tried show business. Maybe I'll tell you about it someday. 'Tain't my label, pards.'

I cleared my throat again but lost my sneer as it was not necessary for what I had to say. 'I wouldn't have thought it was for Cody or me,' I said honestly, 'but it fetches a man, J.B., fetches him like the buffalo herds, or the sun setting over the North Platte, or hearing an elk bugle on the Yellowstone . . .'

'Now you're sounding like Buntline, Jack.' He hooked a thumb at Cody. 'Bad enough him doing it, but you're an educated man.'

I stood a little straighter. Colonel Judson had written an epic about me, well, maybe not really about me if you want true history, but I was the hero of his latest blood-and-thunder novel, published by Street & Smith's Log Cabin Library, and Colonel Judson said he figured it to be his best adventure yet. Maybe he had not paid us the money we thought we were due, but were it not for Colonel Judson's novels and plays, Cody never would have bought a house back East, and I never would have known *Mlle.* Guiseppina Morlacchi.

'All I'm saying, J.B.,' I added in serious quietness, 'is that, if you give acting a chance, you might find you like it. Will here, he was ready to quit at first, but I persuaded him to ride out the storm, and he did. After a spell, it

27

grabbed his heart.'

'That makes my heart happy for my pals. But I still ain't interested.' Wild Bill walked out of Hoff's saloon, and I shot my partner an anxious stare.

'What now?' I asked.

'He'll join us,' said Cody.

'You better hope he does.' Cody had already sent out telegrams to the Eastern newspapers saying Wild Bill would join our new troupe for the 1873-74 season.

'He will,' Cody reassured me. 'I know him better than he knows hisself. Let's see about havin' ourselves a drink.'

The bartender didn't look so jumpy now that Wild Bill had taken his person elsewhere, and he gladly poured us a couple of rounds on the house, as if we had run Wild Bill out of the place, as if anyone could tell Wild Bill what to do. I sure hoped Cody knew what he was doing.

'We're cut from the same cloth, Jack,' Cody told me after our fourth drink—we were paying by then—well, I mean that I was paying. 'Me, you, and Jim. You know what makes us tick?'

'Adventure!' I said.

'Bosh. Well, no, adventure's part of it, but I'm talkin' 'bout somethin' else. I'm talkin'bout what caused us to join up with Judson in the first place.'

I give him the dumb look, which was not

difficult after all those whiskies and the fact that I had nary a notion what he meant.

'Gilt,' said Cody, and called for another round. High time, too, I thought, for him to spend some of his own *gilt*.

Wild Bill had left Springfield by the time we left Hoff's, so we took a train to Nebraska, and from there headed back East to start making arrangements for our next season on stage. We run across a reporter in Omaha, and he made the mistake of calling Cody a scout. That got Cody's dander up, which would not have a year or so earlier. Buffalo Bill Cody was a scout, a mighty fine one, but I had not been lying to Wild Bill when I said play acting got to a fellow. It sure had gotten to me, but Cody even more.

'I'm no danged scout,' Cody told the startled ink-spiller. 'I'm a first-class star!'

Chapter Three

The show baffles description, for it is peculiarly its own kind, but there is plenty of fun to be enjoyed from it. Not the least pleasing feature is the acting, singing, and dancing of Morlacchi.

Daily Beacon, Akron, Ohio
October 30, 1873

Have you ever seen a bald eagle's mating flight? I have. I have propped my head up against a ponderosa pine in the Rockies to watch them fly for hours, admiring their grace, their love for each other, thinking that our Creator is one smart gent, or an even smarter lady, to give these beautiful raptors the talent to dance in the air amidst the sweet smells of summer in the mountains. That might not be poetry, but that is how I felt when I was around Guiseppina Morlacchi. It got my heart pounding when I saw her do the mazurka, the bolero, the sortita, or the caprice schottische, although, just between us, whenever she did the can-can, it got another part of me a-pounding.

I was one jolly scout to be taking that train back East, and got even jollier when Guiseppina met us at the depot in New York City. Since I am being totally honest, though, I admit that when I saw Arizona John Burke holding her arm I was not so jolly. By no means am I saying that I did not cotton to John M. Burke as he could be a right affable fellow who certainly thought Guiseppina should be treated as royalty, as did I. He was a bit stuffy and ate too much, but his girth came nowhere near what Colonel Judson had to carry around on his bum leg. Burke tried to wear his hair long like Cody's but Burke's locks curled up something horrible, and, besides, he had less hair on the top of his head than I did. Mine was just thinning a mite, but our Creator had practically scalped Burke's pate.

Well, Cody rushed to pump Burke's hand once we stepped off the train, and I just swept my hat off my head and muttered something polite—least, I hope it sounded polite—to Guiseppina, who smiled at me. We stared at each other, not saying a thing for a spell, occasionally turning our heads or eyes toward Burke and Cody but not really listening to what they had to say, although I got the gist of it.

Cody had hired Burke to manage our theater troupe that season—of course, my pard had failed to mention that to me. Not that I minded or disagreed. Fact is, it made sense because Burke was an Easterner by birth and had acted and put on plays from *Nick of the Woods* to *Romeo and Juliet.* He said he had served in the Union Army during their tyranny as a major under Grant, but I tended to doubt that as he was not much older than me, yet fellows called him 'Major' when they didn't call him 'Arizona'. I also had my doubts that he had ever seen Arizona Territory except in a stereographic picture. Maybe he earned the rank of major when he had managed his own theater troupe. Anyway, my point is that he was a good theater man who knew the business and knew the East as well as Cody and I knew the border, and he had managed Guiseppina's career and done all right by her, so Cody made a wise choice offering him the job.

Not only that, Arizona John Burke, I believe, fawned over Buffalo Bill Cody more than he did *Mlle.* Guiseppina Morlacchi, and, since Cody had shook the gent's hand, why, Burke had not paid any notice to Guiseppina.

'I want you to meet Fred G. Maeder tonight at the Bowery,' Burke told Cody while Guiseppina and I half listened. 'He wrote the original *Buffalo Bill! King of the Border Men!* You remember, the play Buntline took you to see, and has agreed to let us perform if we'll cast him and his sister in our troupe. But right now, there is another playwright waiting for us at O'Flannery's Saloon.'

'Bully good!' Cody said, referring, I warrant, to the saloon.

'Hiram Robbins, a friend of mine, wants to write a play for you, Wild Bill, and you, too,

32

Jack, called *Scouts of the Plains* instead of Buntline's *Scouts of the Prairie*. Actually,' he said in a whisper, 'it'll be the same damned play Buntline wrote, but, what the hell, it'll pack them suckers in. We'll have an alternate play, which means you'll have to remember more lines, and . . .' He looked around the depot as if he had lost something. 'By thunder, boys, where is Wild Bill?'

I decided to look deeper into Guiseppina's eyes. She smiled at me again, and said: *'Ciao,* Jack. You look well.'

'Howdy,' I said, and tried to think of something to add but come up with nary a thing.

'He'll be along directly,' Cody told Burke.

'Is he still on the train?'

'No.' Cody rolled his lips around. 'No, Major, he's still out on the border. No tellin' where he is right now. Kansas City . . . Ellsworth . . . Cheyenne . . . you know how he likes to travel.'

Burke, of course, did not know a thing about Wild Bill that had not been spread by those nickel and dime novels or that *Harper's* story.

'But you saw him, right?' Burke was sweating something fierce. 'He is coming, right?'

'Like I said, old chum, Hickok will be along shortly. Now, shouldn't we be sociable and not keep Mister Robbins waitin'?'

By then, I had figured what I should tell Guiseppina, but when I opened my mouth, Cody pounded my back and said we had to get moving, so I carried my grip and hat to the hansom cab Burke had waiting for us, and we all climbed in and left the station, clopping along through those streets filled with faces and wool, losing ourselves in the deep cañons with dark buildings for walls.

It was my good fortune that this playwright Robbins chose a saloon to meet us, so when Cody and Burke climbed out of the hack, I volunteered to wait with Guiseppina as she could not enter such an establishment, and Cody found that to be a splendid idea while Burke did not say one thing, but then Guiseppina suggested I escort her back to the Metropolitan Hotel where we were staying, and Cody, God bless him, championed that as a more splendid idea, and even gave me two silver dollars to pay the driver.

Once we got to that fancy hotel, Guiseppina had a suggestion herself, so we retired to the little café where she wanted to hear all about my exploits guiding and hunting since I had left Colonel Judson and her back in June. It was now August, and Burke said we would make our debut on the 25th of the month, which did not give us much time to learn our lines, and gave me cause to fret because I knew what Wild Bill had really told us, and sure did not see him changing tunes.

'You are quiet, Jack,' she told me as we sipped fancy coffee in fancy cups.

I allowed that I was.

She gave me yet another smile that caused my heart to flutter, and I told her what my daddy used to tell me back in Fluvanna County. 'God give me two eyes and two ears but only one mouth, so I guess He wanted me to see and listen twice as much as I talked.'

Sake's alive, you would have thought I told her the funniest joke ever written, she laughed so hard, and reached over and patted my hand, called me a *carino,* and said how much she enjoyed my company. Truth be told, though, that saying held true with my pappy but not with me as I could talk almost as much as Cody after I had loosened my tongue with some fortification. When I fell back to my silent ways, which I tended to do around her, she suggested we go to this fancy place a few blocks away and dance.

Dance? I started sweating like Arizona John Burke. Being Catholic, not hard-shell Baptist, I sure wanted to dance with Guiseppina, but I told her that I was a good horseman but not much of a dancer, at least, not the kind who could dance with a lady who did all sorts of foreign numbers, and she laughed some more.

'I am told, Jack,' she said, 'that you are one of the most, uh . . . popular . . . what is the word? . . . *callers? Si* . . . callers . . . in Nebraska and Kansas.'

'That's square dancing,' I said. 'And I just tell them what to do. I'm not out there cutting the rug.'

'But you are graceful on the stage. And I love it when you do your rope tricks.'

I said something that might have been intelligible but more than likely was buried beneath mumbles and a Southern-turned-Western-plains accent.

She started again about dancing, and me, and, well, jealous as I might have been of Arizona John Burke, I am not one to tread in that direction, so I suggested, since there seemed to be a lot of suggestions going on that evening, that Burke might not be happy and that while I undoubtedly would meet my Maker and say that my biggest accomplishment on this earth was the time I danced with Guiseppina Morlacchi, it would not look right.

She give me a different kind of look and said: 'Jack, John will always be my *amico,* how you say, friend, but he will never be my *marito,* my . . . hus-band. That is the word, no? You understand, *si?* Please. I see him . . . differently than I see you.'

Needless to say, we went dancing after I heard those words.

*   *   *

Later that week, I met our playwrights,

Maeder and Robbins, and by that week-end had copies of *Buffalo Bill! King of the Border Men!* and *Scouts of the Plains* in my hand to learn my lines. *Scouts* came the easiest, because Robbins did not do much other than change a few names and add a few lines to Colonel Judson's concoction. Guiseppina, who played the Indian maiden, Dove Eye, in *Scouts of the Prairie,* became Pale Dove in *Scouts of the Plains.* Buffalo Bill, who went on the vengeance trail after Mormon Ben in Colonel Judson's play, spent most of Maeder's story chasing Colonel Jack McKandlass. That, I figured, would not set well with Wild Bill if ever he found out because, by golly, everyone knows that it was Wild Bill who wiped out Dave McCanles and his Border Ruffians at Rock Creek Station in 1861.

Then we read in the newspapers that Wild Bill was dead, assassinated by some rowdy Texicans, and that left Burke practically in tears. Not that he turned sad, which is how it affected me, but he became overburdened with excitement.

'Don't you see, Jack?' he told me in the dining room where we heard the grim news. 'This is the greatest publicity for our season. Wild Bill dead. Reporters in every city will want to talk to you and Buffalo Bill, to hear the real story from the real men who knew him, and they will also mention how his life is being portrayed on the stage. We'll be rich,

37

lad!'

'I reckon J.B. will be happy for us.' Suddenly, I had a hankering to leave the East, maybe would have done it, too, if not for a certain *danseuse,* and the fact that Cody joined us at that moment, and laughed when I told him what we had read in the paper.

'The only dead Jim has ever been is drunk,' he said. 'Falsehoods,' he added. 'Falsehoods,' he repeated, and wrote Wild Bill a telegram while waiting on our oysters and soup.

Little more than a week later, Cody read me the reply. I was grinning something awful even before I heard the news, but it sure did my heart a world of good to know for certain that Wild Bill still breathed. He said Buntline and the Texicans had failed to kill him.

'Is he coming?' I asked.

'Don't say,' Cody replied. 'What has you so happy, Jack?' He had just noticed.

'Guiseppina!' I shouted. 'Guiseppina and I are getting married!'

I know it sounds like we just got married on a whim, but you have to understand that we had been in close company since I joined Colonel Judson's company in December of 1872, what with her helping me study and rehearse, and us being in the same plays and all, traveling on the same trains, eating together, and for the past week or so dancing together and talking about ourselves more and more. Well, then there is the other point that I

38

had been in love with that woman since December of 1872 but had not realized that she felt the same way about me till August of 1873.

'Does John know?' Cody looked glum.

'Confound it, Will! Arizona John ain't our keeper. I asked her to be my wife, and don't ask me why, but she said yes. We're getting married on the thirty-first.'

He looked glummer. 'Of August?' I nodded. 'Jack, we play in this city through September the Sixth.'

I decided it would not be a good idea to ask him to come to the wedding, but informed him instead about these actors in plays, including ours, that are called understudies. He lifted a cigar from the ashtray, took a few puffs, and suddenly leaped out of his chair. 'Married! By jingo, what great news. Don't worry 'bout the show, pard, just say your vows loudly, get a haircut two days before the weddin', and don't shave that morn, don't even let a tonsorial artist do it for fear of cuttin' your chin or cheek. Wedded! Texas Jack, the lasso king, has got hisself lassoed. I'll send notices to all the newspapers. Burke will be downright giddy at all this publicity.'

Burke, of course, did not speak to me for the rest of that week, but on the day I left New York City for Rochester and an appointment at St. Mary's Catholic Church, he shook my hand and said he hoped we were happy, although I think he only hoped one of us was, and by that I do not mean myself. I thought Cody had forgotten all about me and the wedding, but, as I stepped onto the car, I heard his booming voice, dropped down to the platform, and allowed him to squeeze me like a grizzly. Next, he slapped a piece of paper in my hand, saying he was giving me the best wedding present any pard could. I thought it was a check or some cash money, but it turned out to be just a piece of yellow paper from a telegraph office.

Looking down, I read.

CARDS GONE COLD STOP ACTING LOOKS GOOD WILL JOIN U IN NY NEXT WEEK STOP NEED TRAVELING MONEY STOP PLS SEND TOPEKA STOP JB HICKOK

We had hired an actor who put on a black wig and pasted on a blacker mustache to play Wild Bill, who, by the way, had auburn hair and a blond mustache, but no one had said a thing about it. Sometimes I guessed half the folks in the audience thought we were not real scouts anyway and just Thespians. Bad Thespians at that.

'You were right,' I told Cody, and he slapped my shoulder.

'I know my pards, pard. Give Josephine a kiss for me. Tell her I wish I could 'a been there to see y'all off, but this is a harsh business. The show must be seen.' Stepping back, he held out his hand.

I shook it, and Cody give me a dumb look I thought only I was capable of giving.

'What is it?' I asked.

'We're pards, Jack,' he said. 'Even splits, remember? I need a hundred dollars from you to wire to Jim in Topeka.'

Chapter Four

Buffalo Bill's reception was warm and hearty. The piece itself did not amount to much.
Daily Times, New Brunswick, New Jersey
September 9, 1873

My two Bill pals, *Scouts of the Plains, King of the Border Men,* or J.P. Winter, who was playing the role of Texas Jack in my absence, didn't enter my mind on a beautiful (to me) Sunday at St. Mary's Catholic Church in Rochester, New York. Guiseppina looked like an angel in her white satin dress. I'd never seen her in white, only in red, blue, and black fancy dresses, or those feathered and brocade outfits she wore performing the can-can that would make a Baptist have a conniption fit. Oh, yeah, I can't very well leave out her Pale

Dove/Dove Eye costume with its beads and shells and the silly feather headdress that I'd never seen atop any Pawnee or Cheyenne.

Anyway, while I was exchanging vows with the lady I adored, Cody was killing supes by the scores, and Arizona John Burke was eagerly awaiting the arrival of James Butler Hickok. Meanwhile, we newlyweds took a train to Buffalo from Rochester for our honeymoon. 'The show must be seen,' Cody had told me, and Guiseppina and I figured he was right, planned on staying away only a couple of days, but we soon decided we liked honeymooning even better than acting and dancing, so we spent more time in Buffalo. Besides, J.P. Winter needed practice to perfect the mannerisms and shooting skills of Texas Jack Omohundro. I just prayed he didn't try any rope tricks.

Honeymooning can be expensive, though, and I didn't want Mr. Winter to get too comfortable being me, or let down my pard, Will Cody, so Guiseppina and I left for New York City on Friday, September 5, 1873. We missed Wild Bill's arrival by one day, and, despite my affection for my bride and our honeymooning, I am sorry I missed that occurrence.

Wild Bill took a hack from the 42nd Street depot to the Metropolitan Hotel, where things began to plummet.

'How much do I owe you?' Wild Bill asked

the driver.

'Five dollars.'

Taking the Irishman for a cheat, Wild Bill gave him the eye. You see, he was used to Missouri, Nebraska, Wyoming, and Kansas prices. He set down his grip, and counted out greenbacks he withdrew from his trousers pocket. 'You wouldn't take anything less, would you?' he asked.

'No. That's the charge, bub.'

The hack driver took the five bills offered without another word, mainly on account he didn't get a chance to say anything, not even a 'thank you' or a 'by your leave,' because Wild Bill, in one of his moods, planted a fist in the center of the fellow's face.

I'm told the Irishman was a right solid and tall man, but he rolled into the gutter in front of the Metropolitan and did not stir. A little row like this spread a smile across Wild Bill's face, and he tossed a nickel tip onto the unconscious man's chest, picked up his grip, and walked toward the hotel and a couple of startled employees in red jackets and silly hats who should have been helping with the guest's luggage, but I imagine his countenance petrified them.

Although dressed like a dandy in striped breeches, black Prince Albert, silk cravat, brocade vest, white shirt, fancy boots, and wide-brim hat, Wild Bill was a towering and imposing figure, and the Metropolitan's bellboys and doormen had become wary of any man with long hair for they had seen and heard Buffalo Bill Cody for more than a week, telling stories—all right, lies—of various border experiences that would leave the hair bristling on the backs of their necks.

A few feet from the unnerved boys, Wild Bill stopped, and turned to look down the street. Cautiously the Metropolitan's helpers likewise craned their necks to watch a city policeman making a beeline down the sidewalk, puffing on a whistle, and slapping a nightstick against the palm of a meaty paw.

'What's the meaning of that fracas, dude?' inquired the cop after he spat out the whistle.

' 'Tweren't no fracas,' Wild Bill replied, 'and I ain't no dude.'

'You're one of them Western actors, ain't ye?' the cop said, and Wild Bill snorted his reply, picked up his grip, and headed into the lobby, followed by the furious lawman, whose whistle, now back in his mouth, pierced the ears of every lady and gentleman awaiting a seat in the Metropolitan's restaurant.

'I'm not finished with you!' the cop shouted after removing the whistle once more. Wild Bill did not even turn.

'I am finished with you,' he said, and told a pale clerk behind the desk: 'You have a reservation for me, James Butler Hickok. I'm with the Buffalo Bill Combination.'

Said the policeman: 'Hickok? You're Wild

Bill Hickok?'

Wild Bill didn't answer. Instead, he motioned with his eyes for the clerk to quit dawdling. The clerk turned the registration book toward him and quickly produced a key.

Well, by now the policeman had grown furious, and I can't rightly blame him what with a hack driver lying in the gutter, and two dozen folks inside one of the city's finest hotels figuring him for a coward or buffoon. So, raising that nightstick, he pounced toward Wild Bill, who, without turning around, made a comment just loud enough for everyone in the lobby to hear, but forceful enough to stop the cop.

'I'll make you eat that toothpick.'

'I'm arresting you in the name of the law,' the cop said—after he had stopped, of course, and lowered the nightstick limply at his side.

That's when Buffalo Bill jaunted down the stairs, pumped Wild Bill's hand furiously, swept off his Stetson, and bowed at the crowd of onlookers. 'Ladies and gentlemen, it is my pleasure to present to you, the one and only Wild Bill Hickok, the famous scout and marshal from the plains. We'll be makin' our final appearances in this splendid city tomorrow and Saturday nights before journeyin' on to New Brunswick.'

That was only partly true. Sure, we would play in New Brunswick on the 8th and in West Chester, Pennsylvania, on the 9th, but we would be back in New York, albeit at another location, September 11-13 before taking the rails for Ohio, Kentucky, and Indiana.

'My old comrade, Wild Bill,' Cody announced, 'will only be travelin' with my Combination for this season. His especial duties and destiny await him out West, so this is your once-in-a-lifetime chance to see a true legend, the champion pistol fighter. Major Burke, over there by the balustrade, will be glad to sell you advance tickets.'

Buffalo Bill Cody was more than an entertainer and huckster. He was also a politician, and I am not referring to his brief reign in Nebraska as justice of peace or how he came to be elected to the Nebraska Legislature, which is how he came to add the title 'the Honorable' before his name even though he never claimed his seat on account that it was a joke from the voters of the twenty-sixth district. Whoever said Nebraskans have no sense of humor has never lived in North Platte or Lincoln.

Seeing the red-faced policeman, Cody had to do a little politicking, and, draping an arm around the cop's shoulders while fishing in his buckskin jacket for a cigar, he guided Officer O'Malley—whose name I learned from Cody but it probably wasn't that on account that Cody was something awful about remembering names, but I'll call him that anyway on account that it's better than nothing—outside where a

46

certain hack driver had just begun to return to the here and now.

'Your friend's not on the border, sir,' Officer O'Malley informed Cody after he lighted up his cigar. 'New York does not abide ruffians and rapscallions.'

'And Wild Bill is neither, sir.' He left the cop long enough to help the driver to his feet, gave him a handkerchief to place under the bloody pulp that once had been a nose, and slipped another dollar bill into the driver's waistcoat, saying it was all a misunderstanding and that, if he would give his name, there would be a ticket waiting for him at the Park Theater box office tomorrow night.

'What's the fine for knockin' a cab driver to the ground?' Cody asked the policeman after the driver had driven away in a daze.

'That's up to the judge.'

'Well, I see no reason for Wild Bill to spend no time in your Tombs, sir, nor do I see no reason we can't settle this as men, as Americans.'

'Irish,' the policeman informed him.

'Indeed, and Cody is an Irish name. My father, God rest his soul, hailed from Wexford.' That wasn't rightly true, either, as to my knowledge the late Isaac Cody hailed from Canada, and most of the Codys came from Jersey, the isle, I mean, and not the little state next to New York. 'And you?'

'Kilkenny.'

47

'By the saints, man, we're practically neighbors. Here's five dollars. That's for bail. Tell your sergeant and judge I'll be in first thing in the morn to pay Wild Bill's fine for disturbin' the peace. Do that suit you, Captain?'

'I'm no captain . . .'

'Tell you what, since we're both Irishmen, here's ten dollars for Wild Bill's bond.'

The policeman stared at the $15 in his hand, glanced at the Metropolitan staff, and snarled, shoving the money into Cody's jacket pocket. 'I'll not be bought, mister, and, if you don't watch your bloody step, I'll close your show and send you packing to those sorry plains whence you came. I'll keep Wild Bill out of the Tombs, but only because he's new to the city, but there shall be no more donnybrooks such as tonight's . . . I hold you responsible, sir . . . and none of your graft.'

When he withdrew, however, he had the $15 again and another one of Cody's cigars. Officer O'Malley stepped back, tipping back his cap with his nightstick before strolling into the night.

That's how the story was told to me, anyhow.

*　　　*　　　*

Since Wild Bill had yet to learn his lines, for our final two engagements at Mr. Freligh's

48

Park Theater he just walked on stage a couple of times and shot holes in playing cards. The theater got smoky, and that rotten-egg smell of burnt powder didn't suit everyone, but they surely enjoyed Wild Bill's marksmanship— even more than they liked my rope tricks. But that was all right. We were making money.

There wasn't much for Wild Bill to do in Fred Maeder's play, *Buffalo Bill! King of the Border Men!* as it was mostly Cody's show, and Maeder hadn't written in a big part for Wild Bill—or me. In that play, Maeder played The Old Vet, and his sister, a buxomly, comely red-headed Irish lass almost as fetching as Guiseppina, played Kitty Muldoon, who charmed many a scout. But the main character—not including, naturally, Buffalo Bill and Texas Jack—was Jake McKandlass as portrayed by Alfred Johnson. He kills Cody's pa and is pursued by the play's heroes—just Cody and me before Wild Bill joined us, then he got to run around the stage and shoot and holler, too. Cody wounds Colonel McKandlass, but the vile man kidnaps Cody's sister, Lillie, played by Lizzie Safford. Cody had an army of sisters, but I never met or even heard of one named Lillie. Well, Cody and his pals run a mite off course in their pursuit of McKandlass, fighting Indians, saving pretty actresses from being burned at the stake, saving ourselves from fiery deaths, but finally—I trust I won't be spoiling the play by revealing this—in the final act Lillie is rescued, and the evil McKandlass is killed in a knife duel by Buffalo Bill, our hero.

What confused me, and a few critics, but rarely affected the audience any, was the fact that Lillie's last name was Fielding, and she was supposed to be Buffalo Bill Cody's sister. Her sister's name was Lottie Fielding, played by little Eliza Hudson, and I never met a Cody sister named Lottie neither, and his mother, played by Jennie Fisher mostly but sometimes Mrs. R.G. France when Jennie was in her cups or in one of her moods or had just disappeared for a day or three, was always called Mrs. Fielding, and never Ma.

I liked *Scouts of the Plains* better, mainly because I remembered most of my lines from Colonel Judson's *Scouts on the Prairie,* and the fact that it wasn't just a Buffalo Bill story, even though he got most of the headlines and interviews. In that one, the villains are Jim Daws, played by Hiram Robbins or Frank Mordaunt, and his cowardly companion, Tom Doggett, played by W.S. MacEvey. Daws murders Uncle Henry Carter, played to perfection by Joe Arlington, and kidnaps Ella Carter, his daughter, played by Esther Rubens. Well, Buffalo Bill enlists the aid of his pals, Texas Jack and Wild Bill, and we go after Jim Daws, having some more run-ins with bonfires and the like, Indian treachery, tell some stories around campfires, the murder of Cody's pa, and we finally save Ella, and kill the black-hearts. I forget the total number of casualties, but it's well into the scores.

Another reason I like *Scouts of the Plains* better is because Wild Bill and I get to rescue Cody from being burned alive, and the fact that it also stars *Mlle.* Morlacchi as Pale Dove. In the first act, she puts her hand on my shoulder—I think the way it was written was for her to tell Cody this, but, hell's fire, by then she was *my* wife—and tells me: 'Fly toward the setting sun . . . and save thyself.' Boy, that's poetry to my ears, the way she says it, even if a few scalawag critics sometimes remarked that they had never heard an Indian speaking in an Italian accent. Criminy, them inkslingers had never heard a real Indian say a word, and, if they had, they would have soiled their britches.

Well, by the time the troupe reached New Brunswick, New Jersey, Wild Bill assured us that he had learned his lines, but he forgot them all the moment we arrived at Greer's Hall. The army of men, ladies, and children in front of the box office circled two blocks, and Wild Bill, who always struck me as pale to begin with, turned whiter than my bride's wedding gown. He went more petrified than Cody had before his first night on the stage in Chicago a year back.

'I ain't going out there,' Wild Bill told us shortly before the curtain rose. 'There's a damn' sight of people out yonder. I ain't gonna say things like . . . "Tall Oak is weak. He is like woman. The snake stung him in the back and stole from him the Pale Face squaws." I ain't never said nothing like that in all my days till I read this dung heap.'

Cody, he had turned ashen, too, but not as bad as Arizona John Burke, especially once it got past eight o'clock and the curtain still hadn't rose, and the audience had started to whistle, and shout, and boo.

'Can we do *Border Men* instead?' Cody asked Burke.

'It's too late. The sets are all wrong, the cast all wrong. We have to do *Scouts*.'

'Who's Bill's understudy?' I asked.

'Cunningham,' said one of the supes, who looked downright silly in his tan linens and war paint but without his wig. 'But he run off with Jennie Fisher an hour ago.'

'Why?' Arizona John Burke demanded, and the supe give him the dumb look. So did I. I mean, Burke had seen Jennie Fisher before. She wasn't as pretty as Rena Maeder or my wife, but she wasn't the type of woman you told no. Then he remembered that Jennie Fisher was supposed to play Mrs. Carter in tonight's play.

'Well, she ain't,' Rena Maeder announced. 'I am. Playing an old lady will test my acting, and keep some unwelcome hands off my person.' She gave Cody a villainous look.

Everyone muttered an oath excepting me

and Wild Bill, and Cody whispered: 'For the love of God.' Burke announced that he needed a whiskey, which another one of the supes produced, and then Cody got the idea, and snatched the flask from Burke's hand and give Wild Bill needed fortification, but then some fool raised the curtain, so the actors had to run out to play their scene. While Cody and Burke sweated, Wild Bill drank, and the supe, who got paid only 25¢ a day, scowled at everyone drinking his John Barleycorn.

The play opens at Uncle Henry's cabin, and Jim Daws arrives, pretending to be a good guy. Mostly this first act bores me, and drags on and on, building up, Hiram Robbins explained to me while contesting my notion that it was duller than a supe's knife, anticipation for the appearance of the heroes of the drama—ourselves. On this night, however, with Cody and them sweating, and Wild Bill drinking, it flew by in just about no time, the curtain closed, the workers scrambled on the set for the next scene, and the curtain went back up again, causing Cody and me to race out in front of the false campfire at center stage and start on our lines, most of which were drowned out by the cheers and thunderous applause.

'Where have you been, Texas Jack?' Cody asked.

'I have been on the trail of Jim Daws, that renegade,' I answered.

'By thunder, then we have the same pursuit

for I have been chasin' that murderous fiend and horse thief. If only our old friend, Wild Bill, were here to join our effort. Have . . .'— Cody shot a nervous glance at Wild Bill, swallowed, and continued—'have you seen Wild Bill?'

I was about to answer no, changing my line the way Colonel Judson had done in a pinch on our first night on the stage in Chicago, but the crowd started hooting and hollering, and I looked over, and let out a sigh and prayer of thanks as my pard, J.B. Hickok, wandered onto the stage and quietly mumbled: 'Boys, I'm with you heart and hand. It is I, Wild Bill Hickok, protector of the fair and virtuous.' You could barely hear him, though, and not because of the cheers, but no one seemed to notice or care.

Bad as it was, that performance at Greer's Hall went a whole lot better than the next one the following night in West Chester. This time, Wild Bill got in front of the fire all right, without any fortification, mainly because he knew we would fortify ourselves with a jug we pass around during the scene. The problem that night was his misunderstanding as to the contents of that jug. You see, he drank down that poor supe's whiskey in New Jersey, thus didn't notice that we were just play acting and that the jug did not really contain Old Tanglefoot.

'Tell us a story, Wild Bill,' Cody

commanded, and passed the jug to Wild Bill, who took a swig, stopped, his face a mask of horror, turned his head, and spit out the brown liquid. I would have hated to have been sitting on the front row that night.

'Cold tea don't count!' Wild Bill shouted. 'I ain't telling no story till I get some real whiskey!'

I mean to tell you, the folks in West Chester, Pennsylvania practically raised the roof after that line. When things got quiet, Cody cleared his throat, looked into the audience, and said, real polite: 'Could one of you gentlemen run to the saloon next door and bring my comrade a bottle of rye?'

The roof got raised again, but then one gent volunteered that there was no reason for anyone to leave the opera hall on account that he had brought a bottle in his overcoat and that, why, he'd be happy to share with a bona-fide scout from the plains. So, Wild Bill got his bracer, and the play went on for another night.

Chapter Five

Ned Buntline . . . is simply maundering imbecility.

New York Herald
April 1, 1873

Say what you will about William F. Cody, but savvy this. He thought quick on his feet—not only tracking Indians or hunting game, but on the theater stage as well. He also knew what entertained folks, what made them laugh, what they would talk about in saloons, and parlors, and churches, and on the streets.

As we left Pennsylvania for New York City, he sat beside Hiram Robbins on the train, and told him: 'I want you to write that cold tea line into the play for Jim. We'll do it just like we did tonight.'

'Sure, Will,' Robbins said, 'but you might not have a fellow in the audience with a bottle or flask to share every night.'

'I know. We'll keep one backstage, have a supe rush it out.'

'Real whiskey?' Robbins, who wasn't no temperance man but couldn't put down as much Tanglefoot as we plainsmen, or even Jennie Fisher, sounded incredulous.

'Jim can hold his liquor, and like he says, cold tea won't pry a story out of him.' Cody pushed back his hat, grinning at an idea that just took root. 'Maybe Josephine instead of a supe. Yeah, she can dance, bring out a bottle, hand it to Jim, dance out. Folks'll love it.'

They did, too. So did Wild Bill. I think he enjoyed spitting out cold tea, knowing someone would bring him a bottle of rye in a moment. I think he also enjoyed the laughs he got. You see, most often times men did not laugh at Wild Bill Hickok. They were too afraid of him, but he could be a right funny man. Of course, his sense of frontier humor would get him in mighty big trouble, but that's getting ahead of my story.

Early in our season, though, Wild Bill started to cotton to being a Thespian. Consider the time we played in Dewitt Davidson's Globe Hall in Manhattan on September 12, 1873. Cody had crawled into a hollow log to get some sleep—I'm not joshing you, that's what was written in the play for him to do—but it turned out to be a bad spot to nap because a bunch of Indians—oh, twenty or twenty-five supes, I recollect—come onto the scene, and decide to build a fire. Yep, they throw that hollow log that's not hollow because Buffalo Bill Cody's in it, still asleep, on the fire.

As you know by now, the fire's not real, just more orange and red bunting, and stuff like that. Also, the scene is supposed to be somewhere on the Great Plains, and I can assure you that there are hardly any trees to speak of in that particular country and none big enough for a tall, solid specimen of manhood like William F. Cody to fit in. The audience knows Buffalo Bill is in dire peril, and it's up to his comrades to rescue him at the last moment. I suspect the scene is supposed to be dramatic, but usually I heard a bunch of folks sniggering all the way up in the balconies.

'All right, J.B.' I gave Wild Bill a nudge. That was our cue to run on stage and save Buffalo Bill from a Joan of Arc demise.

'I don't know, Jack.' Wild Bill turned to me with a mischievous grin. 'What say we let him roast this time?'

I hooted in spite of myself, and we stood there. The supes kept dancing around the fire, getting tuckered out in no time, and panting and wondering what was keeping us, and a minute later Cody figured we were funning him, and crawled out of the log—not seeming to mind the hot blaze all around him—and shot one of the exhausted supes, who took to dying with great pleasure. Cody leaped to his feet and started shooting and knifing and knocking down all those little men who hung around the opera halls whenever we came to city for a chance to get killed by a Western plainsman and earn two bits.

'Hell,' Wild Bill swore, 'ain't no need in letting him reap all that glory for himself.'

With that, he rushed onto the stage, drew his Colts from the red sash, and shot with each hand, me right behind him, revolver in my right hand, lariat in my left. The orchestra started blaring murderous music, and our guns popped, Cody smiling at us—he could appreciate a joke, even one on him—and killing Indians galore, although they would be resurrected like Lazarus for several more scenes of battles during the night's festivities.

I should take a moment to explain about our guns, lest you think any actor or patron stood in harm's way during these violent performances. I carried a Smith & Wesson American revolver in .44 caliber, a right powerful weapon, but I never fully charged it, and tapped my cartridges full of paraffin. The gun fired, but there was no lead, nothing that could harm a body. Wild Bill carried a brace of cap-and-ball Colt Navy .36s only without the balls except when he performed his shooting exhibitions, and then he, too, used a light load, just enough to puncture a paste card but not penetrate a fine woolen waistcoat. Likewise, Cody's two little .41-caliber Cloverleaf Colts contained rimfire cartridges always lightly charged and sealed with paraffin. We burned a right smart of powder with each performance, but all was done safely, never harming no persons except for an occasional powder burn when a supe got too close to one of our revolvers or rifles, which didn't really harm him, just gave him a smart and caused him to jump and shout but learned him to keep his distance when we border men went about our killing.

Well, Wild Bill, Cody, and I shot Indians in tan frocks and red flannel, and everyone loved it, although the supes got a little confused at times. By that I mean, I might shoot at one fellow, but he'd keep on standing while another one fell. Wild Bill pulled his trigger once, and three Indians died.

'Shit!' Wild Bill said that night, but no one heard him except me because of the din of gunshots, applause, music, and laughter. 'I'm empty.'

'It don't matter!' I shouted to him. 'The cymbals!'

'Huh?'

'The cymbals!' I waved my gun at the orchestra pit, and accidentally pulled the trigger, somehow killing an Indian standing stage right but sparing C.A. Ortloff's Riverside Percussionists. 'The cymbals are like gunshots!'

'Oh.' He laughed, pulled the trigger, and, although the hammer struck an empty chamber, killed yet another red devil.

The curtain closed after the last supe finished dying, and the stagehands cleaned up the carnage while the supes hurried backstage to adjust their scalps and get ready to be killed again in the next act. A bully good time was had by all.

*   *   *

Back at the hotel, the desk clerk presented Cody with a note, and he read it with pursed lips.

'What is it?' I asked, and he passed me the gilded invitation.

My old chums Cody and Omohundro:
You are cordially invited to my temperance lecture on the evening of the 13th. 7 o'clock, Trinity Church, Broadway and Wall. It's free and open to my adoring public. I trust you can attend and we can talk after the lecture of old times. I have read in the newspapers that your performance that day is a matinee. Per chance you will not depart for your next engagement until after my lecture and a fine supper. Before the performance, you might find the cemetery interesting as it contains the graves of many famous Americans.

Your trusted amigo,
E.Z.C. Judson
(Ned Buntline)

'Well?' I said.
'He ain't mad at us,' Cody said.
'No, but . . .' I tilted my head real discreet at

61

Wild Bill, but he noticed, and snatched the invite from my hand, read it, laughed, and passed the note back to Cody.

'I'd like to meet Judson,' he said. 'Maybe he'd care to write about me, the truth or some semblance to it.' I imagine he was remembering that Cody kills Colonel Jake McKandlass in *King of the Border Men!* while, as I have already informed you, it was Wild Bill who shot Dave McCanles dead in 1861. 'Don't worry, the cemetery don't interest me none. I ain't planning on killing Judson and burying him there.'

* * *

Robert Fulton was born in 1765 and died in 1815, but his steamboats weathered a lot better than his tombstone, which leaned at a bad angle in the cemetery's soft ground. I imagine someone would fix it pretty soon, Robert Fulton being a mite famous. They might even clean off that white paint across the stone that spelled: Bastard & Thief! I don't know what anyone had against Robert Fulton, but seeing that sacrilege made a sometimes good former Catholic altar boy like me a tad uncomfortable, until my wife asked me a question, and I thought up a joke.

'Who is . . . Robert . . . Ful-ton?' Guiseppina inquired.

'Well, if you believe them New Yorkers, he

was a bastard and a thief,' I said, smiling when she covered her mouth and giggled, and then I crossed myself and decided I'd go to confession real soon and told Guiseppina that Fulton invented the steamboat, and I was glad of it because a steamboat had carried her across the Atlantic Ocean, but she corrected me by saying she doubted it was his steamboat on account he died more than fifty years before she came to America.

Holding Guiseppina's hand, I strolled through the cemetery overshadowed by the massive Trinity Church. They say that giant spire and gilded cross served as a lighthouse, a beacon for all the ships sailing into the New York harbor, and I reckon it always will, even though some of its neighbors had started to crowd out the light of this magnificent church. New Yorkers sure liked tall buildings. Me? I preferred mountains.

The church had started way back in the late 1600s, and preached to folks of color in 1705. Wild Bill told me that on account that he and Cody were staunch Abolitionists, and he enjoyed picking at my Southern heritage, but I didn't mind.

'William Bradford's buried over yonder,' Arizona John Burke said, pointing to a headstone that remained white and erect.

'Who is . . . William Brad-ford?' my wife asked.

'I don't know,' I said in good humor, 'but

he's buried over yonder.'

She laughed, squeezed my hand, and we bypassed William Bradford for this tomb that Cody fancied. I had to squint my eyes in the fast-approaching darkness to read the marble, but Cody must have learned it already—he was getting good at learning lines—and he read the highlights to us: 'The patriot of incorruptible integrity . . . the soldier of approved valor . . . the statesman of consummate wisdom . . .' He glanced at Hiram Robbins. 'That'll be what people say about me.'

Wild Bill had wandered over and tried to read the rest, but his eyes failed him in the dark, and he shrugged it off, and lit a cigar, but Guiseppina managed to make it all out, although it was hard for us to understand her in that Italian accent: 'Whose tal-ents . . . and vir-tues . . . will be ad-mired . . . long after . . . the . . . marble . . . shall have . . . uh . . . I spell for you . . . m-o-u-l-d-e-r-e-d . . . what is that?'

'Moldered,' Arizona John Burke said, and Wild Bill started singing: 'John Brown's body lies a-molderin' in his grave, oh, John Brown's body . . .'

'Mo . . .'—she skipped it and finished—'into dusk.'

'Dust,' Arizona John Burke corrected.

'Dust,' she said. 'Who is it?'

'Alexander Hamilton,' I read, satisfied that I had finally beaten Arizona John Burke.

'The patriot of incorruptible integrity . . .

the soldier of approved valor . . . the statesman of consummate wisdom . . . that'll be me,' Cody repeated.

Robbins nodded and suggested we take our seats inside the cathedral to listen to the temperance lecture as the line didn't look so formidable any more, and we all found a place where we were comfortable—on the back pew for us backsliders.

Quite a turnout, mostly ladies of high society in fancy dresses, a few preachers and priests, couple of gents in Navy uniforms, and four men and two women of color. A few ladies curiously glanced at our long locks, but said nothing as they did not recognize us without our heavy buckskins and arsenal. I think we fit in with the Sunday-go-to-meetings we all wore, although it was Saturday night, and those congress gaiters pinched my feet something fierce, and I wished I was wearing moccasins or a pair of John Mueller's boots.

Colonel Judson, however, soon had me forgetting all about my feet. He was some talker, waving his cane like it was a staff and he was Moses. He had passion, especially when preaching temperance, and the Trinity Church soon filled with the sounds of laughter and sobs as he spoke. Colonel Judson could do that, have you slapping your knee at a right funny story of his drinking as a sailor, then make a sharp turn and you'd be dabbing at your eyes with a handkerchief because now you were crying at a sad, sad tale of the evils of John Barleycorn. They don't call the colonel the 'Destroyer of Demon Rum' for nothing. He stood in front of the pulpit, dressed in a Naval officer's frock weighted down with about two dozen medals and ribbons, and a fancy shirt, stopping only to take a drink of water from a pitcher and glass they had set up on a table beside him when his throat got dry, and dry a throat will get with all that fire and brimstone he kept preaching.

During those first two hours of the temperance lecture, Colonel Judson shone as bright as the Trinity Church tower, but the more he helped himself to that pitcher of water, the more confused he seemed to get, and by nine-thirty the only thing bright about the colonel was his nose. He was telling the story of how whiskey ruined many a sailor, a good story, certainly, but he had told the same tale a couple of times before during his lecture, and it got a little different, a little exaggerated, a little more slurred with each telling. He excused himself, and helped himself to another drink.

Cody leaned to me, and whispered: 'What do you supposed he's got in that pitcher?'

When the colonel belched, I said in a hushed but respectful tone: 'By jingo, I think he's destroying demon rum with every swallow.'

A few dignified ladies of Manhattan society

walked out, leading me to suspect they had the same suspicions as us, and before long people started filing out of that church—'their faces masked with indignation' is how Hiram Robbins later described the scene. When a preacher approached the colonel in the middle of one of his slurred stories, Colonel Judson shoved him away, and started singing a tune you didn't sing in church, stopped, excused himself, and resumed his story, only then his words weren't making any sense, and Arizona John Burke allowed that, as those Naval officers didn't look too friendly, perhaps we should intervene before things got out of hand.

So Wild Bill, Cody, and me excused ourselves, slid out of the pew into the center aisle, and walked toward Colonel Judson, who slumped in his chair, then rolled onto the floor. I grabbed the colonel's feet, Cody took hold of the fat man's arms, and Wild Bill helped himself to the pitcher and glass, and we carted the old reprobate outside, followed by a tall parson whose face was also masked with indignation and who carried the colonel's staff, I mean, cane. By then, there weren't many folks left in the church, and we hailed a hack, and the parson announced he would pray for Colonel Judson, and told us the hotel where the colonel was boarding, so Cody handed the driver some greenbacks and asked the man to make sure his passenger got to his room safely.

The preacher tossed the cane in the cab,

then returned to the church, the cab rolled down the street, and Wild Bill took a sip from the pitcher, and passed it to Cody and the glass to me.

'The Destroyer of Demon Rum has been slain,' Cody said with a grin.

'Nope,' Wild Bill announced. 'It's gin.' Cody poured two fingers into what had been Colonel Judson's glass now held by me.

Chapter Six

As it is there is no plot, and the whole performance consists of a succession of raids by the Indians, in which the young ladies are carried off and afterwards rescued in an impossible manner by their lovers, Buffalo Bill, Wild Bill, and Texas Jack.

Kentucky Gazette, Lexington, Kentucky
October 1, 1873

Cody took more from that embarrassing temperance lecture than the evils of John Barleycorn, as we learned on our opening night at the Opera House in Columbus, Ohio. Before the curtain was raised, Arizona John Burke stood in front of the audience to inform the packed house: 'Ladies and gentlemen, tonight you will be witnessing history as we present Frederick G. Maeder's acclaimed drama, *Buffalo Bill! King of the Border Men!*, a true story of the violent border of our frontier of the not so distant past, featuring, as himself the patriot of incorruptible integrity, the soldier of approved valor, the statesman of consummate wisdom . . . *William F. . . . Buffalo . . . Bill . . . Cody!*'

'Reminds me a lot of Alexander Hamilton!' Wild Bill shouted to me above the thunderous reception Burke's words had received, and I nodded.

We sold out three nights in Columbus, and six in Cincinnati. It never got tiresome, play acting, to me, and Cody took to it even more. Well, I think what pleasured Cody was all the money we made. Cody never put much stock in rehearsals, so we studied our lines as we rode the rails all over the East and Midwest. Even Wild Bill never much minded all that tomfoolery we said each night, although that would change real soon, but the parades and speeches we'd have to do when we first stopped in a big city would get in his craw, and he never trusted newspapermen—not after Colonel Nichols made him famous and a target for any fool Texican with a six-shooter—but whenever one of his moods would start to turn him contrary, Cody would become peacemaker, plying Wild Bill with rye whiskey, or having him sit next to Jennie Fisher for a spell.

Wild Bill was in fine spirits, as well as his cups, when we closed our engagement at Cincinnati's Opera House, and I think the menfolk filling most of the seats had also partook liberally of the fine bourbon and barley beverages offered in various saloons of that city because they howled like Comanches during that little ruction.

'That Injun ain't dead, Bill, shoot him again!'

'Set 'em up again, gents, so y'all can kill 'em again!'

'Look out, Buffalo Bill!'

'Bully! Bully! Bully for Texas Jack!'

'Hooray! Hooray! Hooray for the scouts!'

'Jack, you better lasso that gal before she ropes Buffalo Bill into marriage!'

'Think not on him till tomorrow, I'll devise thee brave punishments for him. Strike up, pipers.'

I don't exactly know what that last one is all about, but it sure got Arizona John Burke, Walter Fletcher, and J.V. Arlington to laughing. The thing is, most of our plays went like that. People just acted like lunatics, shouting, urging us on in the slaughter of Indians—and folks say we Westerners aren't civilized.

After the curtain dropped, they kept on screaming and hurrahing, clapping their hands, and stomping their feet till it sounded like I was carrying dispatches for General

70

J.E.B. Stuart back in the war when the Yankees were running all over Virginia with artillery thundering in all directions. Arizona John Burke forced us three actors back on stage, and the curtain rose so that we could take our bows, and bow again, and that only caused the clapping and stomping to get real noisy.

One man tossed us a bottle, which I grabbed out of the air and took a pull, and a lady showered us with roses. Another woman even hurled a flower that hit me in the head and staggered me a mite, and, when I touched my cheek, I wiped away a speck of blood, and that's when I looked down and saw Cody picking up that carnation and noticed that the lady had tied a key to the stem along with a note. Cody read the paper, and slid it and the key into his breast pocket before sweeping off his hat and taking another bow. Me? I took a pull on the bottle, passing it to Wild Bill before he got ugly and ripped it from my hand.

Cody missed our train to Kentucky that night, but Arizona John Burke told us not to fret as it was not a far trip to Lexington from Cincinnati and that trains ran regularly between the two cities. Besides, we did not open at Lexington's Opera House until the 29th of September, and Cody certainly would not miss a performance. He joined us at the hotel the next morning, shortly after we finished breakfast.

'Get lost?' Wild Bill said. We were sitting on the hotel verandah, smoking our morning cigars, and watching the bustle of activity on the street, enjoying the whispers of folks casting curious glances in our direction, wondering if we were the real scouts that would be playing for two nights, Monday and Tuesday, at the Opera House.

'Lost . . . yes, you could say that, Jim.' With a wink, he settled into an empty chair, and bit the end off a cigar Arizona John Burke offered him.

Wild Bill shook his head, and I began to suspicion my pard, Cody, because he was a married man, although Lulu was either in Nebraska or West Chester with the young 'uns, and I guess it would be hard for a fellow like Will Cody to . . . , well, I mean that I was traveling with my wife and, criminy, I don't think I have to say much more on this subject.

Our opening Monday night turned out to be another splendid success. Those Kentuckians, who paid between twenty-five and seventy-five cents per ticket—no extra charge for reserved seats—kept clamoring for us to keep at it, to keep rescuing our damsels and keep shooting down the supes, but we finally escaped back to our hotel, and had a right fine time drinking wine and eating scalloped oysters and sourdough bread.

The next morning over breakfast, Wild Bill read aloud the review that appeared in the

Daily Lexington Press, which did not quite compare any performer in our Combination to Edwin Booth, nor did it rank the author of the drama, Hiram Robbins, as the play had been *Scouts of the Plains,* to William Shakespeare. I somehow escaped the critic's wrath, not that it was really wrath. I mean, *wrath* is a Cheyenne dog soldier on the warpath, or a first sergeant in the 5th Cavalry anytime, but it was more that the writer just didn't understand why this drama captivated so many citizens across these United States. He did call we three actors 'fine-looking men,' but he singled out Cody and Wild Bill as poor actors. That caused Cody to scowl, and Wild Bill to snigger.

'Land's sake,' said Wild Bill, hardly able to control his cackling, 'that's the first newspaper writer I ever knew to write the damned truth about me.'

Cody grunted, and went about his breakfast.

Well, the review did not stop anyone from coming to see us Tuesday night because once more we had to turn people away. Guiseppina was not feeling well and could not dance in either Lexington performance, so she stayed in our room, and we opened with a shooting exhibition by Wild Bill. Then I came out and did some rope tricks, twirling the lasso in a loop, and then stepping into it, roping the trombone player, and pretending I had me a big longhorn, things like that. Sometimes during the play I got to lasso Indians, which

73

the crowd really loved, but mostly they wanted us to kill every supe rigged out as a savage redskin.

From Lexington, we journeyed on to Louisville, and had a fantastic opening night, one of the best to my way of thinking. Guiseppina had recovered, and started the evening by dancing and singing and acting in a little farce titled *Thrice Married,* and everyone screamed and clapped and stood on their feet the entire time we scouts took to the stage. I'm not fooling you when I say that they actually groaned when there weren't nobody left for us to kill on stage.

Yet, I became worried about how we would do the next night after I picked up a copy of the *Courier-Journal.* The review was not bad, by any means. It ran for just a couple of paragraphs, but the writer praised my wife—I decided to save this paper for our scrapbook— and even noted . . . 'we do not remember having seen the Opera House so crowded for years. The attendance fully justified the stock expression "filled from pit to dome." The scouts will continue during the balance of the week and will, if any room is left, draw still more crowded houses.'

That's where I had my doubts because when I turned the page I saw all these advertisements of amusements for that night. Well, there was a fish frying at Shooting Park on the river, and for an old gamesman like myself that appealed to me, and I would have gone had I not had a commitment at the Opera House. Beneath that little notice was a bigger once announcing our play—we were doing *Buffalo Bill! King of the Border Men!* one more time—but the column also listed a fair to benefit the St. Patrick's church and schools, and a race at the Greenland Driving Park Association with a $100 purse, which would appeal to Cody who would likely have gone and bet a few more dollars than he had on his person had he not had another commitment. There was a Vaudeville Theater that proclaimed 'A Carnival of Fun,' all of which sounded like competition to me, but the thing I feared most was an event at the Public Library Hall.

READINGS
FROM HER OWN WORKS BY
MRS. HARRIET BEECHER STOWE

Well, we had played to sold-out houses in New York, but I just didn't see how we could compete will all those goings-on in a place like Louisville, Kentucky. Yes, I was more that a mite nervous when we reached the Opera Hall, got into our costumes, and loaded our revolvers with blank cartridges.

I tell you, my heart felt glad when the curtain rose and I heard all those cheers, the foot stomping, and I quickly forgot about

Uncle Tom's Cabin, which I had never read anyway but always wanted to and probably would have if it had not been for the fact that I was raised a Southerner and served with the Confederate cavalry under J.E.B. Stuart and my parents and most of the folks I had grown up beside in Fluvanna County, Virginia held Mrs. Stowe in the same regard as they held President Grant and the late Mr. Lincoln.

After we killed all the supes six or seven times over, and Alfred Johnson, playing the villainous Colonel McKandlass, was stabbed in the heart by Buffalo Bill and expired as Cody took his sister in his arms and proclaimed all's well that ends well, the curtain descended, and we took our bows several times before retiring to the dressing room, where Wild Bill passed around a jug that did not contain cold tea, and we toasted ourselves and our success.

We were enjoying a fine jollification when Arizona John Burke escorted an elderly woman with spectacles and gleaming gray hair into our lion's den.

'Gentlemen, may I present an especial visitor,' Burke said, and Cody corked the jug, and we all stood and tried to look pleasant and pleased. Arizona John Burke called us by our given names, and we each bowed slightly at the old lady, who must have been sixty. She smiled.

'It is an honor to introduce you to Harriet Beecher Stowe,' he said, and I about choked.

'She watched from the balcony tonight with the mayor and Mister Germain of the city council.'

While I was recovering, Cody kissed her hand and told her it was an honor him—being an Abolitionist whose papa had died for the cause in Bleeding Kansas before the war really started, you see—to meet her and that he had known her son who had died a few years back in a glorious fracas against Roman Nose's Cheyennes with George Forsyth and a bunch of Kansas scouts, none who had been Buffalo Bill, Texas Jack, or Wild Bill. I didn't even know Cody had known Lieutenant Beecher, whose Christian name I disremember, but it was no matter anyway on account that Mrs. Stowe corrected Cody on account that it wasn't her son but a nephew, and she thanked Cody for his sympathy anyway.

Then she turned to me and said: 'Your skills with a lariat are like those of a magician, Mister Omohundro, and your wife is a poet of dance.'

I could only think of one thing. 'But what of your reading at the Public Library Hall, ma'am?' I asked her, and she give me a look like she was my mama and I had just warmed her heart by telling her how much I loved her, which I never really told my mama, although I reckon she knew it, and still knows it on account of the money I send her from time to time since my daddy was called to glory.

Her eyes twinkled, and she announced: 'Why, I rescheduled for Monday night, Mister Omohundro, so I could see the famous scouts.'

We talked a bit, and she gave me a copy of *Uncle Tom's Cabin* in which she signed her name and a sentiment before leaving. I aim to read that book one of these days, even though I'm a Southerner.

I must concede, though, that most of the ladies we attracted were much lovelier and younger than Mrs. Stowe. I call to your attention the fact that my wife told me she noticed a strange woman coming out of Cody's hotel room in Hamilton, Ohio, and Wild Bill himself admitted to me that he had planned on frequenting a brothel the next day in Dayton but was waylaid by a certain temptress outside the hotel and took her for a stroll on the banks of the Miami River, and, well, I need not spell everything out to you.

Naturally I remained faithful to my *Mlle.* Morlacchi. My *compadres* should have restrained themselves.

Chapter Seven

The drama is replete with incident, and introduces almost everything that ever transpired on the plains. It is of the intensely sensational school, and bristles with shooting, scalping, Indian dances, burning at the stake, and so on. It is safe to say you never saw anything like it.

Express, Terre Haute, Indiana
October 10, 1873

Allow me to call to your attention two items that showed up in the local newspaper in Terre Haute, Indiana. The first is the advertisement that appeared on Wednesday, October 8, the day before we opened.

The Originals! Living Heroes!
Links between Civilization and Savagery.
BUFFALO BILL
(Hon. Wm. F. Cody)
Texas Jack!
(J.B. Omohundro)
Wild Bill!
(J.B. Hickok.)
Original Scouts of the Plains.
A Tribe of Wild Indians,
And Full Dramatic Company, in
FRED G. MAEDER'S

Thrilling Drama of Border Life,
BUFFALO BILL!
King of the Border Men.

    This advertisement went on to note the admission prices, 25¢ to 75¢, with reserved seats available at Button & Hamilton's Book Store, which struck me as a bit odd—not that they'd be selling theater tickets at a bookstore, but that William F. Cody and J.B. Hickok would have to rely on a bookstore for their livelihood. Cody often proudly declared to me, when my nose was buried in the latest Beadle & Adams offering, that he had never read a book from cover to cover, not even the ones written about him. Sometimes I don't even think he read much of the plays we kept reciting, either. Hickok allowed that he had read a few books, but couldn't remember the titles (I think he was pulling my leg, but can't be certain). Me? Well, being a former schoolteacher, I had read a score of books, mostly Dickens, Cooper, Dumas, and Colonel Buntline, and had even thought about writing one because I enjoyed doing my articles for *Spirit of the Times,* although my editor often suggested I try to get to the point a little quicker.

    Anyway, when Cody, in full glory, showed me this advertisement, I paused. I had never rightly considered myself a link between civilization and savagery, nor am I sure that the title of living hero applies to me, although, well, perhaps I had done some heroic things out on the border. Cody and Wild Bill, now, they were definitely heroes, and originals, but what struck me about those advertisements— the Terre Haute *Express* is just one example of many that Cody and Arizona John Burke placed during our travels—is the mention of 'A Tribe of Wild Indians'.

To be certain, back in the dawn of my acting career, Colonel Judson had tried to lay his hands on some Pawnee and Sioux braves, but the War Department and Indian agents frowned upon such notions, not to mention the Pawnees and Sioux themselves, therefore the wild Indians the colonel used in our Chicago opening were actors he found wandering along Blue Island Avenue, and ever since that time all the Indians were supes, who were not savage, nor red-skinned, nor had many of them ever seen an Indian at all, or, in the case of the actors we employed in Indiana, been west of the Wabash. These supes, as I have already explained to you, earned 25¢ per performance, but in Terre Haute one fellow would really earn his pay.

The play was going along splendidly that Thursday night, the packed house enjoying our link between civilization and savagery, but mostly our savagery. Buffalo Bill had crawled into that hollow log to take a nap. 'Don't do it!' someone shouted down from the balcony, and I figured he had seen the play before somewhere or had great insight into the ways of a melodramatic playwright, but Cody made his way into it and began snoring loud enough for everyone to savvy that he was asleep, and that's when twenty-eight Indians—$7 in our Combination's expenditures—in tan frocks and red flannel came out from the wings, muttering a blend of German and gibberish that supposedly passed for Pawnee or Cheyenne or Sioux, and one of the extras, the only one with a line said:

'Ugh. Me cold. Let us build heap big fire.'

The supes stopped chanting long enough to throw some imaginary kindling on their imaginary fire—only they never seemed to hear Cody's snores—before hefting the heavy log. I heard a lady in the front row gasp, and another pray for the Lord's deliverance, but most people just laughed. Between Maeder's and Robbins's plays, there must have been a scene where someone is almost burned at the stake, accidentally or on purpose, at least a half dozen times, but in all my years on the plains, while I have seen more than a few burned-out homesteads, and a party of Kiowas once set the prairie on fire while me and some bluecoats were chasing them back to Indian Territory, never have I found anyone, red or white, burned at the stake. In fact, it would take a ton of buffalo chips for the savages to burn anyone in Kansas or Nebraska because of the utter lack of wood.

I digress from my story, though. I did mention this fact to both Fred Maeder and Hiram Robbins, but they told me that folks in the East loved these kinds of affairs, so I said nothing further on the matter. But it did gall me, and it galled Wild Bill even more. Cody, well, he didn't mind it at all, even when he was about to be burned, which is what was about to happen in the scene I am describing again. Well, back to my story, the grunts and grimaces the supes made at that point in the melodrama were not acting, for unemployed Indiana actors are not accustomed to carrying a hollow log filled with two hundred pounds of plainsman, and they dropped it with a thud on the fake fire, and started dancing around the bonfire—to warm up, I imagine.

Someone in the audience shrieked at the plight of Buffalo Bill Cody, but then Wild Bill and I stepped from the opposite wings, and with my trusted lariat I looped a perfect cast and snagged the nearest Indian, pulled him closer, and knocked him out—I didn't really hit him, mind you—with the butt of my Smith & Wesson. Wild Bill was already shooting the supes dead with his Colts, and the band had started a lively number, clanging cymbals almost in time with the cheering and screaming.

Cody crawled out of the burning log that wasn't really burning, fired his Mississippi

Yeager rifle that misfired but no one noticed, not even the supe who pretended to be killed by the shot. After lowering the empty weapon, Cody then pulled his Cloverleafs in a most deliberate fashion, and between Cody's and Wild Bill's Colts and my Smith & Wesson, white smoke hung thick in the Opera House, and more actors fell dead or dropped to the floor in agonizing and exaggerated death throes.

That's when I heard a supe take the Lord's name in vain, and hop around, cursing Wild Bill for a fiend. Of course, I couldn't really understand him, him being a Dutchman, and I turned to see Wild Bill's six-shooters smoking. Wild Bill's lips turned into a sneer, but the Indian finally fell to the ground, and lay still. I understood what had happened. The supe had gotten too close and had been burned by the powder from Wild Bill's Colt. It had happened before, but this time the actor made the mistake of cursing Wild Bill, which one did not do to any border man. The powder burn had been an honest mistake, an accident.

Wild Bill strode over to the dead Indian, and shot him again—in his exposed leg, at close range—and the dead Indian turned into Lazarus, and leaped onto the stage, fell to the floor, holding his leg in agony, shouting words that I hoped the band's brass section kept the ladies and preachers in the crowd from hearing, because even a body who didn't understand German knew what that actor was saying, before limping off the stage and shouting at Arizona John Burke. The curtain closed after we had killed everyone, and we hurried off the stage to get ready for the next act.

The actor Wild Bill had given a bad powder burn kept up his hollering at Arizona John Burke, and Cody and I joined the conversation, although we couldn't understand what the man was saying because it was all in German, which probably explains why he was not getting hired by any combinations or repertoire shows and had to take a job with us for two bits to play an Indian.

'What's he saying?' Cody asked Arizona John Burke, who savvied the Dutchman's lingo. I only knew a couple of words.

'He says he's not paid enough to get shot like that, twice in one scene.'

A glance over my shoulder told me Wild Bill did not concern himself with the incident. He was pulling hard on the jug we had not emptied in an earlier scene.

'Tell him I'll speak to Jim,' Cody said, 'but he must not curse any of us again, even in German.'

Arizona John Burke grinned. 'The only English he knows is son-of-a-bitch and . . .'

'I heard him.' Cody suppressed a laugh, lest the Dutchman turn that wrath in his direction. 'That's all he needs to know. I've met Indians like that. Tell him I'll pay him an extra two bits for his trouble, but only if he behaves hisself. And I'll see that Jim Hickok behaves, too.'

After this was translated, the German bowed graciously at Cody, and said: *'Danke.'*

Cody shook the man's hand while whispering to me: 'What's the response to *danke?'*

'De nada,' I said.

'De nada,' Cody told him, and went to talk to Wild Bill as the stagehands pulled up the curtain, and the actors rushed to their cues.

The second item from the *Express* I want you to consider is a review that ran in the Friday edition. It was a right fine piece, mentioning all the scalpings, and praising Cody, Wild Bill, and me as 'three athletic and affable gentlemen, who, as scouts, have served their country nobly in years past; and not having been over-paid, (and those who serve their country best never are,) and wishing to travel through the States profitably, financially, and otherwise, they take this way of accomplishing their purpose.'

That is not the point, though, and I include it here just because it's the truth. What I call your attention to is this sentence: 'But shooting and scalping and the free use of the cheerful Bowie knife is not all there is of the play; there is a due amount of love making, and throughout it is intensely interesting.'

The reporter left out a lot of details—I

86

imagine Arizona John Burke paid a visit to the newspaper office to talk to the editor and reporter after our performance that night— and I think perhaps you might also find the 'love making' of that particular show 'intensely interesting'.

Late in the play, Buffalo Bill Cody pays a visit to an Irish girl named Kitty Muldoon whom he is sweet on, and tries to woo her into coming out to the plains with him.

'Don't do it!' someone yelled from the balcony, likely the same person who had been shouting down advice all during our engagement. 'You'll lose your lovely red hair!'

That cad was right about one thing. Rena Maeder had lovely red hair. In fact, everything about Rena Maeder was lovely, and Cody must have noticed her beauty because he put his hands on her waist, and pulled her close as he tried to entice her to join him on the border.

Later, when he had come to, Cody said he was just acting and didn't mean nothing by it.

Rena didn't see it that way. Her brother, Fred, who wrote the drama, and also played The Old Vet, an 1812 Pounder, decided it was none of his affair, but rewrote the scene in subsequent plays where it is Wild Bill who tries to lure Kitty Muldoon out West with him. Fred Maeder did that at the insistence of Cody and Arizona John Burke. In this particular scene from then on, Wild Bill always shoved his hands in his pockets.

Cody was still delivering his line, holding her tightly, and, when he pulled away to point at the mountains—a scene provided for all opera houses by the Buffalo Bill Combination's own Gaspard Maeder, belonging to the same Maeder family that produced Rena and Fred—Rena Maeder pulled a Cloverleaf Colt from Cody's sash and hit him with the little pistol as hard as she could. You could hear the *thunk!* way up in the balcony as the butt caught his noggin and the barrel slammed into his temple, and, when he collapsed, I thought he had been killed sure, and Rena hollered at his supine body that he had best keep his hands to himself, and the audience roared with laughter, and Arizona John Burke shouted: 'Close the curtain! Close the curtain! Close the gol-dern' curtain!'

The audience enjoyed it, likely thinking it was part of the play and quite funny as we often billed Rena Maeder in advertisements as 'The Charming Comedienne'.

The curtain closed, and Fred Maeder, J.V. Arlington, and I rushed onto the stage. Fred grabbed his sister, and J.V. and I hauled Cody backstage, and set him down on a buffalo robe.

Wild Bill came over to join us, as Jennie Fisher patted Cody's hands, and Arizona John Burke wondered if we should fetch a doctor.

'If Cody had been packing his Forty-Four Smith and Wesson,' Wild Bill said, 'you'd be fetching an undertaker.' Squatting beside

Cody, he held the open jug underneath Cody's mustache, and the smell of the forty-rod whiskey caused the leader of the Buffalo Bill Combination to squint and moan and move.

'Next time I shoot him in his bloody arse!' Rena Maeder announced, and by then whistling, cat-calling, and hollering came from our patrons, and Cody groaned: 'The show . . . the show . . . get back to work.'

Cody remained game, and he pulled himself to his feet as the curtain rose, staggered a bit, but steadied himself after a brace of whiskey from Wild Bill's jug, and, when it came time for him to go out there and kill more supes and save his sister from Colonel Jake McKandlass, played by Alfred Johnson, he did so. He never even reprimanded Rena Maeder, and did not forget to pay the German extra his bonus 25¢. Cody also continued to appear in Terre Haute, despite the ugly bruise on the side of his head.

What I did not remember until we were back in our hotel room was what Guiseppina had told me after Rena had knocked Cody unconscious: 'I should remember that . . . trick.'

I thought about asking her what she had meant now that I recollected it, but she was asleep, purring like a little old kitten, and she looked so pretty when she was asleep, I figured it would wait, and I'd just ask her about it over breakfast if I remembered to. I would have

gone to sleep, but it had become right noisy—I
didn't even know how Guiseppina managed to
get any shut-eye—on account that Cody,
having recovered from his close call with Rena
Maeder, had invited Jennie Fisher and some
other ladies to share a bottle of champagne he
had been given by the owner of our hotel.

I reckon I finally drifted off around four
o'clock, and didn't think to ask my wife about
her comment. The way things turned out, I
didn't need to ask her. I learned it myself
during our final performance in Terre Haute.

Chapter Eight

Buffalo Bill, the king of border men, the
dashing Texas Jack, and the great
plainsman, humble scout, and law-
preserver, Wild Bill, created a decided
sensation in the drama, and gave a
realistic rendition of scenes in the Western
wilds that called forth enthusiastic plaudits
from the entire assemblage.

Cleveland *Leader*
October 28, 1873

The more Wild Bill drank intoxicating liquors,
the more amorous he became with the
actresses in our plays, with the exception of
Rena Maeder, who no one ever bothered after

her little row with Cody. Jennie Fisher did not seem to mind Wild Bill's embraces or lengthy kisses, even when they were not called for in Fred Maeder's or Hiram Robbins's directions, but Esther Rubens kept shoving him away, and once even remarked that his breath smelled like a whiskey keg worse than had her first husband's—which it did, I mean smell like a whiskey keg, because I never met any of Esther's husbands. She said this loud enough that it caused the Indians filling Colerick's Opera House in Fort Wayne to applaud and hurrah.

By then the whole Combination was beginning to bore Wild Bill. He started shaking his head at all the burnings at stakes, and various Indian massacres, calling them 'shameless falsehoods', and no longer appreciated all that laughter. As I might have mentioned before, early on Wild Bill enjoyed the humorous condition of our plays, enjoyed making people laugh, and he had always certainly enjoyed a good joke, but he started thinking that these people coming to see our plays were not laughing *with* him, but *at* him, and you never laugh at a shootist. So, he drank more frequently and harder, and began wooing a number of our actresses. Which would have been fine, except the time in Terre Haute when he hugged Guiseppina a bit too tightly and a bit too long for her comfort, as well as mine. When she began wiggling and writing at his embrace, I stepped forward to pull him away, and he raised his hands as to offer no fight, and swept off his sombrero, addressing Guiseppina: 'My apologies, ma'am, but rare is your beauty, and you can dance with me anytime.'

There was nothing like that written in Mr. Robbins's play, but the audience loved it. If Arizona John Burke or Cody suggested they write that into the show as a permanent feature, the way they had done the whiskey/cold tea scene involving Wild Bill, I vowed to raise a furious objection. It never came up, however, and Wild Bill apologized afterward to both me and my wife, and swore that he would never do such a thing again.

He was a man of his word, too, until we played in Sandusky. Then I had to step in again. That was on October 25th. Wild Bill had been with us for just over six weeks. We had performed only eight shows since his Terre Haute dalliance with Guiseppina. I began to question the wisdom of staying in the acting business, and wondered if Wild Bill or I could last the season, not scheduled to end until next June. Cody had much on his mind, and I did not want to complain to him. Besides, what kind of husband would I be if I could not take care of my Guiseppina myself? It's not that Wild Bill struck fear into me, even though he had killed several men handy with guns—hundreds, if you believed the newspapers, novels, and Wild Bill himself when he was pulling a greenhorn's leg, but only forty or so when he was just plain lying. I figured the actual number totaled maybe fifteen or twenty, about fifteen or twenty more than I had sent to St. Peter's gate. But Wild Bill and I were pards, and I know he did not mean anything by his unwelcomed advances. It was just a potent mixture of Old Tanglefoot and Old Beelzebub.

Anyway, Cody had been nursing a broken rib since Indianapolis when a supe got too close to one of his Smith & Wesson .44s, Cody having replaced the Cloverleaf Colts on account they only held four rounds each and our public wanted more shooting on stage, and he had presented them to Arizona John Burke as a token of his friendship and appreciation but more on account that he was a right superstitious fellow and didn't want to see the damned things again after Rena Maeder practically cracked open his skull with one of them. Well, Cody had fired the Smith & Wesson right at the moment one of the actors playing a wild Indian walked into the path and got a powder burn across his left wrist, and he, the Indianapolis actor, hollered and, enraged even more than the Dutchman in Terre Haute, slammed his oaken war stick against Cody's exposed side, cracking a rib. Cody grimaced and cursed, but kept his feet, and slammed the Smith & Wesson against the supe's head, dropping him in a heap.

Roared Cody: 'Such abuse will I take from a redheaded Irish actress, but by thunder if I will from a mendicant I found in the Indianapolis gutter!'

The 500 souls filling Shakespeare Hall shouted with glee, even if I reckon many did not know what 'mendicant' meant. In fact, I had to look it up in Guiseppina's *Webster's Common School Dictionary,* and I warrant Cody had picked it up from Fred Maeder or some newspaper reporter. Anyway, the supe recovered and was paid an extra 25¢ for his headache.

Having been assured by Wild Bill that his hands would not embrace my bride's waist any more after the Sandusky affair, I decided to take necessary measures at Brainard's Opera House in Cleveland two nights later. In this particular scene, Guiseppina, as 'Pale Dove, a child of the forest', warns Wild Bill, Cody, and me of impending peril, that wild Indians are about to be on us, and we thank her, after she puts her hand on my shoulder, begging me to take flight and save myself. Cody and Wild Bill are only supposed to shake her hand, but Wild Bill had twice taken it upon himself to give her a fare-thee-well embrace. I was watching him with much suspicion for a third such attempt, and, before he could take my wife in his arms, I pulled my Smith & Wesson, and fired. Not at him, mind you. At the wings, stage left.

'Indians!' I screamed, and shot again.

The supes weren't supposed to come out, and the band did not know exactly what to do, but Hiram Robbins yelled at the Indians to charge on stage and die, and the musicians figured it out and started blaring 'Garry Owen' while Cody drew his .44 and started shooting. So did Wild Bill, as Guiseppina danced away, stage right.

'I wasn't gonna do nothing,' Wild Bill told me as he killed a couple of Indians.

I said: 'Well . . .'

Cody didn't say anything, but held his arm tightly against his busted-up side, biting his lip, and blasting away with his brace of .44s. The curtain closed after we had slain the last of the Cleveland supes. Only then did Cody collapse in a rocking chair and bend over laughing. He looked up at me, tears streaming down his face, and said: 'Jiminy crickets, Jack, don't do that again. I'm about to bust my other ribs laughin' so hard.'

He handed his big revolvers to a stagehand, who set about reloading them for our next scene, which reminds me of another story. This one happened a few nights later in Akron, Ohio. I figured it was a good idea, letting stagehands load our pistols between scenes, for we actors had enough to do already, and it worked fine when we opened at the highfalutin Academy of Music, filling all three and a half stories of that fancy brick building on October 29th. The next night, however, did not go so fine. Oh, we had another sold-out house. That wasn't the problem. We were performing *King of the Border Men,* but, because folks had so enjoyed my wife, Arizona John Burke had us toss in a scene from *Scouts of the Plains* to let the Akron ladies and gents see Guiseppina on stage some more, and I had no objections, because it was the scene where Pale Dove warns the scouts of the approaching Indians. She put her hand on my shoulder, her eyes full of love that came not from acting, and told me in that thick Italian accent as she always did: 'Fly toward the setting sun . . . and save thyself.'

I kissed her, spoke my bit of flapdoodle, and stepped back, allowing Cody and Wild Bill to thank her, and studied Wild Bill hard as he had that look in his eye and gripped the butt of my .44, waiting. When it looked like he was about to pounce on her, I drew the revolver as I had done in Cleveland, and fired a round.

'Indians!' I shouted, thumbing back the hammer.

'Oh, the devil . . . ,' Cody said underneath his breath.

Akron performers ran out to meet their deaths, and Wild Bill, howling like a coyote, drew his Navy Colts. White smoke filled the building.

I knew something was wrong with my Smith & Wesson, something did not feel right, because, although I am more comfortable with a rifle or shotgun, I am well acquainted with revolvers. When I fired again, I put on a really good show. All the remaining five rounds went off, showering the stage, supes, front row, and myself with sparks. I dropped the hot revolver and yelped. Everyone from the second row on up to the balcony laughed, hurrahed, and applauded.

The scene, of course, had to go on, and the Akron crowd did not know anything had gone wrong, thinking my fireworks exhibition as just part of the show, and they just hollered and begged for us to keep on killing the Indians, although I decided some of the paying customers knew the supes by name because they yelled things like:

'Kill Preston, Cody! Shoot him again!'

'Look out, Wild Bill, or Joey Bryant will knife you in the back!'

'Stab my brother, Texas Jack. Stab Robbie and take his scalp!'

This last shout was directed at me because I had drawn a knife and had engaged myself with a supe in mortal, hand-to-hand combat as my Smith & Wesson lay smoking on the floor. My fingers ached, some covered with melted wax that took off the hair on my knuckles, and I felt for those actors we had accidentally or on purpose given powder burns, but I managed to carry on and pretend to stab in the breast the supe named Robbie, who looked ashen as a

97

dead man and frightened almost to death that I really would kill him and lift his hair.

The curtain dropped, and I picked up my .44, examined it and my right hand closely before making a beeline toward the stagehand who had loaded my revolver.

'Are you trying to get me killed?' I demanded, and shoved him, a boy of no more than sixteen, against the wall, practically mad enough to plow up Market and Main streets with his face. 'You're supposed to use paraffin in each cartridge! This gun's covered in melted wax! What did you use, you blasted idiot?'

'C-c-c-candle grease,' the fellow stammered.

'Candle grease!' I shook my head. The first round had melted the candle topping, and the second shot had caused all the wax in the cylinder to melt and spark, setting off every unfired chamber. 'Candle grease!' I repeated.

'It was a right pretty show,' Wild Bill said from his corner. 'Thought it was the Fourth of July.'

I give him a snarl, and released the boy. 'Don't you know the difference between candle wax and paraffin?' As dumb as these Yankees were in the ways of firearms, I wondered how we had lost the war.

'Y-yes . . . yes s-sir,' came his response, 'but he said it would be all right.'

'Who?'

Criminy, I knew who before I heard the answer.

'Him . . . M-m-mister H-Hickok.'

Well, that also got Cody to laughing and wheezing one more time, pleading with us to stop with the capers lest he break all of his ribs.

'I might break them all for you,' I said, but Cody howled even harder, and pretty soon everyone backstage began cackling, except me and my wife and the boy who had mistakenly loaded and damned near ruined my favorite revolver.

The show went on, though, as Will Cody always seemed to make it do, and we closed our two-night engagement and left Ohio, heading East again until the train reached New Castle, Pennsylvania.

In this part of the country, it became hard for Arizona John Burke or Cody to round up men to dress up as Indians and be killed several times a night. Towns were smaller—not Nebraska or Kansas small, but not New York City, and, while much of the East was smarting because of the Panic, here work could be found in the oil fields, factories, and canals, which is where all the actors had gone to. I thought these Pennsylvanians might take exception that we killed only six or seven savages, but they liked it all nonetheless, especially when Wild Bill shot a 'dead' Indian in the knee or ankle, giving him a burn that set him screaming. My Smith & Wesson worked fine for this performance, and Wild Bill did not molest my bride at all, having gotten his fun by shooting a supe.

The fun of Wild Bill's antics had worn straight through Cody's nerves, though. Cody grew sick of hearing the complaints, and even sicker of having to pay a supe an extra 25¢ in goodwill. Right before *Scouts of the Plains* opened in Meadville for one performance only a few nights later, Cody addressed Wild Bill: 'Jim, this is a special performance for a special audience. None of your shenanigans, all right?'

'Who are we playing for?' Wild Bill asked. 'President Grant?'

A one-armed man rigged out in our Indian costume answered: 'Students of the Meadville Theological School. It was founded by Harm Jan Huidekoper.' He sounded right proud.

Wild Bill snorted, and I almost did myself, but the one-armed man's face got all red, and redder when Wild Bill added: 'If someone saddled me with a handle like Harm Jan Hooo-hell, reckon I'd become an atheist instead of a Bible-banger.'

'Sir, Harm Jan Huidekoper was my grandfather.'

'Jim,' Cody cut in, 'this is General Shippen of the Pennsylvania National Guard. He's playin' one of our Indians, free of charge, as a special request of the students of the Meadville Theological School.'

'An honor,' Wild Bill said. 'I'd shake your hand, but . . .' He nodded at the pinned-up right sleeve.

That, quite naturally, only turned General Shippen's face even more crimson. I expected the man to keel over right there of apoplexy or challenge Wild Bill to a go at bare-knuckles boxing. 'I lost this arm at Gettysburg, sir.'

Well, Cody started getting a mite red in the face himself, fearing that General Shippen and his ten little Indians would walk out, along with half the audience filling Meadville's tiny Opera House, but Wild Bill laughed it all off, and patted General Shippen's shoulder.

'Just funning, General. I'm a Yank myself. So's Cody.' He hooked a thumb toward me and lowered his voice, but he knew I could hear him anyway. 'It's him that you must watch, sir. He's a Secesh, and unreconstructed.' The general stormed off to the other supes, but he appeared not to be leaving the theater, and Cody relaxed.

'Don't worry, Cody,' Wild Bill said. 'I won't put the fear of God into our God-fearing public tonight.'

He didn't, either. He simply mumbled his lines as he always did, barely loud enough for anyone to hear, fired his Colts, and never questioned the wisdom of sending a bunch of young theologians to witness such a sordid melodrama as ours. After the show, which delighted everyone in Meadville, we headed for the depot to board the next train to Titusville, but before we got on, Arizona John

Burke, looking about as grim as General Shippen, handed Cody a telegram.

'What is it?' I asked while Cody read.

'The manager of the Parshall Opera House,' Cody said. 'Just a warnin'. Some rough and ready men from the oil fields are in Titusville, itchin' for a fight.'

'Who do they want to fight?' I asked.

'Us, Jack, us!' Cody shook his head. He had gotten to be in poor humor the past few days.

'I was just funning you, Will,' I said, and Cody balled up the telegram and tossed it underneath the nearest car. He was staring past me, and, when I turned, I saw he was looking at Wild Bill.

'I say we oblige 'em,' Wild Bill said. 'Wipe 'em out.'

'By my boots and socks, Jim, this is serious business!' Cody had had enough. 'You're makin' a right smart of money. We all are. You're not on the border any more, pard. We're east of the border, and we have to behave ourselves. It's different here. People are civilized, so start actin' civilized till we're finished with this season. That's all I'm askin' of you. That means keep your hands off Josephine, and stop shootin' our Indians at close range, burnin' 'em apurpose. I mean it, Jim. I'm askin' you as a pard. Will you behave yourself?'

'I promise,' Wild Bill said with a sad-dog look before he boarded the smoking car.

I doubt if Cody believed him. As for me, hell, I had done stopped talking to Wild Bill already.

ACT II

Hickok

Chapter Nine

Wild Bill, Mr. J.B. Hickok, is also very handsome, but no actor at all. His part seems to be to do the bloody work and say as little as possible.

Daily Press, Lexington, Kentucky
September 30, 1873

'Fear not, fair maid! By heavens, you are safe with Wild Bill, who is ever ready to risk his life and die, if need be, in defense of weak and defenseless womanhood!'

That's the shit I had to say, so, hell, the only way I could get through play acting was to be roostered. Two reasons made me join the Buffalo Bill Combination: I had lost my stake playing poker in Topeka, and I needed a change. Everything from Mennonites to unreconstructed Rebs, mostly Texicans, had started crowding up the West, and I reckon about nine-tenths of the latter wanted me dead. It got to be where I had to sit with my back to the door in every groggery or gambling parlor. I couldn't even walk down a street in broad daylight, had to hug buildings along the boardwalks so tightly that, if the walls had been freshly painted, my sleeves would likewise get whitewashed. My eyes burned half the time so that I could hardly see the hand in front of my face. After marshaling in Abilene and killing a damned fool deputy, no town wanted me for a lawman. Truthfully I didn't want to wear a star again, become a target for every drunken fool with a six-shooter, and after a bloody row with some 7th Cavalry fools over at Hays, no officers desired me as a scout. Don't matter. I didn't care much for that job, either. My right thigh still throbbed at night after a dog soldier had tried to tear it off with a lance, and my back ached considerably from too many days in the saddle. *Sans* marshaling and scouting left only gambling, but the cards turned colder than a February norther.

Luck had shied away from me. Don't blame her none. I felt like Methuselah, and I ain't but thirty-six. Maybe I had been out West too long, having left Illinois for Kansas back in 1856, fighting one war to preserve the Union, and other wars to put Indians on reservations or make drovers and cardsharpers respect law and order. Bone-tired, half-blind, with no woman excepting some rawhide whore who'd slit your throat or pick your pocket if you weren't careful. It was no life for a plainsman, not any more. Play acting looked good, I told myself, but I knew it was a mistake even when Cody kept promising we'd all make our piles.

We were pards, Cody, Jack, and me. That's why I floated my stick with them. Fred G. Maeder, Esquire, and Hiram Robbins, however, weren't any better than Ned Buntline with all their shameless falsehoods. They always called us 'scouts' and 'trappers', and, while I had scouted, as had Cody and Jack, none of us had ever done any trapping to speak of. Texas Jack had suggested they call him a cowboy and scout because he had cowboyed a lot—how he came to be so handy with that lariat—but Arizona John Burke slammed the door.

'No, no, no, Jack,' he had told him. 'No one in the East knows what a cowboy is, and they never will. The cowboy will never be a hero to Easterners the way a scout or trapper is.'

Reckon he had a point, and I sure didn't want to glorify drovers when half of them weren't worth spit, Jack Omohundro being an exception. I like Jack, like his wife, and never meant anything by giving her a squeeze or a kiss in *Scouts of the Plains*. That was just to rile Jack, add a little fun to those miserable nights and matinees. That's what I was looking for: FUN. Life on the border hadn't been fun the past year or two, and I needed to laugh. What I should have recollected before I sent off that telegram to Cody was my previous experience in a similar Eastern enterprise. Cody's claim that he was the first fellow to bring the West to the East is bogus. Months before he had joined that lying rapscallion Ned Buntline, I had been engaged in a similar damned fool venture.

Colonel Sidney Barnett had rounded me up in the summer of 1872. I didn't know Barnett from Adam's house cat, but the wad of greenbacks he flashed in my face at Cotton's Beer Garden in Kansas City commanded my attention. The colonel's pap was Thomas Barnett. The colonel had said this as if it were a letter of introduction from General Samuel Curtis, but Thomas Barnett meant nothing to me. The elder Barnett owned a museum on the Canadian side of Niagara Falls, and Colonel Barnett planned on staging a true-to-life buffalo hunt and Western exhibition to lure tourists from the American side of the spectacular waterfalls.

'I see,' I said, but I didn't.

Buffalo, the colonel explained, were being shipped by rail to Ontario at that very moment, along with Texas longhorns, Mexican *vaqueros,* and Sac and Fox Indians. The Barnetts would put on a grand show, bringing in tourists by the thousands (children admitted free).

'I see,' I said, but I still didn't.

'That's where you come in,' the colonel went on.

'Uhn-huh.'

'You're our master of ceremonies. You'll introduce what is happening, tell a few stories about yourself, maybe give a display of your prowess with your revolvers. A man of your reputation, why, Mister Hickok, you'll be an even bigger attraction than the buffalo and Indians. I'm also thinking of staging a lacrosse match between Cayuga and Tuscarora Indians.'

'I see.' Hell, I didn't know what lacrosse was, not to mention Cayuga or Tuscarora Indians.

'I'm willing to offer you a railroad pass to Niagara Falls and a contract that will pay you one thousand dollars, two hundred dollars upon signing and the balance after the two-day show.'

That I saw clearly, and quickly signed the deal.

*　　　*　　　*

If anyone can put on a Western exhibition successfully, he's a better man than me. I did get to see Niagara Falls, which is spectacular, but the 'Grand Buffalo Hunt' (as the Canadians called it) did not amount to much. Horn tooters and drum beaters of the 44th Regiment from St. Catharine's played music at one end of the arena till the Barnetts turned loose the buffalo. Then the entire band scrambled and fled for safety, escaping unharmed, except for a trumpet that got flattened by a bull buff. The Sac and Fox Indians rode after the herd, shooting arrows

111

that had been blunted for safety measures. Soon the Indians became bored with the whole affair, so the *vaqueros* charged out with their lassos, and tried roping the buffalo. Only one of them got hurt, a broken leg, I think. I'm referring to the Mexicans. The buffalo were all healthy, last time I saw them. They broke through the fence, and did considerable damage in the residential part of town. The *vaqueros* finally quit the chase after the buffalo disappeared in the woods.

Oh, yeah, I didn't mention the bear and the monkey, mainly because I didn't know about the bear and the monkey till I was in Canada. The Barnetts had added a bear and a monkey to the show, the bear in a cage that advertised the Barnett museum, and the monkey on a rope held by a Tuscarora Indian wearing his lacrosse uniform. The monkey broke free, or the Tuscarora set him loose, and that smelly bastard started throwing everything—corn, trash, buffalo dung—at the crowd, which wasn't much of a crowd, maybe fifty or sixty men, women, and children.

About that time a twelve-year-old boy opened the bear cage, and that big old cinnamon sow headed straight for this gent cooking and selling Italian sausage. The puny little vender and his vendees disappeared like the buffalo while the cinnamon destroyed the cart and cook fire, and ate about everything. The Mexicans, who returned a few minutes later, roped the sow and eventually managed to get the bear back in her cage, but no one ever caught the monkey. That was pretty much it. Most of the crowd left, and that was a shame because that lacrosse match between the Tuscaroras and the Cayugas turned out to be pretty good. The Tuscaroras won; I forget the score.

There was no show the second day. Nobody came, except the *vaqueros,* me, and the Indians, except the Cayugas. They had gone, mad, I heard, about the lacrosse score. The Tuscaroras left a short while later.

Naturally Colonel Barnett and his pap went the way of the buffalo and monkey when I tried to collect the rest of my money. I gave up after a while, tired of the whole thing, had a dirty Italian sausage the bear had missed for supper, and went to bed. The next day I learned the Barnetts were held in jail, but when I explained my plight to the constable, he just shook his head. He told me I'd have to wait in line, and, being an American, it was doubtful I'd get any money from the Barnetts because he doubted the Barnetts would have anything left after the law and citizens of Ontario got through with them.

I wasn't about to beg, and Canadians ain't worth killing, so that afternoon the Sac and Foxes, *vaqueros,* and I stole aboard a freight train, and made it to Buffalo, New York where we eventually parted ways. The Mexicans, I

113

guess, made it back to Mexico, the Indians to Indian Territory, and me to Kansas, sick of the whole affair. The Italian sausage wasn't bad. I don't know what happened to the longhorn cattle that were supposed to have been there. I heard the Barnetts had to sell their museum. I'll never go back to Canada as long as I live.

*   *   *

Cody, Texas Jack, and Buntline, however, made a lot of money play acting in opera houses, and I dreamed that maybe things would turn out better as there were no bears, monkeys, buffalo, and Barnetts associated with American stage productions. That's what I told myself when I left Topeka for New York in late summer, 1873.

The first time I saw Cody and Texas Jack on stage, they looked like haunts. The limelight shining on those two made them glow. Damnedest thing I ever seen, and the damnedest thing I ever heard were the words they said. People don't talk like that on the frontier. They don't talk like that anywhere, and it embarrassed me when I had to step in front of hundreds or even thousands of folks, and drivel. Cody and Burke kept urging me to speak louder, but I couldn't make myself do it. Two weeks of train travel and cramped cities had me longing for the plains, but I had told Cody I would give him one year and wanted to keep my word. To fight boredom and embarrassment, I went about making things a little more fun. First thing I tried was kissing Jennie Fisher, but I took the joke when she rammed her tongue down my throat, practically to my stomach, and I about choked. Then I fooled around with Texas Jack's wife. Mostly, though, I just gave some idiot playing an Indian a powder burn to remember me by. A supe would be lying still, eyes shut, breath held, and I'd shoot him in his leg, just so the blast from my Navy's muzzle would make him dance and holler. I liked it immensely, but it irked Cody and Burke more than my hugs had festered Texas Jack and Josephine.

Which brings my story to Titusville, Pennsylvania, a town that stunk of oil and oil men. The proprietor of the Abbott House, a pasty, sweaty little gent named Mathews, approached us as we registered and politely—or, shall I say, *cowardly*—expressed the same concerns as the dude at the Parshall Opera House.

'Over there is our billiard room, and I beg you to stay out of it, at least tonight.' Mr. Mathews dabbed his forehead with an already sopping-wet handkerchief.

'What is this?' Texas Jack demanded. 'You let us rooms, but deny us a game of billiards?'

'Please, you are heroes to our entire nation,' the gent said, and I rolled my eyes. 'I say this because I fear for your safety. Several vermin

115

are in from the oil fields, and quite in their cups. All night they have been drinking Demon Rum, bragging that they will wipe out the famous scouts.'

'Then, by Gawd, let us start the ball!' I said, and started for the room, but Cody, ever the peacemaker, put his hand on my shoulder.

'Old chum, 'tis not the way in these parts.' Cody sounded like he did when he was treading the boards. 'We must abide the landlord's wishes.' He spoke next to the nervous proprietor. 'You have my word, sir, that we will avoid any confrontation. There is nothin' to be got from violence but more violence.'

'Thank you!' Mr. Mathews boomed. 'Thank you kindly. I hope you enjoy your stay in Titusville.'

'We shall,' Cody said, and I nodded in agreement, signed the register, and carried my grip to my room.

Hell, I was going to have a rollicking good time. There's something about fisticuffs, and I longed for one friendly fight. As a peace officer in Abilene and Hays, there was nothing friendly about fights. My predecessor, Tom Smith, never held much truck with pistols, preferring his iron fists, but that's why he was my predecessor because he got his head chopped almost clean off trying to serve a murder warrant. Nice fellow, Tom Smith, but dumber than a Texas drover. I would have shot the sons-of-bitches dead before they even twitched. East of the border, however, in civilized states like Pennsylvania, men didn't carry axes, pistols, or Bowie knives, so I was none too feared for my safety. Fighting oil workers sounded like a fine frolic.

After being warned by the manager of the Parshall Opera House and the Titusville hotel owner of these hard rocks wanting to waylay us, Cody, Texas Jack, and I promised to behave ourselves. We'd go through the side entrances to the hotel and theater, keep out of sight. Mind you, Cody and Texas Jack ain't yellow—far from it—but they were turning into paper-collar men. They'd spent too long in the East, forgotten their true roots. They didn't want to stir up trouble with the locals, wanted things to stay peaceable so they could keep earning tidy profits. I had a much better idea.

Chapter Ten

The boys—Buffalo Bill, Texas Jack, and
Wild Bill—are as lively as crickets, killing
everything right and left. The galleries
enjoy the wholesale slaughter, and only
seemed to regret that they couldn't take a
hand in the tussle. If the company would
just elect a coroner, we think it would
make the combination complete.

Courier-Journal, Louisville, Kentucky
October 4, 1873

Another thing I disliked about play acting was
our costumes. Cody and Texas Jack preferred
buckskins with fancy embroidery, but, if you
were to inquire about my impressions, those
outfits made them look like painted-up whores
from the Devil's Addition. Don't get me
wrong. Buckskins are fine on the prairie. I'd
wear them and duck pants when scouting, but
they were greasy, smelly duds as earthy as
Kansas sod—not loaded down with beads and
porcupine quills that turned deerskin heavier
than Sir Lancelot's chain mail. As soon as I'd
finished scouting and immediately before I'd
perched myself in front of a deck of Lawrence
and Cohen playing cards, those buckskins and
duck pants would be set afire. Reckon you
could call me fashionable.

One thing I did like about the East, especially as I was making good money with the Combination. The tailors, emporiums, and gentlemen's shops could outfit a fashionable gent, and most of those businessmen certainly desired the business of J.B. Hickok. I smoked a cigar while taking a hot bath in my room in the Abbott House, toweled myself dry, and got dressed after tossing my cigar, now only a stub, and towel into the bath water, just to be ornery. I wore black striped trousers of the finest wool, which I stuck into my fanciest pair of Kansas-made boots, electing not to wear city shoes on this joyous occasion. Besides, you can't put spurs on Bloomingdale alligator operas, and I wanted to show off my Kansas City pair with the jinglebobs. I donned a white silk shirt with Myrtle collar and diamond-studded cufflinks and buttons—all presented to me by the owners of Modory's & Serur's Gentlemen's Clothing store in Indianapolis, dealers of nonpareil shirts and accouterments, or so said their sign. To this I added a brocade vest the color of a fine burgundy wine, black handkerchief tucked into the pocket that didn't hold my gold Waltham repeater watch. A black silk Windsor tie, tooled leather suspenders, red silk sash, white Boss of the Plains, and tight-fitting kid gloves concluded my outfit, along with a pair of .41-caliber Williamson Derringers I dropped into the inside pockets of my black Prince Albert. I didn't think I'd have need of the Derringers, but I have always been a cautious, fashionable fellow.

After perfuming my hair with a bottle of tonic I had purchased at a Fort Wayne tonsorial parlor, I waxed and combed my mustache, fired up another cigar, and headed downstairs. The lobby clock chimed three-quarters past midnight.

Thick smoke clouded the billiard room, which reeked of tobacco, sweat, whiskey, and drunken men. I could barely make out the mirror or cherry backbar as I hooked a boot on the brass foot rail and ordered a gin and bitters. Behind me came the curses of men, laughter, the crack of billiard balls. As Titusville, Pennsylvania was not much of a town, the billiard room was not much, either, just a low pit with an even lower clientele. The mustached bartender watched as I sipped my drink, practically all gin and no bitters. I smiled, enjoying myself. Unlike on the stage, here I felt at home.

'Well, I'll be good and damned,' a nasal voice sounded behind me. 'Boys, we got company.'

I turned around, setting my empty glass on the bar. No one asked if I cared for another round.

'Hello, Buffalo Bill,' said a red-bearded man with a face dirtier than a coal miner's. 'We've been looking all day for you.'

Eight men stopped their drinking and billiard games to take a stand on either side of the tough. All were big men, the smallest of them about the size of Cody, and he's only a hair under six foot one. The largest of them towered over me, and I'm taller than Cody. A chair scratched the floor, and on came another one, ready to join the crowd, I thought, but he stopped only briefly, looked me in the eye, then trotted for the lobby.

'Where you goin', Karl?' asked a black-bearded Irishman with fewer teeth than brains.

'*Ach!* His eyes,' came the reply.

The barkeep cleared his throat and followed the quick-footed Dutchman. That left the billiard room to me and these gents.

As soon as the door had shut behind them, everyone stared into my pale blue eyes, but I just stood at ease, sizing up my prey. My eyes burned from all the smoke, but I didn't blink, lest they not get a good idea of what they were up against. One fellow wised up, and hurried out despite catcalls and curses from his friends. The rest strained to make out my eyes through all that smoke.

I knew what the Dutchman, barkeep, and other roustabout had seen. Even Will Cody had remarked that just before a fight, either with guns or fists, you could see the fires of perdition in my eyes. But I said casually: 'They're blue.'

'Right pretty, too,' some fool said, and that

even took me by surprise. 'Almost transparent.'

'Shut up, you . . .!' the Irishman snapped. (Whereas the Irishman finished the sentence, I have chosen not to, by the way.) Someone sniggered, and all went quiet for a few ticks of the clock.

Then the red-beard: 'I asked you a damned question, Buffalo Bill. Where you been?'

'My name is not Buffalo Bill,' I said calmly. 'You are mistaken in the man.'

I tossed a silver dollar on the bar, and walked easily toward the billiard tables as if a game interested me. I put my hands on the back of a chair, waiting with anticipation.

The red-beard led his entourage after me. 'Don't turn your back on me, Buffalo Bill.'

I kept my back turned. 'As I said, you are mistaken.'

'You are a damned liar!' he shouted.

Eight oil men, every one of them a bruiser, against me, but, since this was a game of billiards, and I was challenged, I got to break. When I turned, the chair came with me, and I lifted it and swung before those rowdies knew they were overmatched. The chair busted the red-beard's head, knocked out the Irishman's remaining teeth, and scattered three more gents before turning into kindling. Quickly I replaced the chair with a billiard cue, whacking it across a barrel-chested fellow's nose. One piece of the cue went sailing to the backbar, but did not break anything. The barrel-chest

122

dropped to his knees, holding his nose in both hands, but not the pouring blood. I jammed the remnants of my cue stick into a blond-mustached man's stomach, then tried to shove the cue down his ear, but it bounced out of my hand as he fell onto a table, which overturned. I let loose with a Johnny Reb yell even though I am a Yankee by birth and temperament. This being Pennsylvania, I figured a Rebel war cry might rouse up those boys to putting up a better fight.

Perhaps it did, for my nose stung, and I tasted blood. Someone had hit me, but I did not know who. It didn't matter. It just made me happy. Still, I retreated, overturning a chair to trip up anyone close, and took refuge behind a billiard table. My closest pursuer probably wished he had been toppled by the chair because the red ball I rifled dented his forehead. He leaned against the table for support, stared at me briefly before his eyes rolled up in his head, and a pair of cue balls stared back at me before he dropped on the floor. I wanted to shout out something witty—like 'Anyone for a game of American Four-Ball?' or 'You boys should stick to snooker!'—or send a guy sailing onto a nearby table and have his head break the stacked balls. That's the way a numskull like Ned Buntline would have written this, but in a fight, even a friendly one such as this, you do not have time for such Homeric sentences or dance routines. This is

Wild Bill in a brawl, not Josephine Morlacchi dancing the sortita. I did straight-rail a couple of gents, caromed a few shots, and scratched three or four times, but I didn't have a chance to say anything. Those boys kept me busy.

You probably think my story is growing a tad tall. How can one man whup eight? Let me take a break from this bloody spectacle to explain my advantage. You see, I had taken a few unsuspecting boys out of the game with my handy chair, not to mention cue sticks and billiard balls. Luckily the table I had used to fort up behind had been set up for a game of the relatively new American fifteen-ball pool and not four- or three-ball. Not only that, but while I considered this a friendly fight, Pennsylvanians had a different viewpoint.

A tall fellow with hands the size of hams wailed after I introduced my knee to his crotch: 'Damn . . . you . . . Buffalo Bill . . . you ain't . . . fightin' fair!'

'These are Western rules,' I said, 'and I told you . . . I ain't Buffalo Bill.' My knee made his head's acquaintance, and he joined the parade of boys on the floor.

Besides, it wasn't like they weren't getting their shots. One boy busted a cue stick over my head—I don't know when or where I lost my Stetson in the little row—and that hurt. Someone had stomped on my right foot, and then tried to pull my hair from behind, but he paid for that error. When I kicked him in his

124

shins with my boot heel, he cried out like a stuck pig. I had forgotten I was wearing spurs.

So, the Pennsylvanians got in their licks. The outside pockets of my Prince Albert had been torn, and the buttons ripped off my vest. I made sure my Waltham repeater was all right when I stopped to catch my breath. A couple of knuckles were jammed, and all were scuffed and swollen, despite my kid gloves. My nose still trickled blood. My lips had been split.

The last man still fighting threw a bottle of bourbon at me, but missed, and I pounced on him like a catamount, slapped him a time or two, maybe thirty, banged his head against the bar, drug him across the floor, and threw him over the battlefield. He landed with a thud, giving a pocketless billiard table a pocket. This, by the way, was the guy about my height, but he weighed about as much as a plug of tobacco. Don't know how he kept a job in those oil fields down south.

By then the commotion from the lobby drowned out the moans and groans from the billiard room. As I did not want to wind up in the Titusville jail, I buried my fist into the red-beard's noggin—he was still kneeling on the floor, hadn't moved since I bashed that chair across his face—and he sank into slumber. I found my hat under one slippery roughneck, dusted it off, drained a mug of stout that had survived the affair, and left $10 for the barkeep or whoever had to clean up this mess.

I opened the door, stepped into the lobby, and put on my hat, whistling 'Tenting Tonight'. Quite a turnout greeted me—the hotel owner, a gent whose name I had already forgotten, sweating more than the boys I had left behind in a heap; some gentlemen hotel guests, one in his nightshirt; two women, fully clothed; a couple of clerks not old enough to go into a billiard room; and my old pard, William F. Cody.

No Titusville law. Cody had probably stopped our landlord from summoning the authorities. Bully for him. I stopped whistling—'Tenting Tonight' is Cody's favorite tune—long enough to wipe the blood off my face with a handkerchief. Hooking a thumb at the closed door, I explained: 'I've been interviewing that party . . . the ones that wanted to clean us out.'

Cody didn't look to be in a jocular mood, but I suspected I could chisel off that granite false front. 'I thought you promised . . . ,' he began.

I shrugged, and headed him off. 'Aw,' I said, 'I tried to follow that trail, Billy, but got lost among the cañons, ran into some hostiles.' To me, that sounded like something Maeder or Robbins would have us say, only they would dress it up with a lot more flowers and sauce. 'You always were better at following a trail than me.' This, I said loud enough for our audience to hear. Arizona John Burke would

126

have been right proud of me seeing how I never spoke—*enunciate,* he kept telling me—loud enough in our plays. Billy Cody wasn't as vainglorious as some people make out, but the Lord had blessed him with a good dose of haughtiness, and I thought that compliment might make him happier, or at least tolerate my behavior. 'But all is right now,' I added, spitting out blood that caused one of the women to gasp but the other to grin and give me a suggestive wink. I began to have a better impression of Titusville, Pennsylvania. 'See you in the morn, pard.'

I meant what I said. Cody could do a better job tracking than me on my best day, but he never played poker worth a tinker's damn. Didn't know the meaning of the word bluff. He fought that smile, but the smile whupped him in a moment. Deep down, I think Cody envied me. Like I've told you, neither him nor Texas Jack ever showed yellow, and Cody would have loved a sporting chance at laying a ton of bruises on those Titusville bruisers himself. I'm not sure he would have won that fight as his fisticuffs morality differed from mine—he had never been a lawman except for a time or two when I hired him to help escort prisoners—but each and every one of those rowdies would have been begging for water after the spat.

I told a clerk I desired another hot bath, repeated my room number loud enough for

127

the lady who grinned to hear, and, before I wandered upstairs, I gripped our landlord's shoulder, and waited for him to lift his sweat-glazed face and look me in the eye. He did, ever so timidly, and I gave as fine a smile as my busted lips could manage.

'Those the fellows who were looking for us?'

His head bobbed ever so slightly.

'They've found us.'

I was whistling 'Tenting Tonight' as I went to my room, and whistled it while taking another hot bath that night, or rather, morning, but started a bawdier tune when I heard a discreet tapping at my door.

Although he had been upstairs snoring like a lumberjack, a week or so later Hiram Robbins described the fight this way to a reporter from the Buffalo *Daily Courier:* 'Wild Bill is a gentlemen, but if provoked can turn as savage as a meat axe. Just ask any Titusville b'hoys who assaulted him. Twenty of them, against him, unarmed. Why, they didn't even cut his lip bad enough to stop him from whistling.'

Now, if Mr. Hiram Robbins or Fred G. Maeder had written more lines like that, I might have taken more of a liking to being a Thespian.

Chapter Eleven

The *Scouts of the Plains,* the enlivening drama that is now holding the boards here, is drawing large and enthusiastic audiences. Buffalo Bill, Wild Bill, Texas Jack, and the other scouts, each take their number of scalps every night, and a fair number of Indians are slain, and people in danger, rescued. *M'lle* Morlacchi's beautiful dancing forms no small feature of the entertainment.

Pittsburgh *Gazette*
November 20, 1873

The *Morning Herald* contained no mention of my skirmish with the roughnecks, a disappointment to Arizona John Burke, who had slept through the match. He thought the publicity would have guaranteed a sold-out performance, and thereby asked me to let him know the next time I planned to go brawling. What a saphead. We didn't need any publicity. I couldn't recall us ever not turning away paying customers, and Titusville proved no different. A crowd of enthusiastic ladies and gentlemen filled the Parshall Opera House. Even a score of oil men, who had overcome their fear of lye soap and hot water, put on their best bib and tucker, and paid 35¢ to see us living legends. None tried to clean us out, and I never again saw any of the rowdies who had entertained me so at the Abbott House.

Rebecca Gentry, the lady who had grinned and not gasped, had cleaned up my cuts and bruises, but she couldn't do much for my lips, which remained busted and ugly when I stepped into those blinding calcium lights. Slinging the dung I had to say seemed even more painful, and I kept messing up my lines. None of that mattered to me, and I don't think it bothered Cody or Texas Jack, for even as professional as they were, they botched their banter oftener than I did. Despite the pain, I felt happier than a pig in a poke, especially when the supes ran on stage to meet their deaths, and even more so when Josephine Morlacchi brought out that jug of whiskey. I had just spit out the cold tea, with a bit of blood, and shouted for the umpteenth time: 'Cold tea don't count! Either I get real whiskey or I ain't telling no story!'

The denizens of Titusville laughed like madmen, and Cody lifted his head and pleaded for someone to bring out a jug of Taos lightning. Josephine danced out, and everyone applauded as she waltzed with that brown jug, which she handed me. She pirouetted, and, before I took a swig, I slapped her fanny.

That's when Texas Jack knocked me off the fake log with the butt of his rifle. 'Damn you, J.B.!' he shouted. 'Stop funning with

Guiseppina!' She didn't seem to mind—never breaking character, Burke would say—as she fluttered and flew toward a wing. Titusville hollered and laughed. Cody helped me up.

'Wild Bill! Wild Bill! Wild Bill!'

The chant went on for minutes, and my fellow actors just stared in wonderment. I don't know if the crowd had heard about my brawl, or if they just enjoyed my consorting with Josephine Morlacchi that way. When the roar died down, I shook my head. I hadn't even had a sip of whiskey, unless you count the bracer I had that morning with Rebecca, or the three rounds I had before the curtain rose that night.

'Boy,' I said, 'this acting is as easy as rolling off a log.'

Our audience laughed again, and I took a sip, the whiskey burning my lips, before passing the jug to Texas Jack. 'Here,' I said, 'so there's no hard feelings between us pards.'

Texas Jack looked like he needed that rye more than me, and I warrant Cody needed it even worse. After we had passed it around three more times, Cody heard Burke's urgent direction from the wings: 'The story . . . tell the story . . .'

Cody cleared his throat and head. 'So, Wild Bill, what have you been doing?'

My memory misfired. I couldn't remember a thing. 'I . . . uhhhhhhh.'

Burke groaned.

'Have you seen any wild Comanches?' Cody prodded.

'Uhhhhhh. I can't remember,' I confessed.

Cody leaned forward, and whispered: 'Just make up something. Like I do.'

I took another drink, but nothing came to mind. The audience grew quiet, waiting. I shot Texas Jack a glance, hoping he would pull out his .44 and start killing Indians, but he ignored me. Reckon he was right mad.

Well, I started to tell them about my affair with the Titusville boys in the billiard hall, but decided against it, figuring it could madden a few friends of the boys I had pounded and lead to a riot. Nor could I very well tell them about Rebecca Gentry as I had seen her in the fifth row with her husband. So I retreated: 'Why don't you tell us a story, Buffalo Bill?'

I don't know if Cody turned white, or if it was just those damned calcium lights. He blinked, wet his lips, and the audience started calling out his name over and over again.

'You look constipated,' I told him.

'It's consternation,' he corrected, and stood, walking to the center of the stage.

Billy Cody is a showman, and a master. I give him that. He had shunned his buckskins on this performance for black *vaquero* pants, an embroidered shirt, fancy vest, watch chain the length of a boy's jump rope, wide-brimmed hat, and a brace of Smith & Wessons tucked into a wide—and I mean WIDE—belt with the biggest dad-blasted square forged buckle I had ever seen. It must have weighed five pounds. I couldn't see how he breathed, but he took a deep breath, exhaled, and spoke with a quiet confidence.

'Boys, and dear ladies.' I swear I thought he winked at Rebecca Gentry. 'I've just returned from the Rockies.'

'Hunting elk or Injuns?' asked Texas Jack, ever Cody's helper.

'Neither,' Cody said with a smile. 'Huckleberries.'

The Titusville citizens giggled politely.

'You'd think there is no danger in pickin' huckleberries, and in most cases you would be right.' He paced the stage as he talked. I think he had been taking lessons from the Combination's Walter Fletcher. We billed Fletcher as 'The Great Dutch Comedian' because he had made a name for himself playing Falstaff and Benedick, and he got plenty of laughs pretending to be Snakeroot Sam and Nick Blunder for us, but he had also been well-received as Hamlet and Richard III. Even Edwin Booth said Fletcher was a fine dramatic actor, but I figured, if he was that fine, he'd be acting in a real theater company and not with us fools. Cody looked like he knew what he was doing, even though Texas Jack and I knew he didn't.

'I had my oaken bucket practically full of huckleberries, ready to eat till my goatee turned purple. And then . . .' He jumped and turned, pointing at the left wing. I gripped my Colts, expecting him to start slaying Indians, but he didn't. He looked back at the crowd, and said: 'A grizzly bear charged out of the brambles.' Shaking his head, Cody went on: 'Well, I had left my Mississippi Yeager and Colt revolver at camp, so I ran straight down the mountain, clingin' to that bucket full of huckleberries. I could hear that silvertip grizzly chargin' me, could feel its rancid breath. I dared not look over my shoulder lest I be paralyzed by fear. I thought I was dead for certain, but I kept on footin' it, the bear right behind me. It soon occurred to me that the silvertip sought my huckleberries. He was hungry. All I had to do was drop the bucket and save my life, but I couldn't. I know it sounds outrageous, but I had spent hours pickin' those berries, and I had picked them for me, Buffalo Bill Cody, not for a mad, thousand-pound silvertip. I kept runnin' down the mountain, over boulders, dodgin' trees and other obstacles.

'Yes, I ran. I ran to save myself and my plunder, and I thought the grizzly would lose interest, but on he lumbered. Thunderation, he must have been as hungry as I! Gladly would I have traded my bucket for a Testament, but I just couldn't let go of those berries. They are so delicious. The bear got closer. I tried to run faster. Suddenly I burst through a clearin' and found myself slippin' and slidin' on a frozen lake. Somehow I managed to keep my balance, and so I run across the ice and snow, but on charged that bear. Now, the ice was thick . . . enough to support this leviathan . . . and as a lake in the Tetons is quite large, I didn't know if I could outrun a grizzly on a frozen . . .'

'Just wait a dad-blasted minute, Buffalo Bill!' a man shouted from the second row. He stood up, angrily pointing a finger at Cody. The gent looked like he might have been kin to one of the roughnecks I had met at the Abbott House. 'I've been tryin' to catch you in a lie, mister, and now I have. You say you was out pickin' huckleberries, right?'

'Yes, my good fellow,' Cody answered.

'And a griz' charged you?'

'You've heard my story correctly.'

'Well.' The man put his hands on his hips. Sarcasm scented his voice. 'If you wuz pickin' huckleberries in the summer, how could you be runnin' 'cross a frozen lake?'

Cody didn't even crack a smile. 'Son,' he said in all seriousness, 'that bear chased me from July to November.'

Hell, even I laughed at that one, practically doubled over on my fake log, forgetting all about my aches and pains. Everyone in that theater hollered with delight, and, when they had about calmed down, Texas Jack drew his revolver and shouted: 'Indians!'

We started slaying a score of supes, trying not to laugh at Cody's joke.

Titusville might have been the high point of my acting career, and it had to rate up there for Billy Cody, too.

We played only one night in Titusville, then took an eastbound for another solo show in Jamestown, New York. Next, we had a long stay in Buffalo before arriving in Erie, Pennsylvania for two performances at the Park Opera House.

As I had been on my very best behavior since Titusville, I shot an Erie supe in his buttocks, mainly to see if the powder flash would set those smelly garments on fire. I don't know why Burke never saw the need in washing the outfits we provided for those extras. I mean, there are laundresses in cities, even in Pennsylvania. Well, this 'Modoc'— apparently Cody had changed the tribe from 'wild Comanches' to those poor Indians recently hanged in Oregon—went into conniptions, as did Cody, after the curtain closed.

'By my boots and socks, Jim, you're 'bout to bust my boiler with your antics!' he roared. 'You stink of whiskey, and, if you don't behave yourself, I won't allow no more rye on the stage. You must stop your drinkin' and, for the love of God, stop tormentin' my Modocs!'

I looked shameful—and Walter Fletcher, Josephine Morlacchi, Burke, and folks of that ilk said I was a horrible actor. After I offered my hand to the 'Modoc' who spoke in one ugly accent, I told Cody I would try to behave myself and would limit my drinking to my morning bracers and just one drink before going on stage. I also said I would take only two or three sips from Josephine's jug and no longer would pat her fanny or rile Texas Jack, who hadn't spoken to me, except when called to in a play, since Ohio.

I kept my word about the enchanting Josephine, and never much fondled her again, although she was tempting. Sometimes I am too ornery for my own good, and it began to weigh on me that I had come close to severing my friendship with Jack Omohundro, one of the finest barkeeps and square-dance callers ever to set foot in Kansas and Nebraska.

To show my sincerity, I visited Eugene Metz's Housekeeper's Emporium and purchased a Burdett Cooking Stove, which I had shipped to the newlyweds' summer home in East Billerica, Massachusetts. Perhaps they had no need of a stove, but I got the price halved by cutting the jack of clubs to the owner's nine of diamonds. I also bought Jack a fancy shirt and Josephine a pretty brooch at a couple of shops on Park Row. I presented the gifts and the receipt for the stove to my friends at the Park Opera House before pouring my bracer.

Texas Jack shook my hand, without any

begrudging, and, when Josephine hugged me, I did not molest her in any way. Cody simply stared at my drink.

'That's a mighty big glass,' Cody told me.

'Well,' I said, 'I told you I'd limit myself to just one drink before the show.'

He let out a lion's laugh, found a glass of a similar size, and finished off my whiskey. Cody and I were in a right joyous mood when we took the stage, although I gave him an awful fright later in our performance.

We were engaged in the slaughter of Modocs during the second act, right after I declared: 'I would face a hundred Comanches for that girl.' No one noticed that I had botched my line—hell's fire, I doubt if they even had heard me as soft as I talked on the stage—because we had changed it from Comanches to Modocs, and I had forgotten. The girl, of course, was Kitty Muldoon, played by Rena Maeder, sometimes as cantankerous as me. To save her, we had to kill twenty out-of-work businessmen, the Panic being in full force by now, enticed by the 25¢ we paid our extras to play our wild Indians. Well, there lay a supe playing dead, his buttocks sticking up over a fake boulder. And there was Will Cody, staring at me with murder in his eyes. I placed the barrel of my Navy a few inches from the Modoc's hindquarters, and pulled the trigger.

Click.

I howled with laughter while shoving the

138

empty revolver into my sash. 'Fooled you, fool!' I cried out, before becoming engaged in mortal combat with another Erie Modoc who held a hatchet so dull it wouldn't even split a hair of my mustache.

Later, as the train sped to our next show, the entire Combination, those who partook of Pennsylvania ale, enjoyed what Cody called 'one of the grandest beer jollifications in history.' We all felt in fine spirits, but those tumbled upon reaching Pittsburgh.

Well, everyone's but mine dropped a notch after a haggard V.E. Beamer, manager of the Academy of Music, greeted us with the grim news that he had sold only half the tickets for our Monday night opening and even fewer for the Tuesday show. Burke and Cody sobered right up. Walter Fletcher and Texas Jack got into a debate as to whether we scouts had lost our appeal. Gaspard Maeder cried out that the show was about to close. Personally I did not give a fip.

Chapter Twelve

The 'Wild Bill' now playing here is the identical scout that has been so famous on the frontier. Those who desire to learn more of the history of 'Wild Bill' would do well to consult *Harper's Magazine* of February, 1867 in which the leading article is devoted to an account of Bill's remarkable adventures.

Express, Terre Haute, Indiana
October 10, 1873

Pittsburgh was deader than Davis Tutt, who I killed back in 1865, and almost as ugly. Several businesses had been boarded up, and many of the folks walking along Liberty Street looked mighty glum, but that was to be expected. On October 1st the Jay Cooke & Company had failed, and people started holding onto shinplasters like skinflints. I had never heard of Mr. Cooke or his company, but I imagine both were right powerful on the East Coast because things quickly went from a calamity to national financial ruin. Banks fell faster than the Indians we killed on the boards, businesses closed, people turned sullen. Of course, that had been more than a month ago, and we were still getting our free railroad passes. People kept coming to see our silly melodramas.

Nobody in the Buffalo Bill Combination ever gave the Panic a thought till we reached Pittsburgh.

We had booked the Academy of Music for the week, Monday through Saturday, with matinee and evening shows on Wednesday and Saturday. Pittsburgh was a big city, far bigger than Erie or Titusville, and Burke and Cody had expected to do roaring trade here, especially since the Cody-Texas Jack-Buntline play had done so well here back in January. Of course, all opinions had changed once we reached the city. It was like we were at a funeral.

During our hack ride to the Academy of Music, Texas Jack suggested perhaps we had nothing to fear. He pointed out the fact that we had been delayed several times by men and equipment grading streets and alleys.

'If the city's spending that much money on streets, the Panic can't be as bad as everyone's making it out to be,' he said hopefully.

'Hell, Jack,' I fired back, 'that fella on the corner holding the shovel used to own the First National Bank of Pittsburgh.'

Of course, I did not know if there even was a First National Bank of Pittsburgh, but I got a good laugh from my joke, although nobody else did.

Arizona John Burke snorted something rude, and, if we had been in Kansas, I would have shot him dead. Instead, I gave him what turned out to be a right fortuitous lecture: 'If you're so jo-fired concerned about this Panic, put it in your advertisements. *Scouts of the Plains* will cure the nation's money woes.' This I said partly in jest, but Burke, being a shyster, and Cody, being greedy, took me at my word, and thus our advertisement in the Pittsburgh *Gazette* declared:

Attention! Attend!! The Event!!!
'A HIT, A HIT, A PALPABLE HIT!'
The Panic Dissolved 'Into Thin Air'
by the resumption of payments to see
BUFFALO BILL, TEXAS JACK,
WILD BILL, THE WILD INDIANS,
THE GREAT MORLACCHI,
In the new Drama,
SCOUTS OF THE PLAINS.
Replete with Thrilling Scenes,
Startling Situations, Songs,
Dances, and Mirth.

Sumbitch, it worked, and after I studied on it, maybe this shameless self-promotion did not lie. Men, women, and young 'uns packed the Academy of Music during our stay in the city. Maybe they needed a laugh to take their minds off their miseries, and for a couple of hours they forgot their depression. We made them happy, and they made Cody and Texas Jack happy. I was the only one in the Buffalo Bill Combination who did not care about the money I was making. Whenever I got paid, I'd spend it, and Cody had started making me buy the rye for my jug and before-curtain bracers— his, or Burke's, idea of punishment for all of my theatrical transgressions. Money did not mean to me what it did to Cody and the others. After our shows in Pittsburgh, I would toss my change to the dirty waifs in the alley. They had more need of a coin than did I.

Of course, at our Wednesday matinee not everyone laughed. I am to blame for that, but so are Cody and some fool who paid 75¢ to see us. Once again, I had forgotten my lines. I was supposed to tell some outlandish story of me fighting Comanches, the Modocs having been replaced as no longer topical. I just sat on that stump, trying to think of something.

'Just make something up,' said Texas Jack, who had resumed conversations with me after our truce.

'Tell them a true story,' Cody whispered. 'That's what I did in Chicago with Judson.'

I wet my lips, and wished I had not taken that pledge to limit my drinking on stage. Then someone in the crowd yelled out: 'Tell us how you sent the McKandlass gang to glory, Wild Bill!'

Encouraged by cheers, I told them.

'Well, firstly, it wasn't Mac-KAND-lass. It was McCanles, and, Christ Almighty, there wasn't no gang to speak of, and I guaran-damn-tee you Dave McCanles didn't go to

143

glory, not that miserable bastard. *Gang?'* I snorted, trying to envision how Cody had made up that story about huckleberry hunting without any rehearsal. 'Hell. That *Harper's* story that ran six or so years back wasn't the gospel truth. Fact of the matter is it was nothing but a slew of son-of-a-bitching lies.'

'Don't curse,' Cody admonished me.

Laughing, I hooked a thumb at Cody. 'Billy Cody, folks, is the only man I know ever employed by Russell, Majors, and Waddell to abide by their rules. We all had to sign that pledge . . . "I agree not to use profane language, not to get drunk, not to gamble, not to treat animals cruelly, nor to do anything else that is incompatible with the conduct of a gentleman." I signed it. I just didn't quite follow any of the rules except the animal one.'

When I heard all those giggles, I thought there was nothing to this at all. It was one of the few times I felt all right being on the fool stage.

'Cody signed it, too, but he followed all of the rules, except the one about getting drunk. He's the only man, or boy, I ever knew who could work as a muleskinner or cavallard driver and not swear.' I winked at Cody, who did not wink back. 'I had gotten into a bit of a row with a black bear on my way to Santa Fé. Hadn't been picking huckleberries, though.' That left them Pittsburgh folks all struck dumb, and I figured out my error. They hadn't

144

heard Cody's huckleberry joke. I went right on, though. 'While leading a train over the Raton Pass, I got ambushed by this bear. I put up a fight, but the bear won.' That did trigger a few nervous laughs. 'Bears don't follow those newfangled Marquis de Queensbury rules.' More laughter. 'Well, I had been cut up and mauled, but I lived, and they carted me back to Rock Creek Station in Nebraska Territory to recover. Wasn't a bad place to get over my wounds. Jane Wellman, she was living with the stationkeeper, fellow named Horace, was a mighty fine nurse. I got better.

'Well, Russell, Majors, and Waddell had bought this relay station from Dave McCanles to use for their Pony Express. I was tending stock at the station, and tending to Jane Wellman and Sarah Shull when I could. Sarah, she had been consorting with Dave, but Dave's claim went bust when Missus McCanles arrived from North Carolina and made him kick the concubine out.' One man laughed, but he had to stop when his wife punched his ribs with her elbow. I figured I had done enough explaining. It was time to get to the blood and thunder. 'Horace Wellman owed McCanles money. Or, rather, Russell, Majors, and Waddell did. They had been a little delinquent on those payments for the relay station. That's what brought McCanles to Rock Creek on that July morning back in 'Sixty-One. McCanles came with his son, a twelve-year-old kid who

145

looked like a girl. He also brought a couple of hands with him, and one of the riders brought his bloodhound with him. That dog was so gentle, she wouldn't even scratch a flea. *Gang?* If that was a gang, then I'm not a horrible actor.'

I reckon that got the most laughs of the matinee.

'The two hired hands stayed at the barn, tending to their mounts and the dog, while McCanles and his boy went to the station and called out to Wellman . . . they didn't know I was inside, consorting with Missus Wellman, Horace only charging two bits a poke . . . to pack up and get out. He, McCanles that is, was evicting them. That got in my craw. McCanles was a man, wore a revolver in his britches, and he brung a boy, snot-nosed kid, with him to do a man's job. It riled me, especially since I had little regard for a piece of Southern trash like Dave McCanles. Honestly, though, he wouldn't vote me into Congress as I had whupped him at poker and had practically stolen Sarah from him, too. Well, while I was finishing my consorting, Horace stood on the porch, and had a few words with McCanles. Horace said he had talked to some lawyer who said McCanles had no authority to evict him. The cussing got louder, and Jane Wellman got angry, finished consorting with me, and threw on her unmentionables, and went outside to tell McCanles a thing or two while I pulled on

146

my clothes. It took a while, me still a mite stove up from that Raton Pass bear.

'Jane Wellman told David McCanles he was a sorry so-and-so to come cussing her man, said if he wanted to fight somebody, he should ride over and fight Russell, Majors, and Waddell. Horace Wellman had retreated like a damned coward into the house, pulled down a Kentucky rifle, started loading it.'

Damn, I should have said Wellman loaded a Pennsylvania rifle, but I was so engrossed in telling my story, telling the truth for once, the way Cody had suggested, that I forgot we were in Pittsburgh.

'"You expecting a fight?" I asked Horace. "He's got a shotgun!" Horace told me, over all of Jane's shouting going on outside. McCanles cussed right back at Jane, so I stuck my Navy Colts in my waistband, and stepped outside.'

Things got quiet for just a few seconds, like every man and woman at the Academy of Music was holding their breath.

'"Go inside," I told Jane, and she did.

'"This ain't your affair," Dave McCanles told me. He didn't have a shotgun. His boy, Willie, did, but it was a single-shot scatter-gun, and the nipple wasn't even capped. Rusty as it looked, I doubt if it had been loaded in years. Just a kid's toy.

'"I am employed by Russell, Majors, and Waddell," I said. "I reckon it is my affair. I'm paid to protect their property."

' "It ain't their damned property, *Duck Bill,* till I get paid for it."

' "You call me Duck Bill again, Dave, and you'll get your payment, sure enough."

'I guess McCanles got cotton mouth, because he asked if he could come in for a drink of water. Asked real polite, too, and I stepped aside, let him in.

'McCanles had just got his foot in the door when Horace Wellman shot him in the chest. I reckon it was Horace. He had the rifle last time I saw, but I wouldn't put nothing past Jane. McCanles come staggering out, collapsing by his son, who dropped the shotgun, and just stared, mouth open, drawing flies, eyes not even blinking. Pathetic sight. It would have sobered me up, but those two men who had ridden in with McCanles come running from the barn.'

I laughed, without any mirth, and shook my head. Didn't notice it, but the gallery had gotten mighty quiet again.

'That was a damned fool thing to do, because them boys had guns, so I drew my Navy, and shot them both. Didn't kill them, mind you. I just shot to defend my person, lest they . . . Woods and Gordon were their names . . . think I had done in their boss, who had rolled over on his back, and now begged for water. I hit Gordon in his shoulder, Woods in his hip. Gordon took off running for parts unknown, leaking blood. Woods dropped to

148

the dust, tried crawling to the barn, crying and praying. I spit in McCanles's face. "There's your damned water, Dave," I told him.

'About that time, Jane Wellman come out charging like a Kiowa buck, grabbed a hoe leaning against the side of the house, and chased down that poor Woods fellow. She was screaming, swinging that hoe, pounding Woods's head like there was no tomorrow. I didn't think a grub hoe could do such damage, especially with a woman wielding it, but damned if she didn't plow in that man's head, sending blood, chunks of bone, hair, and finally his brains all over the ground. Chickens had a feast, sure as Sunday, for the next week. Just watching Jane, hell, it practically turned my stomach.'

It practically made a handful of ladies and gentlemen in the audience sick, too, because I heard some gagging, and praying, and vomiting. But I was enjoying telling this story, didn't even feel Cody tugging on my buckskins, or hear his pleas. Later, when I pictured them folks in the front row at the Academy of Music, they looked as white as the limelight made us up on the stage.

'Horace, having reloaded his Pennsylvania rifle'—I got it right, or stretched it just a mite, that time—'ran out of the house, too, and took off after Gordon, who had taken to the little mess of timber on the creek. I looked at McCanles's son, who still hadn't moved, and

149

told him . . . "You best get out of here, boy." He wised up, come out of his shock, and ran. Jane was still beating Woods with that hoe, and McCanles had stopped his begging, and gone ahead and died. I stepped down as a bunch of Pony Express riders and other folks ran over to see what all the commotion was about.

'"What's happened?" Doc Brink asked. He wasn't a doctor, just a puny Pony Express rider, but he had more sand than a dozen Horace Wellmans.

'"McCanles come to kill us all," I said. Wasn't exactly a lie. He had brought guns and men.

'"One of 'em's gettin' away!" Horace shouted from the edge of the yard, and Doc Brink led a handful of men that way.

'"Wait a minute!" Jane yelled. She tossed the bloody hoe aside, and ran to the barn, untied the rope securing the bloodhound that Gordon had raised from a pup, and sent the bitch chasing after her owner. Dog didn't know any better. I felt sorry for the dog and Gordon.

'I just waited by the corrals, wondering how Sarah Shull would take to the news that Dave McCanles was dead. An hour or so later, Brink and the Wellmans come back, grinning like they had found Jesus. Of course, I knew that wasn't who they had found.

'"Jim Gordon won't be raidin' no more stations!" Brink happily informed me, but I got

150

angry.

'"If you sons-of-bitches hurt that dog, there will be hell to pay."

'Well, the dog come trotting behind them, and I relaxed. Dog looked mighty sad, and wouldn't let nobody, not even me, come close to her. Started growling, barking. Finally we had to shoot her, too. I mean, Brink did. I can't bring myself to harm a dog. Now, cats, cats I'll kill with pleasure. And snakes. And drovers, cardsharpers, and pistol fighters. But not dogs. And not children, even them raised by a skunk like Dave McCanles. Hell, I didn't kill a soul that day, just shot two men to protect my person. I did ride to the nearest settlement that had a lawyer, and paid him in case things got ugly. And there was an inquest, but the Wellmans and I got freed. Self-defense. No-billed. So I went back to tending stock while recovering from my bear wounds, but I stopped consorting with Jane Wellman, even though Horace said I could have her for ten cents rather than two bits. Just couldn't do any consorting with that lady. Every time I saw her, I pictured her covered with Woods's blood and brains. So I consorted with Sarah Shull, instead. Then she left, the telegraph wire got strung up, the Pony Express bit the dust, and I went to fight the Rebs, mostly as a scout and a spy. After the war, I hung my hat in Springfield, met Colonel Nichols, and he wrote up that story of me in *Harper's*. Damned lies, and I hate that rapscallion almost as much as I despise Ned Buntline. I told Nichols not to write anything that would upset my mother. And I'm telling you folks, too.' I pointed my finger in their general direction. 'If any one of you tells my mama what really happened at Rock Creek Station, you'll all pay.'

The curtain closed, and I went to get ready for the next scene.

Cody almost forgot his vow, and almost cursed Burke and the stagehands for not dropping the curtain sooner. He also tried quarreling with me, but I reminded him that I had just told a story, told the truth, like he had suggested.

'Thunderation, Jim,' Cody said, 'I always tell the truth. You know that. But there are layers of truth! We're not treadin' the boards to make people cry, to lose their supper. We're here to make 'em laugh. By my boots and socks,' he said as he stormed off to find some John Barleycorn, 'if I make it through this season without losin' my head or hair, it'll be a miracle.'

Chapter Thirteen

The drama has scarce the shadow of a plot and is like an animated dime novel with the Indian-killing multiplied by ten, but for all that it was enjoyable and heartily enjoyed, and the bloodier the tragedy the broader was the comedy.

Morning Dispatch, Erie, Pennsylvania
November 15, 1873

The sickness caught up with me in Wilkes-Bane, Pennsylvania, after completing our stands in Pittsburgh, Johnstown, and Williamsport. By sickness, I don't mean the cold that had been plaguing me since around Pittsburgh, but homesickness. Everybody around these parts talked about the Wyoming Valley, and the name alone got me to thinking about, and longing for, Cheyenne. Or Fort Fetterman. Or some other place on the Great Plains where men of my class frequented gambling dens and buckets of blood, not highfalutin academies of music and opera houses. Pennsylvania's Wyoming Valley is pretty, I guess, a lot greener than the prairies that I frequented out West, but it wasn't home. Not to me. And it was damned hard to find a whorehouse there.

153

Folks at the opera house and hotel on Hazel Street said we could have all the beer we could drink, on the house, compliments of a famous and wealthy local brewer named Charles Stegmaier, which was all well and good. But after Cody, Texas Jack, and me had consumed a keg or two, I got to hankering for female companionship. When I asked the fellow at the hotel's front desk for directions to the nearest brothel, he turned white as linen, stammered, and quickly disappeared without giving me so much as a suggestion as where I could find a soiled dove.

Mind you, I do not like whores. Don't trust them, especially the Kansas species, but it seemed that every night I was bunking next to Texas Jack and his wife, or Billy Cody and either a strumpet or an actress—I'll give you a dollar if you explain the difference to me— who had become enraptured with the great scout. Sumbitch, you would think the carpenters would make the walls a little thicker in a cold place like Pennsylvania, but the noises proved distracting. I reckon I could have wooed Jennie Fisher again, or risked my manhood and flirted with Rena Maeder, but I had grown sick of my comrades by now, so, after enduring two and a half hours of foolishness, murdering supes, speaking idiocies, and playing the fool one more time on the night of November 28th, I went whore hunting.

154

I don't know what those poor blokes mining anthracite coal, or the factory workers, or the mill workers, or any man in Wilkes-Bane do in the way of horizontal refreshments, but it would take a great scout to find the tenderloin in a Pennsylvania burgh. They hide their prostitutes better than a Kansas cardsharper can conceal the tools of his trade. It started snowing, turned downright miserable walking along those cold, dark streets. Didn't help my cold, either, and I thought I'd practically die of pneumonia before I found a whore, but at last I stumbled onto a little crib by the railroad tracks, saw a man leave a dark-haired vixen in the doorway, and I decided she would serve my purpose. The location of her business also proved beneficial, as I would not have far to walk to the depot. Our train was leaving for Scranton shortly after breakfast.

The whore, who called herself Courtney, took my money, and asked me if I wanted her to undress me. I told her I did my own undressing, and asked her to turn down her lantern, which she did, and which I regretted as that lantern was about the only thing heating her crib, not counting the act of fornication, of course.

Cold as it was, I wasted no time in joining her beneath her quilt, coughed a bit, and slid my Williamson Derringer underneath the pillow.

'You're one of them scouts!' she exclaimed.

155

'Yes'm,' I said.

'Well, I'll be damned. Are you Buffalo Bill?'

My first thought was to become insulted and incensed, and to get dressed and take my whoring business elsewhere, but it was too cold, and she had started twirling my long locks in her fingers while rubbing my chest, and then my stomach, with her other hand, and I got a mite more comfortable, and told her: 'Yes, ma'am, I am the honorable William F. Cody, better known as Buffalo Bill.' I started thinking about all the stuff Cody said each night as a Thespian. 'I will save my friend Texas Jack or die in the attempt.'

'Huh?'

'Nothing.'

'I ain't never bedded no living hero before,' she said.

Arizona John Burke calls it being in character, so I tried to stay in the character of Buffalo Bill Cody, at least the theatrical Cody, when I said: 'It's my deepest regret that our show sends us to Scranton tomorrow, or I would pass on a ticket to see our show. Maybe next year when we pass this way again.'

'Won't be here. Looking to move to West Chester.'

'I . . . I see.' Actually, I saw a lot more, despite the darkness. I only hoped she couldn't see my grin. 'I have a home in West Chester. Per chance you might pay me a visit?'

'Hell, yeah,' she said, and kissed me hard. I

156

don't fancy kissing whores, don't like to think where all, who all, and what all whores have kissed. Her breath stank of cigarette smoke, but I reckon mine smelled like Charles Stegmaier's beer, and I was more interested in her hands than her mouth, but mostly interested in a plan I had just concocted.

I gave her Cody's address—at least, I hoped it was Cody's address, having never been invited to his estate—and she said she most assuredly would pay a visit, and I tried to picture how Louisa Cody would look when this vile little creature knocked on their front door of that fancy house Cody had bought for his family. Since he had been hornswoggled by Ned Buntline into thinking he was an actor, and not a scout, Cody had been bragging about his glorious parlor, his immense wealth. He had become a man of property, and not a man of principle. My joke would teach him an important lesson. Of course, there was a good chance Louisa would have taken the young 'uns off to North Platte, and the whore would visit when nobody was home, or would learn my deceit beforehand, but this little plan certainly improved my mood, and the whore named Courtney excitedly got to her business.

It was one relaxed and happy James Butler Hickok who stepped outside into the miserable dawn, leaving a contented whore snoring on her cot. I practically had forgotten

157

my cold, kept picturing Louisa Cody, or better yet, Billy Cody, if and when my mischief played its hand. That is when I spotted the waif by a stack of ties by the rail yard. He was asleep, a ten-year-old boy covered with grime and frost, a mangy dog serving as his quilt. Pity soon soured my good mood. Both boy and dog awakened when I cleared my throat.

'Why aren't you home?' I demanded.

He shrugged, brushed the frost off his hair, and pulled on a woolen cap he had been using as a pillow. 'Why don't you get your hair cut? You look like a girl,' he said.

'Boy,' I said sternly, and was tempted strongly to introduce him to my .41-caliber Derringer, not to shoot him, mind you, but to scare him into respect for his elder, 'I've seen men killed for insults less than that.'

'Yeah.' He rose with a nonchalance, and the dog yawned, circled around, and went back to sleep. 'Well, shoot me, hairy sister. You'd be doin' me a favor. Be quicker, too, than freezin' to death.'

That struck me tough, and my pity hardened.

The kid asked me: 'You gonna kill me, Buffalo Bill?'

'What makes you think I'm Buffalo Bill?'

He shrugged. 'You're one of them scouts. Ever'body in town's been talkin' about you heroes.'

'We ain't heroes,' I said. 'I'm Wild Bill.'

'Pleasure.'

'Let me buy you breakfast?'

He started to turn protective again, but I gestured at the dog. 'I'll treat your pal, too.' Lord knows, both of them looked like they could use some hot food.

The kid snorted. 'This is Wilkes-Barre, Pennsylvania, mister. You can't get no restaurant to serve no dog.'

'Wild Bill Hickok can,' I told him, and pointed at a café across from the depot.

Wild Bill could, too, especially when he introduced himself to the proprietor of the Depot Café with a firm grip, firmer voice, and firmest Williamson Derringer. The owner waited on us himself, and the few railroad men drinking coffee and smoking pipes did not say a thing about the dog, the waif, or the famous scout.

The dog ate a mess of ham and eggs, the boy drank coffee and wolfed down a bowl of oats, and I had a gin and bitters, a cup of coffee, and some hot cakes. When the boy was on his second cup of coffee, I asked him again why he wasn't home.

'Home?' He snorted again, and motioned for a refill on the coffee.

'That'll stunt your growth,' I told him. 'You should be drinking milk.'

'You shouldn't be drinkin' whiskey. You got any more advice?'

'Yeah. Watch your tone with me or you'll be

159

eating your teeth along with them oats.'

The kid grinned, and I'll be damned if he didn't even mutter something of an apology. With a smile, I gave him some more advice.

'Don't play cards. There ain't no future in it. Don't wear a gun. The odds are against a pistol fighter worse than a crooked deal. And don't become no damned actor. There's less of a future in that, and not a whit of self-respect.'

'You're one to talk.'

'Yeah.' I had another drink, finished my breakfast, and told the kid we had best move on, because I had a train to catch. I tipped the owner a nickel for feeding the dog, and we walked into what passed for morning on a Wilkes-Barre day. Smoke from the locomotives mingled with smoke from the factories and the thick fog. About that time, Cody, red-eyed but bushy-tailed, strolled over, and introduced himself to the boy, who still had not given me his name. My first suspicion was that Cody had been visiting Courtney, but then I realized that couldn't be, as I had paid for her all night, and Cody would not have frequented such a rough-hewn place when he had a fancy hotel room available on Hazel Street.

'He looks like a girl, too,' the boy told me.

Cody laughed. 'Son, girls do not have mustaches and goatees.'

'Some of 'em do,' the kid said, ' 'specially 'round here.'

That got Cody to cackling like a hen. 'I was gonna have breakfast, Jim,' Cody told me. 'Join me?'

'We done et,' the boy said.

'I can walk you home,' I told the boy, but he shook his head, and started to pull on his cap. Then he stopped and plucked out a grayback, which he crushed with his dirty fingernails.

'Ain't no need, hairy sister.' He flicked the grayback away, and pointed to the crib of the whore Courtney's. 'I live right over yonder.'

'Here.' Suddenly feeling tremendously guilty, I fished out all my change, plucking out the token from an Ellsworth bawdy house, and dropped the money in the kid's woolen cap. He looked at it with a right smart of suspicion, but said nothing. Next, I gave him all my paper money.

The boy stared at the offering, sniffed, and started off in a hurry, hollering for the dog, which he called Hank, to come on.

'Wait up, there!' Cody hollered, caught up with the waif, and proceeded to empty his billfold of greenbacks into the kid's cap.

'Thanks, Buffalo Bill,' the boy said, and walked toward the crib.

'Might I have your name?' Cody asked.

'Archibald!' the boy hollered back. 'Just Archibald. I was a mistake.'

I warrant that Cody and I both felt mighty long, and as Archibald and Hank disappeared inside the miserably shanty, we walked to the depot, and I started feeling more like the skunk I am.

'Thought you was going to eat breakfast,' I told Cody.

'I'll eat in Scranton,' he said, but he wouldn't. He had given the waif all of his money, and I decided that Cody had not forgotten all of his principles. The joke I had played on Cody and Courtney didn't seem so funny now, and I felt bad, downright ashamed of myself, which is something I seldom feel, even when I should.

Pretty soon Arizona John Burke and others from the Combination arrived at the depot, and Burke started talking about some parade he had managed for us in Scranton, and Rena Maeder started cussing the weather, and Joseph Arlington and Alfred Johnson began arguing over who had botched whose line last night.

I just stared at Courtney's crib and my old friend, Buffalo Bill Cody, whose stomach started rumbling louder than the whore Courtney's snores. At last, I excused myself, and went to the ticket office, where I borrowed a pencil and piece of paper, and began writing a note.

Dearest Courtney:
    I thought I was playing a joke on you last night by telling you that I am Buffalo Bill Cody. I am not. So please do not visit

that home in West Chester, Pennsylvania, as you would be embarrassed.

John Burke came up to me and asked what I was doing, and I told him to go to hell, and took my note to the crib, but, of course, by then my morning bracers had started swimming in my veins, and I remembered that Archibald had thanked Cody for his generosity, instead of thanking me for mine, and had told Cody his name, and related hardly a thing to me but rude insults. Hell, it was me who had bought the kid and mutt breakfast, had given him my sage advice, not Cody. 'Course, I couldn't blame Cody, who had showed true grit by forfeiting his breakfast for Archibald.

Inside, I heard the dog and Courtney snoring, and wondered if the boy was asleep as well. It didn't matter. Ungrateful bastard. I finished the note.

My real name is John Burke, although I am called Arizona John. It would be my greatest desire to see you again. You can write me in care of the Brevoort Hotel, New York City, or next month meet me in Bethlehem, Easton, Pottsville, Reading, Lancaster, or Harrisburg. You can find the dates of our appearances at the Opera House here. Tell the manager that I sent you.

Thank you for a wonderful night. I hope to see you again.

Major John M. Burke
'Arizona John'

I pinned the note to a splinter on the front door. My glum faded away, and by the time I settled into my seat in the smoking car, I felt rather jolly as the train pulled out of the station and steamed toward Scranton.

Chapter Fourteen

Then came the new drama entitled *Scouts of the Plains,* founded on the lives of the three principal actors. This was, of course, full of the sensational, of gunpowder and the knife, of open fighting and of treachery, and of Indian torture and the white man's bravery and nonchalance, and suited the audience thoroughly. There is a naturalness about these performers which commends itself at once to those who hear and see them.

Journal, Providence, Rhode Island
January 15, 1874

I don't remember the supper after our show in Port Jervis, New York on December 2nd, so I have to rely on Texas Jack Omohundro's version of the events that transpired. Others were there, of course, but most had become too flabbergasted with my lack of social graces, and Texas Jack is trustworthy, at least since we made amends after my transgressions with his pretty bride.

We hung our hats at some boarding house, a quaint little place overlooking the Delaware River and, in the words of Arizona John Burke, 'just a short buggy ride out of town.' Burke had arranged these accommodations, figuring the quietness would be a blessing, getting us away from the big city. Big city? Port Jervis has maybe 6,500 souls, which is a sight more than places like Ellsworth and Abilene, but nothing like Pittsburgh and New York. Burke is a numskull, because he had not figured on just how long a 'short' buggy ride can seem when it's ten degrees and sleeting. So, if I must blame someone for my drinking, it's that cad Burke. I had to consume both of my flasks—just to keep warm—and had shared several sips from W.S. MacEvey's by the time we reached our destination.

The opera house's furnace was broken, and it's a wonder anyone came to see us that night. I emptied a jug on and off stage so I wouldn't freeze. The point I'm making is that I was roostered by the time Cody took the entire cast to a garish restaurant on Pike Street after the show. Cody had invited all of Port Jervis' leading authorities—the opera house manager and his wife, the mayor and his wife, and assorted members of the Order of the Eastern Star, Orange Chapter Number 33, whatever that is.

After a waiter took orders, I decided to roll a smoke. I had never been much of a cigarette man until I joined the Buffalo Bill Combination, but I took up the habit after my visit with the Wilkes-Barre whore and saw how it relaxed her, even if the smoke pestered my eyes. The smell of the smoke, at least, overtook the stink of her crib. Besides, cigars do not come cheap east of the border, and my money kept disappearing. Since becoming an actor, my nerves had frayed, and the cigarettes relaxed me like they relaxed Courtney. On this night I did not fare well in rolling my smoke since the cold I had contracted in Pittsburgh was still tormenting me and I came down with a sneezing fit. I claim it was the cold. Esther Rubens said too much tanglefoot will do that to a man, but she ain't no doctor.

Leaning over the table, concentrating on getting the tobacco in my paper, I suddenly sneezed, and blew the flakes all over my place mat. No one even God-blessed me. Next, I carefully raked the scattered tobacco into a pile at the edge of the table, and brushed the flakes back into my crinkled paper. I lifted the smoke, and sneezed again. Once again, I gathered the blown tobacco into a pile, dropped it into the paper, lifted the paper, and—sneezed. This went on for four or five more times till at last my sneezing fit caused the mayor's wife to giggle like a mad hatter. She started exclaiming that Wild Bill Hickok was the funniest actor she had ever seen, even funnier than our own 'The Great Dutch Comedian', which caused Walter Fletcher, 'The Great Dutch Comedian', to grumble.

Mind you, this is all from Texas Jack. The last thing I remember is complimenting W.S. MacEvey on filling his flask with Old Tom-Cat Gin. Anyway, Jack says I never got that cigarette rolled. Finally I gave up, and tossed paper and flakes into Burke's cup of tea, then reached for my drink. Never got it, though, because, according to Jack, I leaned forward, and planted my head on the table. They left me like that all through supper, then hauled me off to a hack.

Awakened during the ride back to our boarding house, I protested when Texas Jack gripped my shoulder, and escorted me to my room.

'Jack,' he says I slurred, 'if you don't let go of my arm, I'm gonna punch you in the mouth.'

'J.B.,' Jack says he told me, 'that would be a big mistake on your part.'

He got me to my room, tossed me on my bed, and I slept off a mighty fine drunk, had a dozen scrambled eggs and hash browns for breakfast, and we proceeded on to

Poughkeepsie for another one-night show, which is where Cody confronted me.

'You made a fool of us all, Jim!' he shouted.

'You don't need my help to make you look like a fool,' I said, being in another mean mood. 'You act like one every night you tread them boards.'

'No more whiskey for you!' Cody said. 'You must promise me that you'll stop your drinkin' this instant!'

I waited for the *or else,* but damned if Cody didn't just stop right there. *Or else you're fired!* That's what I wanted to hear. You see, even Texas drovers who wouldn't piss on me if I was on fire will tell you that Wild Bill is a man of his word. I had told Cody I'd give him one season play acting, but I was fed-up with the whole shebang. Wanted out, but, I guess, I wanted the easy way out, wanted my old friend Billy Cody, who I've known since he was just a kid, to throw me out on my arse. That's what I deserved.

Yet Cody looked as if he were about to cry, so I pushed aside my rowdy intentions and agreed to his demands. You can add that to all the other mistakes I had made since joining the Combination. I tried, though, tried hard. I behaved myself in Poughkeepsie, and did not drink on stage, shoot any supes at close range, or torment anyone for the next week. Of course, that was the week Cody disbanded the troupe, sending everyone to rest and recuperate before resuming our schedule in New Jersey. Cody went back to West Chester to see his wife and family, Texas Jack and Josephine returned to Rochester, and the rest of the Buffalo Bill Combination departed for parts unknown. Nobody invited me to accompany him. Can't say I blame them, but that hurt. After all, Cody, Texas Jack, and I were staunch pals. At least, we had been.

I was a lost soul this far East. Thus I had planned on spending my time gambling until I read a short notice in the Poughkeepsie *Daily Journal*, so I caught the next train to Richmond, Virginia, and took in a circus.

Back when I was marshaling, the Hippo-Olympiad and Mammoth Circus had once played in Abilene. I don't care much to see animals abused, or caged, but the star of the Hippo-Olympiad and Mammoth Circus was a fetching creature named Agnes Thatcher Lake. Maybe she's not fetching if you compare her to Josephine Morlacchi, but she looked like a swan when she took to the high wire or trapeze.

Agnes probably would have wedded me in Abilene if I had asked her, but I didn't, my mind preoccupied on things like drinking and marshaling and gambling and staying alive. We dined a few nights at the Drovers Cottage, then parted ways. 'She blew her way, following the circus, and I blowed mine, following the wind.' That's not my line, by the way, just

169

something I had to say in *Scouts of the Plains*, although in the play the woman follows the wagon train and not a circus. But it's about the only line Hiram Robbins ever wrote that I actually cared for and didn't mind saying, stupid as it is. Sakes alive, if I'm not getting as windy as Jack Omohundro.

I had been thinking about Agnes more than a little, and now our paths crossed—well, as a scout I admit it wasn't exactly a crossroads considering the distance between Poughkeepsie and Richmond. You've seen circuses before, so I won't tell you what went on. After the show, part of me said to go down and call on her, *and I was sober.* Yet I couldn't brace myself for that. Newspaper scribes and shameless liars like Nichols and Buntline will tell you that Wild Bill Hickok knows no fear, but I can personally attest to the veracity of the fact that James Butler Hickok was scared to death that night.

It had been an expensive performance for me, considering the train ticket to Virginia, and I had barely enough money for supper. I couldn't very well ask the widow out, and make her pay. So, I turned craven yellow and departed the big tent with nary a word to the Widow Lake. Instead, I took a street car to The Gentlemen's Club of the Old Dominion, a big name for a tiny gambling parlor near Virginia Hall, where I convinced a blue-suited man at the door to invite me inside for a game of stud poker. These Southern gentlemen looked me over with some suspicion before pointing to a vacant chair.

'If you don't mind,' I said, 'I'd prefer yours.' I pointed at a gent with a silk hat and gray Dundrearies.

'Why?' asked a fellow missing an arm and an eye. Dundrearies simply stared.

'Because I don't want to get my head blowed off. I'm Wild Bill Hickok.'

'The actor?' the one-armed man asked excitedly.

I refrained from slapping him, and Dundrearies, who introduced himself as Dr. Dorsay Cullen, stifled a laugh, and vacated his seat.

'Would you care for a drink of whiskey, Mister Hickok?' another man asked.

'No,' I said, silently cussing Cody. 'I've taken the pledge.'

Sometimes I feel as if I am straddling a fence between society and the border. I wear the best clothes and boots a body can find, keep my hair clean and perfumed, yet by nature I am what you would call a brawler, and, when surrounded by men like those playing poker in Richmond, Virginia, I feel as uncomfortable as I do on the stage with Cody and Texas Jack.

'Is it true you've killed one hundred men?' the one-armed man asked.

'No,' I said flatly. 'At last count, it was only

eighty-six. White men. Now if you count Indians, I could not fathom a guess.'

'That many?' said a bald fellow who whistled when he talked.

'My abacus broke,' I explained. I think they took me serious.

As Dr. Cullen dealt the cards, he said that he had watched Ned Buntline, Buffalo Bill, and Texas Jack perform at the Richmond Theatre last year, and, having heard that I had joined the troupe, wondered if we would be performing in Richmond soon.

'Not this year,' I said. 'The yellow fever outbreak has scared our lot.'

'But not you?' said the one-armed man. He had introduced himself as Captain Lee, but I figured he had taken the handle of Lee for the same reason you find so many Buffalo Bills on the plains.

'I'm fearless,' I said.

The bald whistler, a gent named Simpson, then said he thought we were all actors, and there were no such plainsmen as Buffalo Bill, Texas Jack, and Wild Bill.

'I'm no actor,' I said, revealing my Navy Colt.

He whistled, saying there was a city ordinance against carrying concealed weapons, and, besides, members of The Gentlemen's Club of the Old Dominion did not come heeled.

'It's not concealed . . . now,' I said, and

172

folded a miserable hand.

They laughed, but I don't think they found any humor, and the game continued. About this time, our poker table had attracted quite a crowd of Virginians who looked to number the size of unemployed actors we'd find up north and who looked to sport a similar temperament to Titusville oil toughs. I guess The Gentlemen's Club of the Old Dominion had some loose standards for membership. Else I wouldn't have been here.

Dr. Cullen asked me to relate a story of my bravery on the border. The crowd around the table encouraged me as well, but I could read those toughs. They weren't itching for a story, but a fight.

'Hmm,' I said, 'there was the time I was scouting for the Fifth Cavalry after some Cheyenne dog soldiers had committed ghastly depredations in Kansas. I was looking for signs on my trusty steed, Old Brigham, probably five miles ahead of the troopers I was scouting for.'

Old Brigham, you recall, was one of Cody's horses, but I had determined that, if Cody could take events from my life and manufacture them into his own life story, then I damned sure could steal his horse.

'Well, Old Brigham snorted a warning, and I looked up just as an arrow parted my hair. Boys, there must have been fifty of those savages if there were a hundred, their coup sticks showing many scalps, and my locks would make a fine trophy for one of those bucks. There were too many to fight, so I leaped into the saddle, and off went Old Brigham and me. When they gained on me, I would fire a round of my Navy Thirty-Six, but I don't think I hit a one. Cheyennes have a way of leaning over the side of their horses, so it is almost impossible to hit one of those devils, and I am not a man who will kill a horse, even one ridden by a dog soldier.

'I was drenched in sweat, but thought I might make it back to the command when suddenly Old Brigham stepped in a prairie dog hole, and down we went. I got up, beating and blowing sand from my Colt, then fired my last two shots. I was only carrying one revolver, and it being of the cap-and-ball model, I had no chance to reload. My rifle was in the scabbard, out of reach, and I had lost my trusty Bowie knife when I jumped clear of the saddle when Old Brigham fell. There I was, boys, unarmed, alone against fifty of the fiercest warriors this side of the Army of Northern Virginia.'

That got a few smug smiles, and I paused, waiting.

'Well,' said Dr. Cullen, 'how did you get away?'

'I didn't,' I said. 'Them dog soldiers killed me.'

The gents playing poker laughed good-naturedly, but the toughs surrounding their table snorted with vile, Secessionist contempt and called me a long-haired fraud, liar, and Mormon-lover. They expected me to challenge them to a duel, I guess, but I don't duel with fools, I pummel them. There were only six, and I flew into them with one mighty fine war cry, clubbed the ugliest one of them with the butt of my Navy, questioned the parentage of Stonewall Jackson, boasted about all the inhuman atrocities I had performed on scores of Rebels I had killed at Pea Ridge, and began crushing furniture and heads. Some of the card players joined the fray.

When they backed me against the bar, I gripped a bottle of Scotch, and hollered for them to stop. One kept right on with his charge, but I lifted him over the bar by his waistband, and flung him into the backbar, rendering him soaked, cut, and useless.

'Hold on! Hold on!' I said, and they stopped. Stupid Secessionists. No wonder we won the war. I glanced at the Scotch with a twinkle in my eye. 'Old Buffalo Chips Smith, a scout I knew back on the prairie, and a former Reb like you boys, he once bragged on how, if he slammed a bottle down hard enough, it would pop out the cork but not break the glass. Easy on the teeth, you see. I've always wondered if it worked.'

They watched as I gripped the bottle by the neck. Only instead of slamming it against the bar, I planted the base in the nearest Reb's

175

forehead, and he dropped like a Titusville rowdy. The cork remained in the bottle.

'Buffalo Chips, you was wrong!' I hollered, and smashed the bottle against another man's head. Hated wasting whiskey, but it was Scotch, and I prefer gin.

The remaining Rebs, even Captain Lee, leaped on me, and we had a mighty fine frolic before the Richmond constabulary came in and carted my carcass off to the calaboose.

Next morning, the bald whistler named Simpson, who happened to be a lawyer, paid me a visit. He first asked if I had any funds, and I said they had busted me in that poker game. He said he would not charge me a dime, but could not post bail himself on my account. He asked if I knew anyone who would go my bail, or act as a character witness on my behalf. Immediately I suggested the Widow Lake of the Hippo-Olympiad and Mammoth Circus.

I regretted those words the moment they left my lips, and my heart sank, fearing what Agnes would think to find me in this condition. My heart sank even further, though, when Lawyer Simpson sadly informed me that the circus had headed north, trying to avoid the yellow fever epidemic.

'Is there anyone else?' he whistled.

'Hell,' I said, 'wire the Honorable William F. Cody, West Chester, Pennsylvania.'

I expected Cody to let me rot, but he showed up, a bit late, but he showed up, confounding me again. Needless to say, he was not happy when he posted my bond for disturbing the peace, paid for my supper, paid The Gentlemen's Club of the Old Dominion for damages, and grub-staked me a train ticket to Newark.

'This has to stop, Jim,' he admonished me time and again on the rocky ride north. Having heard this many times before, I simply nodded. No fighting, Cody ordered. No tormenting the supes. No getting drunk. Well, I hadn't powder-burned any actors or swallowed a drop of John Barleycorn, and I still say those Virginians started that row in Richmond.

We reached Newark in time for our show, and Cody immediately sent a supe off to fetch him a bottle of whiskey. That must have been a funny sight: a red-headed actor dressed in one of our Indian costumes by now stinking to high heaven, covered with the actor's expensive Grand Ducal overcoat, and buying a bottle of rye at the nearest grog shop. When the supe returned, Cody was already on stage, acting his part, and I started thinking again that I needed to be fired. I could also blame this on Cody, tormenting me by having a supe bring whiskey to the wings. But, as I have told you, no one will ever say I go back on my promises. I keep my word, as long as humanly possible. Thusly I stunned the Newark actor by handing him my Navy Colt, butt forward. I had to order him to take it, which he did, tentatively, holding the .36 in his right hand, Cody's rye in his left.

'Give me the bottle,' I said, 'and point that gun at me.'

He gave me a Texas Jack Omohundro dumb look.

'What?' he stammered. 'Why . . . ?'

'I want you to point that gun at me.' I stared at him with malevolence. 'Now.'

He obeyed. 'Why?'

'I want you to make me take this drink.'

Chapter Fifteen

At the Academy of Music, this evening, W.F. Cody, J.B. Omohundro and J.B. Hickok, better known as 'Buffalo Bill', 'Texas Jack', and 'Wild Bill' will make their appearance in a drama entitled *The Scouts of the Plains*. The first two of these gentlemen will be remembered as having made a decided sensation and achieved a marked success, financially, in this city in a kindred drama last season.

Philadelphia *Inquirer*
December 29, 1873

The Sioux and Cheyennes will be among the first to tell you that William F. Cody has a big heart. Cody didn't fire me for drinking half his rye at Newark, just laughed, held his hands up in defeat, and the heartless bastard forgave me.

On we traveled—Trenton, Bethlehem, Easton, Pottsville, Reading, Lancaster, Harrisburg, and, the week before Christmas, Baltimore. That's when I saw a doctor about my eyes. Actually, I went about the snakebite, but I asked about my eyes anyway. The rattlesnake was Cody's idea. You see, a saloon stood across the alley from Baltimore's Academy of Music, and Cody went over there with Jennie Fisher before our second performance for a bracer or four. Well, on the backbar sat a glass case, and behind the glass rested a lazy rattlesnake, which the bartender fed mice and stout to entertain customers, Baltimore being populated with more ornery, uncivilized men than even Hays.

After a couple of whiskies, Cody decided that having a live rattlesnake—this one, well fed on mice and beer, was four feet long if it was a inch—on our stage would be a great addition. He asked the bartender if he'd rent out his snake, but got told no. Jennie Fisher, however, started honey-fuggling the barkeep, and a man can take only so much sweet talk from a woman like Jennie Fisher.

The long and the short of it is that Cody walked out of the saloon holding that old rattler. He took the snake in his hands, the case being too heavy to tote. Having done her

179

part, Jennie made a beeline to warn everyone that Cody was bringing in this killer viper. It seems that Jennie had found Cody's idea splendid until Cody lifted the hissing snake out of its home. By the time she found Texas Jack, Burke, and me, the snake was forty feet long with horns and clawed feet. Burke figured Jennie had consumed too much liquid courage, but Texas Jack and I knew Cody too well.

Rumor of an approaching snake sent several supes heading for parts unknown, and sent Texas Jack, Burke, and me outside to head off Cody. Hiram Robbins joined us a few moments later. Fred Maeder stayed inside to keep the rest of our 'Indians' from scattering. We wouldn't have much of a show if we had nobody to slay.

'Have you lost your mind?' Burke yelled. 'Get that snake out of here!'

'Listen to me,' Cody said. 'We'll bring the snake out for the first act. I'm thinkin' of havin' a Comanche shaman come out, holdin' the snake in both hands, offerin' a prayer to his god to kill his enemy, Buffalo Bill. Hiram, you can write it, can't you?'

Before Robbins could answer, Texas Jack informed his pard: 'Comanches hate snakes, Will.'

'Well, then we'll make it a Mormon,' Cody said. 'Better yet, it'll be Jim Daws.'

That got Robbins's attention because

180

Robbins played Jim Daws, and he vowed that he would never touch a real snake on stage or off stage, no matter how much money Cody offered.

Cody sulked. The rattler, its head and tail pinned in Cody's hands, twisted and turned like a thick jump rope.

'First,' Burke said, 'no one in the Combination will hold a serpent. And, second, man, think what would happen if the snake got loose. This isn't Bunnell's Dime Museum, and you aren't P.T. Barnum. We'd have bedlam!'

At last Cody retreated, saying all right, if everybody found it such a poor idea, he'd return the snake to the saloon. That's when a feral cat raced down the alley chasing a rat, and the cat starting screaming. For once, that slink Burke was right. It was bedlam. Perhaps sight of the rat excited the rattler. Cody, turning around to see what the commotion was all about, tripped, and, as he fell with the writhing snake, fear overtook him, and he flung the old mice-eater as far as he could.

Sight of the flying snake sent Hiram Robbins racing to the back door, while John Burke went to rescue his friend, Billy Cody. Texas Jack drew his Smith & Wesson, then cursed, realizing his weapon was loaded with blanks. I wasn't paying much attention to all of this, because of the cat. I had pulled out a Williamson Derringer, and had drawn a bead on the cat—I hate cats—when the snake landed, coiled, and struck my forearm, spoiling my aim.

The cat got the rat, and I cussed Cody and the entire Combination while ripping off my buckskin shirt. Meanwhile, Texas Jack clubbed the snake, but it got away, slithering underneath all the trash and offal that fill Baltimore's alleys. I hope the snake got the cat.

Suddenly sober, Cody came to my aid, moving like a velocipede. He slit the punctures with his knife—it's a wonder he didn't cut off my arm, nervous as he was—sucked and spit out the poison, and practically carried me from the alley to the street, shouting at Burke and Texas Jack to carry on the show without us. He commandeered a cab, and we raced ten blocks before Cody hollered at the driver to stop, paid him handsomely, ignoring the hack's protests, and shoved me through a door.

Lucky for us, it being a night performance, the doc lived above his office, and he shrugged before going to work on my arm. He seemed much more interested in Cody's teeth than my snakebite, telling Cody stories of rattlesnake poison killing Good Samaritans with bad teeth.

'I brush my teeth every morn,' Cody informed the doc.

'Yeah,' I said, 'with whiskey.'

'Then you two must share the same habits,' said the doc, staring at me. 'You both smell like whiskey vats.'

The doc bathed my wound, put some salve on it, wrapped it up, threw my arm in a sling, and told me to keep the arm immobile for a few days. He allowed that I might run a fever and could get sick to my stomach.

'But you'll live,' he told me. 'I don't know about the snake.'

Cody's ashen face gathered its natural color at the news, and he started begging for my forgiveness, saying how truly sorry he was for coming damned near getting me killed by a rattler. 'Anything you want, Jim, it's yours,' he told me. 'Forget what I said about you not drinkin' before the shows! Forget about you buyin' your own personal whiskey. By jingo, I'll fill your jugs with Old Tom-Cat myself!'

I wished the rattler had killed me. Cody would never fire me now. Maybe I should have taken him up on his offer. *Anything I want? I want to go home.* Pride, naturally, kept me from doing that.

Cody took his leave to race back to the Academy of Music, telling me not to worry, and telling the doc to send him the bill. After Cody had gone, I asked the doctor to check my eyes.

'They've been paining me,' I said.

The doctor told me he wasn't an eye doctor.

'What are you, then?' I asked. 'Other than a snake doctor?'

'I'm a veterinarian,' he said.

I laughed.

'I tried to tell your friend, sir,' the doc explained, 'but he wouldn't listen.'

'He can be single-minded,' I said, 'but that's all right. I'm half mule myself.'

The doc, being a good Yankee, offered me a drink, and I accepted. He asked about my eyes, and I told him they burned a lot, and my vision got cloudy. He had me look up and focus on a light, and examined my eyes while sipping his gin and bitters.

'Your eyelids are red-rimmed,' he said. 'Your eyes bloodshot.'

I could have told him that.

'It could be opthalmia,' he said.

I didn't like the sound of opthalmia, and liked it even less when he asked if I frequented the tenderloin, as gonorrheal opthalmia could result in permanent blindness. After adding things like granular conjunctivitis and trachoma to his list of afflictions I might have, he suggested I see an eye doctor.

'I liked you a lot better, doc,' I said, 'when you were just a snake doctor and a veterinarian.'

'You can wear protective lenses,' he said, 'and stay out of the light.'

I partly took his advice, staying out of the light for the final two shows in Baltimore. I sat up in the balcony, my arm in a sling, and watched them fools make bigger fools of themselves. My eyes, however, weren't so bad

184

that I didn't notice something peculiar and vexing. The fellow working the big calcium light shined it on Cody and Texas Jack a lot more than he shined it on everybody else, including the idiot pretending to be me. I soon forgot all about my eye troubles and wondered if my pards always hogged that limelight. I made a vow to fix that in Philadelphia. But first came Christmas.

Cody invited the Omohundro family to spend the holidays with him and his family. He also invited me, but I declined, saying I'd meet him in Philadelphia. The invitation did make me feel better, but I needed time away from those Thespians, so I took the train to Philadelphia, arriving on Christmas Eve. Despite the snow and cold, I decided to walk to my hotel from the depot.

On a bridge over the Schuylkill River, I noticed a young lad in front of me, carrying a bucket and a long, sharp stick. Once we crossed the bridge, the boy leaped over the railing, and started making his way to the banks of the frozen river.

'Hey, boy, where are you going?' I called out to him.

He said he was gigging frogs.

I followed him.

He walked along the bank, me a few rods behind. Although I had never gigged frogs, it struck me as something one did not do during the dead of winter. Just then, the boy stopped,

185

crouched, and thrust his stick into a snowdrift.
He pulled out the stick, and whooped like a
Reb.

Squinting, I saw the stick was empty, and,
likewise, figured so was the kid's head.

'Practice,' he told me. 'You got to practice
to be good.'

I grinned. 'Reckon so.'

'I'll be eating frog legs all summer 'cause I
practiced all winter.'

'That's right smart,' I said.

'You want to gig a frog.'

'Sure.'

'It'll be hard,' he said. 'What happened to
your arm?'

'A dragon almost bit it off.'

He whistled. 'Golly. You still want to try?'
I nodded.

He grinned back at me, and we crept along
the slippery riverbank.

'There.' He pointed at the neck of a beer
bottle sticking out of the snow.

Quick as lightning, I reached into my sling,
pulled out the Williamson, and blew the bottle
to bits. Like the kid said, you had to practice.
Since I had stopped shooting supes to pacify
Cody, I wasn't getting much target practice.

The boy whistled louder, and I put away the
Derringer. 'Your turn,' I said.

'You mean I get to shoot?'

'Hell, no. Your mama would likely nail my
hide to the barn. You gig. I shoot.'

I've spent many fine Christmas Eves, but that was my favorite. The kid—I never knew his name—would gig a make-believe frog with his stick, then I'd shoot one with my pistol, replacing the empty Williamson with my Colt. In West Chester, Cody and Texas Jack spent the holiday fox hunting with wealthy social types, warming themselves with hot brandies and cozy fires. I would not have traded places with any of them. Which got me to thinking there was something about this play-acting business, too. I never would have gone gigging frogs with a thirteen-year-old back in Abilene for fear that the thirteen-year-old might want to make a name for himself by gigging Wild Bill. My eyes didn't even hurt, and, as darkness approached, the kid said he had best go home. We shook hands, and he scurried into the darkness, hollering back at me to have a merry Christmas, and I hollered back at him to do the same. Then I climbed up the snow-covered bank to the street, slipping, sliding, struggling with my one good arm, but laughing all the while. I remained in a mighty fine mood when I finally reached the street, even when I saw the Philadelphia policeman tapping a nightstick against the palm of his hand.

'And just what do you think you are doing, lad?' He pointed the stick at the butt of the Colt, sticking out of my greatcoat pocket.

'Gigging frogs,' I merrily told him.

That's how I spent Christmas Day in the

Philadelphia City Jail. They thought I was staggering drunk, but they were wrong, and, still in the holiday spirit, I didn't complain when I paid a $5 fine.

Cody thought I was drunk, too, when we opened at Philadelphia's Academy of Music on December 29th, but he was likewise wrong. How that came about went like this: I remembered seeing Cody and Texas Jack bathed in all that limelight back in Baltimore, so, my arm out of the sling by now, I climbed the ladder to where this gent sat away up in the rafters. Almost frightened the poor fellow off his perch.

'I'm Wild Bill Hickok,' I said.

'Er, yeah, I know.'

'You shining that contraption tonight?'

'Yes, sir.'

'Well, I want you to shine it on me. I'm tired of Cody and Jack getting more light than me. Directly on me.'

'But . . .'

'You just do as I say.'

'Mister Hickok, I can't. I can't do that, sir, not without Mister Cody's direction.'

I showed him the Navy Colt. 'I can kill you nine times out of ten from down yonder,' I said. 'Now, do we have an understanding?'

'Yes, sir, Mister Hickok.'

It was one prig and smug James Butler Hickok ready to step onto the stage in Philadelphia for his first scene with Texas Jack

188

and Buffalo Bill. So eager was I, John Burke commented that he had never seen me look so excited.

On the stage, Cody said: 'Where have you been, Texas Jack?'

To which Texas Jack replied: 'I have been on the trail of Jim Daws, that renegade.'

'By thunder, then we have the same pursuit. For I have been chasin' that murderous fiend and horse thief. If only our old friend, Wild Bill, were here to join our effort. Have you seen Wild Bill?'

I ran onto the stage, shouting: 'Boys, I'm with you heart and hand! It is I, Wild Bill Hickok, protector of the fair and virtuous!'

That's probably the first time I ever said my lines loud enough for the folks in the rafters to hear. It even got Burke to applaud. Of course, I just wanted that light manipulator to know I was on stage and he had better do what he was supposed to do. He did, and I staggered back, blinded. I lifted my hands to protect my burning eyes.

'Turn that blame thing off!'

He didn't.

'Stop it, damn you!'

When the light didn't move, I drew my Williamson—my Colts being loaded without balls—ducked, swept off my hat with my left hand, blocked the blinding light with my hat, and fired. No, I wasn't shooting at the gent working the contrivance, but the light itself.

Hit it, too, scaring the hell out of the light manipulator, not to mention Cody, Burke, and many in the audience. Several others, however, started applauding my marksmanship, and before long even those I had scared witless smiled and clapped.

In the darkness, I just stood there. I turned scared myself when those Philadelphians started shouting: 'Wild Bill! Wild Bill! Wild Bill!' They thought this was part of the show.

'Say somethin',' Cody whispered urgently.

'Just not about Rock Creek,' Texas Jack added. *'Uhhhhhh.'* The place turned quiet after a while. *'Uhhhhhh.'*

'How'd you learn to shoot like that?' a man finally asked.

'Gigging frogs,' I replied.

Everybody laughed, only they didn't know why.

Chapter Sixteen

We might mention a slight incongruity in the piece and that is, the frequency with which the same tribe of Indians are wiped out, but the oftener they were shot down, the better the audience liked it, and roared with laughter in unison with the sparks of artillery exploding on the stage.

Morning Dispatch, Erie, Pennsylvania,
November 15, 1873

And I thought Kansas was cold. I don't know how people live in Maine. Obviously those January and February nights froze more than the mercury. It froze the population's tongues, because damned if I could understand their lingo. They talked worse than the Pawnees or a Texas Secessionist in his cups. The thing is you could always shut up a Pawnee by offering him a chaw of tobacco, and silence a Texican by clubbing him with a pistol barrel. Damn me to perdition if those Maine boys ever shut up.

Our Philadelphia run had brought in the year 1874, and afterward the Buffalo Bill Combination spent most of January in Connecticut, Rhode Island, and Massachusetts. I had hoped I would get to meet the writer Samuel Clemens, alias Mark Twain, when we visited Hartford, but the *Daily Courant* reported that he was enlightening the good folks of England and Scotland. So without the 'distinguished American humorist' to entertain me—for I had sure enjoyed his book about the frogs, at least the parts of it that I had read—I entertained myself by giving a couple of dying supes a powder burn or two. I had been denying myself far too long.

It taxed Cody so much his face turned crimson, and I almost regretted backsliding to my bad intentions. After all, Cody had sucked out that rattlesnake venom in Baltimore, and long before he had ever dreamed of acting, he had saved my hide from freezing to death when we were both scouting in Indian country. Thinking about those days, I showed yellow in Hartford, again vowing to behave myself. I caused no more trouble until we arrived in Portland, Maine, on January 29th, and that wasn't my fault and didn't affect the play.

A slew of b'hoys had gathered in the hotel room across from mine. The colder and later it got, the louder they got. We had a matinee the next day, and I needed some shut-eye, but just when I started to doze off, somebody would let out a Yankee hurrah. I cussed them, hollered at them to stop that infernal racket, and pulled the covers over my head. That didn't work, so I plowed a pillow into my ear. The tempest continued. I gave up on sleeping, and tried to read.

A body can't concentrate on written words, though, with all that noise. From my bed chamber, I again pleaded with them in my most demanding voice, but the only answer I got came from Alfred Johnson, pounding the wall, begging me to go to sleep. At last, I tossed off the covers, threw on my necessities, left my room, and knocked on the opposite door.

The man greeting me wore a plaid shirt and massive beard, and smoked a long nine cigar. He gave me a curious stare, which I deserved. Must have been a sight in nightshirt, boots, hat, and Navy .36 stuck inside my robe's sash.

'May I help you?' he asked.

Behind him rose a thick cloud of cigar smoke, the clinking of glasses and coin, blended with the pouring of whiskey. Someone yelled out: 'What's the hold-up, Sam? You in this game or not?'

'Fold me,' my greeter called back, then directed his gaze again at me. 'Is there a problem?'

'I was trying to sleep.' I wasn't tired any more. My intentions had been to clean out this nest of birds, teach them a lesson, but suddenly I had other notions. I tugged on my mustache.

'You're Hickok, right?'

'I am.'

'I thought so. Saw you in town this afternoon. Hope to catch you in the play

193

tomorrow night.'

'We have a matinee . . .'

'Yeah, but I'm a working man. Name's Sam Bradley. I'm a cobbler here in Portland.' He offered me his hand, which I took. Next, he offered me a cigar, which I also took. Finally he invited me in, asked if I'd care to join their poker game. I accepted.

Inside, he introduced me to the other players: Gary Whyte, who owned this very hotel; Jeff Patrick, a Portland haberdasher; M.D. O'Brien, a local tailor; and D.B. Higginbotham, city editor for the *Daily Advertiser.* It was a good thing I had decided not to whup, or shoot, these boys. It wouldn't look good for a member of the Combination to injure some of Portland's leading merchants. Cody would have had thrown a fit over that. All smiled, but nobody outright laughed at me, and, after all the handshakes were done, I was provided a glass of whiskey.

'So you're the actor,' Higginbotham said. 'What's it like pretending to be a man-killer?'

'Indian killer,' O'Brien corrected.

'Been reading about you scouts in the papers,' Whyte said. 'It's amazing what gets published these days, right, D.B.? Don't you wish you were performing Shakespeare instead, Mister Hickok?'

'Have you ever performed with Forrest?' Patrick inquired.

'Do people who attend your plays really
194

believe you've done all these things?' Higginbotham said.

'Never asked them,' I finally got to answer. After they offered me a chair, Whyte picked up the deck, and began shuffling.

'Do actors know how to play poker, Mister Hickok?' Whyte asked.

'I'd be interested in learning.' I yawned.

'It's a simple game,' Whyte said. 'And a friendly one. We play for the camaraderie, once a month, in this hotel room. O'Brien don't even charge us rent.'

They laughed.

'Damn the camaraderie,' Bradley said as he refired his cigar. 'I'd just like to see Gary lose for once.'

Whyte grinned. 'I've been on a roll the past few months.' He offered O'Brien the cut, then began dealing. 'It's five-card draw, Mister Hickok. We'll explain the game to you as we go along.'

'If you gentlemen are playing for money,' I began, 'I need to go across the hall, and collect . . .'

Bradley waved his hand, and scoffed. 'No need, sir. Your credit's good with us. It's not every night we get to socialize with an actor.'

On that night I, indeed, became an actor. I was the tenderfoot, trying to learn the game of poker, and my new comrades kept my whiskey glass full. I lost at first, intentionally, making foolish mistakes, asking stupid questions about poker. A couple of times, I reached over and picked up the discards in the center of the table, and took a lectured chastising.

'You can't do that!' I got told.

'Really?' I apologized. Truthfully I tried that every now and then out West, too. It wasn't exactly cheating, and not everybody I played with objected to my taking a peek at the deadwood on the frontier. That was because, out West, I was Wild Bill. In Portland, Maine, they considered Wild Bill to be a fictional falsehood, and Mr. Hickok to be a Thespian.

After an hour of losing, I decided I should start winning some modest pots. That proved a bit harder than I expected, but I soon learned why. No wonder the landlord had been winning of late. Gary Whyte kept cheating. That suited me all right, too. Often when Gary Whyte dealt, he dropped a card into a bowler hat in his lap, fetching another in the same motion, concealing his movement by wiping his face with a scarf that he likewise deposited in his upturned bowler. I had played against better sharpers in Abilene. I let the game progress, realizing after a while that he had kept the queens. I guess aces would be too obvious.

Long about five-thirty, Mr. Whyte dealt me two kings and two aces. He smiled when he dealt, too. The betting began, and I asked: 'Now, what does two pair beat?' When Bradley answered with a chuckle, I shot out another

196

question: 'And aces, they are like ones?'

'They're better than ones, James,' Patrick said. 'Aces are the highest card in the deck.'

I nodded at the good-natured funning that circled the table.

'I guess I know what Hickok has,' Higginbotham said, and folded his hand.

The betting went around to Gary Whyte, who raised a hundred bucks, double the amount that had been bet all night. I called, as did Patrick and Bradley. O'Brien also folded.

When I drew another king—which Whyte dealt me off the bottom—I knew it was time to play my hand. Patrick drew two cards, and Bradley asked for three. Whyte took three as well, and wiped his face with his scarf. The betting and raising started again, forcing Patrick and Bradley to fold. That left a bet of $175 to me. I called.

'I think this is a good hand, isn't it?' I said, revealing my cards.

'You're calling Gary,' Bradley said. 'He's supposed to show first.' Then Bradley almost dropped his cigar as he looked at my full house. He laughed heartily. 'Yes, that's a good hand. Right, Gary?'

Whyte shook his head. 'Yeah, it's a good one. But not good enough.' With a grin, he showed four queens, which I had expected. When he reached to pull in the pot, however, he found himself staring at my Navy Colt.

'You misunderstand, Whyte,' I said. 'I'm

197

calling the hand in your hat.'

That finally silenced them boys, especially Whyte, and, when his associates found the cards in the bowler, I lowered my revolver, raked the pot into my own hat, which I put on my head, and rose. I didn't know how men in Maine dealt with cheats, and didn't care. I could catch a few hours' sleep now, I figured, and, as I walked out the door, I said: 'Gents, next time you had better think twice before waking a man and asking him to play poker.'

They don't lynch cardsharpers in Portland. Or shoot them. I learned that much when the members of the Combination checked out of the hotel the next morning. Mr. Gary Whyte was working the desk, explaining to an elderly woman that his hotel was the finest in the state. She didn't believe him because of his black eye, crooked nose, and swollen lips.

'I fell down the stairs, madam,' he explained. He took our keys without a word, and never once looked at me.

I loitered around the desk.

'Your beds aren't ticky?' the lady asked. 'I'm traveling with my sisters, Mister Whyte. All seven of them, and we won't stay in a place that . . .'

'I assure you, madam,' Whyte said, 'that our chambers are the finest. Our linens are the whitest you'll find, washed every day.'

'That's a good thing,' I said real loud. ' 'Cause I pissed in mine last night.'

198

That lady pivoted like a West Point cadet. You've never seen such indignation, and she stormed out of the hotel to take her business and her sisters' business elsewhere. Well, you can bet that Mr. Gary Whyte looked at me then. Phil Coe had given me a look like that, right before I killed him. I looked back at him, and Whyte's gaze lowered. I reckon by then he understood that Wild Bill wasn't an actor at all.

There were no more poker games in Maine, just blustery days, frigid nights. The coldest came in Gardiner in February. I mean to tell you it was colder than a witch's teat, and I asked the boy at the desk to light a fire in my room, so it wouldn't feel like I was naked in the Big Horns when we returned from supper. The boy said he would take care of it, and I gave him a pass to the following night's play at the Opera House.

He lied. There was no fire in my room when I returned, and I had no whiskey to keep me warm. I ran downstairs to find a new clerk.

'I'd like a fire in my room,' I said. 'Now.'

'We'll take care of that, sir,' I got told, and I hurried upstairs, jumped in bed—still wearing my winter duds, including my great coat—and buried myself under the blankets and quilts.

People in Maine got no sense of time. I waited, and froze. I froze, and waited. Then I got ornery. Hell, I knew if I went downstairs again, somebody might get hurt, or killed, so I

199

opened my window, and hollered at the snowy street: 'Fire!'

I kept yelling that, too, and pretty soon, people began opening their doors on my floor in the hotel.

'Fire!'

Next, they ran down the stairs.

'Fire!'

They wandered outside, looking up, pointing, talking.

'Fire!'

Ten minutes later, the Gardiner Fire Company arrived with a horse-drawn heavy steam fire engine—right pretty, too, all that red paint, shiny brass, and gold trim. Fine-looking horse, I'll say. There followed more wandering, more looking up, more pointing, more talking.

'Fire!' I yelled.

Finally somebody saw me, and, after another round of pointing the ramrod of the Gardiner Fire Company shouted up at me: 'Where's the fire?'

'That's what I'd like to know!' I answered. 'I ordered a fire six hours ago, and it ain't been built yet!'

That just about ripped Cody's insides out. He—and me—got cussed out by the Gardiner Fire Company, the hotel landlord, half the guests, and, especially, Jennie Fisher, with whom he had been 'acting' when I started with the fire. What frustrated Cody most, though, was that our show in Gardiner got canceled. Seems the owner of the Opera House turned out to be kin to the landlord of the hotel and the chief of the Gardiner Fire Company, Gardiner being a right small town.

So, on the train ride to Bangor, I got another talking to. Got yelled at. Would have gotten cussed at if Cody cussed.

'Confound it, Jim, you can be so tarnal notional!' Cody said. 'You're a rabble-rouser. That's what you are, Jim.'

'I'm no such thing, Billy,' I said.

Cody spit out some more phlegm, threw up his hands, mumbled a few more things that served as cusses for Cody, took a seat by Jennie Fisher, demanded that I behave myself, and called me a rabble-rouser one more time.

Again I denied his accusation. Then I wrote Louisa Cody, posted the letter in Bangor, allowing how she might want to see a show, see how her husband acts, see how popular he is with the ladies, how he'd make her children proud. She might even, I wrote, travel with the Combination for a spell. This, I figured, might be my best joke ever.

Cody sure hit the nail on the head. I am a rabble-rouser.

ACT III

Cody

Chapter Seventeen

Buffalo Bill has won a host of friends in this city during his short sojourn. He is not the rough, uncouth specimen of humanity that many might imagine him to be, but a gentleman in the true sense of the term, and will be warmly welcomed if he should return. The same may be said of Texas Jack and Wild Bill.

Gazette and Bulletin
Williamsport, Pennsylvania
November 28, 1873

The Father, Son, and Holy Ghost had all conspired against me. So had Lucifer, my wife, and Wild Bill Hickok. When you manage a theater troupe, you feel like an unarmed scout afoot in the middle of Indian country, surrounded by a hundred red devils painted for butchery and ghastly depredations. You got about as much of a chance as that scout, too.

I was all alone, even when surrounded by members of the Buffalo Bill Combination. Oh, sure, Major John Burke, alias Arizona John Burke, had been hired to manage things, but it was my show, by thunder, and folks always came to me with their woes and complaints. Burke didn't do a blasted thing except book the theaters and hotels, work with newspapermen, arrange parades and such, handle all the finances and transportation, hire supes, and so forth. Mostly he just pined over Josephine Morlacchi. Buffalo Bill Cody did all the work, and it weighed heavily upon that poor soul.

Naturally I can understand why God frowned upon me, what with temperance and fidelity never being my strongest characteristics. I could even reason with my bride, Lulu, if she ever turned reasonable. But my friend, Jim Hickok, had begun to fray me down to a frazzle, although I'd never admit that to anyone. There are times when I'd shuck the whole thing—all of it, the money, champagne, adoring children, adoring ladies, the money, the buffalo head stickpin made of diamonds and gold and matching gold cufflinks, the money—to be alone on the plains with nothing but Old Brigham, Lucretia Borgia, and a gallon of King Bee Whiskey. Worcester, Massachusetts was one of those times.

I stepped onto the platform and helped down the lovely Jennie Fisher just in time to hear the enraged voice of my wife.

'Who the hell is this strumpet?'

'Mama,' I said, soon as I had collected my wits. 'It is bully good to see you.'

Lulu, on the prod, focused her wrath on poor Jennie. 'I am Missus Cody. Would you remove your arm from my husband, or shall I remove it?'

Naturally Jennie Fisher fled, leaving me alone to deal with my bride's rampage. Of course, I could not let her belittle one of my actresses, not seeing how the depot suddenly seemed chock-full of the members of the Buffalo Bill Combination and the press.

'Mama, rudeness ain't needed,' I mustered. 'That was just Jennie Fisher, an actress. I was merely helping her onto the platform. I . . . uh . . . I thought you'd be in West Chester.' I sought out refuge. 'Where, pray tell, are the little ones?

'In the hotel.'

'Why . . . ?'

'I have decided to travel with you, Will, to see what I have been missing, to see how good of an actor you have become. Your man-killer friend, Hickok, was right. I have been missing a lot.'

I choked down a curse, a desire to murder, and glared at my old pard, Jim Hickok, as he tipped his hat, mumbled something, and walked past Lulu and me with a widening grin. I muttered something back—*Et tu, Bruté?*'— but nobody heard.

Damn the theater! Money had lured me to the lime footlights, but I had not been thinking of myself when I accepted Judson's invitation. I had not been thinking of myself when Texas Jack and I parted ways with Judson and lit out on our own. Always my precious Arta,

207

handsome Kit, and little Orra Maude—even Lulu—occupied my thoughts.

I married shortly after the War of the Rebellion. Married more on a whim, which is how I did practically everything. I reckon I loved her, or perhaps I loved the idea of being married, but Lulu and I come from different worlds, see things differently. I will be the first to admit that I am not the easiest person to be hitched to, what with me riding off with the Army, hunting buffalo for the railroad, or enjoying Old Tanglefoot with pards. Lulu came from money, and she wanted the best for her and me and our young 'uns. So did I, the problem being that I fizzled at making my family rich. I had failed at everything, financially speaking, betting on the wrong horse, investing in the wrong town. I laughed at my follies and foibles, but it troubled me, seeing my precious ones in homespun and hand-me-downs.

It's hard to make a go of things on the frontier, so when Judson offered me a chance to tread them boards, and when Texas Jack and I saw just how well folks back East cottoned to our shows, well, I felt like one of the Indian chiefs who had been transported by rail from his hunting grounds to see the Great White Father, an Indian who had been awed and practically struck dumb by the great cities, who returned to his tribe to tell his people of the unfathomable things he had seen, to beg for peace because they could never defeat a race with such power, with such numbers. Although I am and will remain to my death a Westerner at heart, I saw my future in the East, not the West.

I also recollect back in March of 1873 when Texas Jack, Judson, and me toured the U.S. Treasury Department while in our nation's capital. The Washington politicians and Treasury folks had shown us a vault, and our guide remarked that the vault contained $600,000,000. I had perhaps $4,000 to my name—1873 being a fairly good year as I can also recall when I had my 40¢ on my person and was on tick to the sum of $300 at the post sutler's—and said: 'Lock me up and let me die here.'

No way I could give my family everything I wanted for them out on the border, but here, in the East, I could be the hero to them in a way I never could be out West, where everyone else saddled that hero handle on me. Lulu didn't see things that way. She figured I'd just make a fool of myself on stage, and perchance I did, but I got a fair share of greenbacks for playing that part, greenbacks that kept my family's bellies full. Lulu didn't see that, either. She just saw those greenbacks keeping my belly full with John Barleycorn. I can't argue with that, either, but I certainly needed a bracer. Nobody ever told me how vexatious this acting business can be. I learned, though. I am a right quick learner.

As troubling as things had gotten, I had started rehearsing more with Jennie Fisher to take my mind off my woes. She'd read me some sonnets, teach me about play acting, and pretend that she was Josephine Morlacchi doing the can-can before we got ourselves all entangled in each other. She even gave me some sonnets to read, and then some of Shakespeare's plays. I wish she had given me some of his comedies, but, alas, 'twas not my luck. Although I mightily enjoyed *The Tragedy of Macbeth,* Jennie Fisher kept saddling me with other depressing accounts: *The Tragedy of King Lear, The Tragedy of Othello, The Tragedy of Julius Caesar,* and even more gloomy titles like *The Most Lamentable Tragedy of Titus Andronicus* and *The Most Excellent and Lamentable Tragedy of Romeo and Juliet.* I started dreaming of asking Fred G. Maeder or Hiram Robbins to write us a new play: *The Tragedy of Buffalo Bill!*

Nothing helped much. I found myself arguing more with Jim Hickok, whose jollifications once would have made me howl with laughter. I needed an extra bracer each morning just to face the day. Over the past couple of nights, I imagined what things would be like if I let one of those supes rigged out in a tan-colored frock and a red-flannel scalp Buffalo Bill Cody on the stage. Then Lulu and my family showed up. Major Burke said they

came at the most inopportune time—Jennie
Fisher put it another way, but not with all the
calamitous words my Lulu used—but I didn't
see things that way. To be honest, after Lulu
and I went through about twenty-seven rounds
in Worcester's Waverly House, I felt a joy and
peace I had not felt since sleeping off a five-
day drunk in North Platte back in 1869 after I
won a buffalo-shooting contest with Billy
Comstock (or maybe it had been in 1868 and a
six-day drunk). Anyway, I got to see my
children, got to bounce them all on my knee,
and sing 'Shoo Fly' to them a time or two,
making up words because I hadn't gotten a
chance to sing to them for a spell and had
forgotten most of the words anyway after
pouring a quart of John Barleycorn down my
throat, it being particularly dry after my scrap
with Lulu.

About that time, the theater pulled me from
my family again. Major Burke tapped on the
door, pardoning his intrusion, but desiring a
few minutes of my time. I kissed my children
good night, said good bye to Lulu, and joined
Burke in the hotel's saloon. I had hoped Major
Burke wanted to discuss more about my desire
to perform Shakespeare. Thanks to Jennie
Fisher, and after gaining needed experience
with our melodramas, I had suggested we try a
hand at the Bard. Everyone in the
Combination had practice saying that sort of
poetry—except we scouts—and I thought it

would be a hoot. The major, however, must have forgotten all about *Macbeth*. After a couple of beers arrived from a right handsome barmaid, the major took a sip, cleared his throat, leaned forward, and whispered: 'I think it's time you let Hickok go.'

'Go where?' I inquired.

'To the blazes!' Burke shouted. He killed the rest of his beer. 'Confound it, man, you have to fire that rapscallion before he ruins us all!'

'He promised to behave,' I said. 'Jim's a square deal.'

'He's promised that before. And before. And before. He quits for a few days, then starts up again. Listen, Will, we'll be back in New York at the end of the month, and it's going to be hard to find any actors to fill those parts. It's hard enough here in New England. Even with the Panic. Word has spread how your pard torments the supes.'

I gave the major a fabulous Buffalo Bill grin. 'He hasn't shot you, has he, John?'

Major Burke snorted. 'It's serious business, Will. Hickok must go.'

'I'll talk to him . . .'

'Talk? Damnation, Will, you've talked and talked and talked. That man doesn't listen.'

'He's been good.'

'Good? Burning supes with powder, getting our show canceled in Maine, almost getting us thrown out of the hotel after his mischief in

212

Gardiner? Bringing your wife here? That's being good?'

I waved the barmaid over for some more ale. 'He got my kids here, Major. Ain't seen them since Christmas. Besides, I think Jim would make a good King Duncan.'

The barmaid brought us another round and gave me a friendly smile. Worcester, Massachusetts began looking a tad finer.

'Forget *Macbeth,* Will. Forget Hickok. He's trouble. You must fire him.'

I sighed, saddened that Major Burke had shattered my vision of the barmaid, roped and pulled me back into the drudgery of the Combination. 'That's what you said 'bout Jack Omohundro, too, Major,' I said, 'especially when he started courtin' Josephine.'

Land sakes, I've never seen ears turn that shade of red. 'She has nothing to do with this, sir.' The major got all indignant. 'I was not jealous of Omohundro, and I am certainly not jealous of Hickok. I dislike him because he is uncouth, vile, mean-spirited, and a cold-blooded assassin.'

'He's my pard, Major, and I wouldn't make a habit of sayin' things like that 'bout Jim. He hears real good, and has shot men for less. But he ain't cold-blooded, vile, or mean-spirited, and he sure ain't uncouth, not that way he dresses and perfumes his locks. He's a good man. I'll talk to him.'

'He won't listen.'

213

'Well, I've known him longer than I've knowed you. Sure, he's as notional as most scouts I've rode with, but he's a staunch friend, and I ain't gonna turn him loose in this wilderness. He's part of the Buffalo Bill Combination. He stays. You gonna finish your beer?'

The major grumbled something I took as a no, so I picked up his glass, and drained it. Burke allowed one more time that he didn't see why I stuck by Hickok, and left the saloon. Alone, I got to thinking.

Things had been a whole lot easier back when Judson managed everything, and I just had to massacre Indians on stage. Managing a troop is hard business, even tougher than serving as chief of scouts or justice of the peace. Actors and actresses ain't like Westerners, ain't tough at all but fragile. Actors and actresses get upset at the silliest things, like getting upstaged—I haven't learned exactly what that means, but Walter Fletcher, Alfred Johnson, and W.S. MacEvey, on a regular basis, threw conniptions over who did what during a performance—or being burned by a pistol shot at close range.

While Jim Hickok could be contrary, he never shirked his duty. Back when we were both working for Russell, Majors, and Waddell, when I was knee high to a locust, he had whupped a burly bullwhacker about to whup me, and I wasn't about to forget that no

214

matter how many blasted supes he made hopping mad. I thought about that before returning to *Macbeth*. When the barmaid brought me another beer with another smile, I considered how she would make a fine apparition.

I would play Macbeth, Texas Jack could be Malcolm, and Jim Hickok would be King Duncan no matter what the major said. Jennie Fisher would make a perfect Lady Macbeth, and I'd make Major Burke happy by casting him as MacDuff, although that certainly wouldn't please Alfred Johnson, actors being actors and all. I was trying to figure out who'd play the witches when Lulu arrived in the saloon, and started her tirade again.

Chapter Eighteen

Messrs. Buffalo Bill, Texas Jack, and Wild Bill devoted two and a half hours to killing off Indians. During the four acts 300 Indians must have bit the dust. Some of these days the material will give out, and there will be no Indians left to exterminate. When that event occurs, these scouts of the plains will find good substitutes for red men in the police court rabble.

Daily Times, Troy, New York
February 25, 1874

So vexed was I by my two tons of trouble that, when we performed at the Springfield Opera House, after two rousing shows at the Worcester Hall, I forgot my lines. Naturally even the greatest Thespian blunders on stage. Why I have even heard of Edwin Booth botching a Shakespeare soliloquy, and, anyway, our talk seemed as worthless as an old buffalo bone. Half the time we made up the things we said, or I recited Texas Jack's line, and he said mine, and Jim Hickok said nothing (or when he did say something, you couldn't rightly hear him). Folks didn't ante up 50¢ to see the living heroes talk; they wanted us to kill Indians. Which is what I should have done.

Oh, how many times have I chuckled as Texas Jack or Jim Hickok forgot what they were supposed to say, then simply drew their six-shooters and filled the theater with gunsmoke and noise as our score of supes rushed on stage to be mercifully, or unmercifully when Hickok felt so inclined, slain? On this night, after a slight pause, I reached for my Smith & Wesson, thinking to escape my blunder with some boisterous shooting, when I perchance looked up in the balcony and spotted Louisa Frederici Cody, my wife.

'Mama,' I said, 'I'm such a horrible actor.'

That line excited those New Englanders more than killing and scalping savages could have. They laughed, applauded, cheered, and everyone turned to search for Mrs. Buffalo Bill. I doffed my hat, bowed, and joined the commotion, calling out: 'Be honest, Mama, does this look as awful up yonder as it feels down here?' Pretty soon, everyone started hurrahing, screaming for Mrs. Buffalo Bill to come on stage and say a few words.

'Come take a bow, Mama!' I encouraged.

A portly usher appeared beside her, and the fuss became deafening. Lulu resisted at first, but eventually fled the balcony with the usher, who led her downstairs, down the center aisle, and around the orchestra pit, where I helped her onto the stage. Even with the limelight, Lulu looked redder than Major Burke's ears had the other night, only she wasn't raging, but downright humbled, embarrassed.

The crowd quieted, and Lulu cleared her throat. 'I . . .' She shot a glance back at me. I grinned. 'I . . . thank . . . er . . . I . . .'

I walked up beside Lulu, and put my arm around her shoulder.

'This is my wife, mother of my three darlin' children, a grand woman from Saint Louis, Missouri, Louisa Cody,' I announced, and kissed her cheek, which caused quite a stir in the audience and in Louisa. I mean to tell you, she shied away from me like a green filly. She wanted to stampede like a frightened buffalo calf, only her legs wouldn't work. Almost like she had buck fever. I couldn't help but giggle as I went to comfort her.

Behind me, I heard Texas Jack, ever the true friend with theater savvy, whispering some lines to Lulu. 'It is a pleasure to be here . . . I wish to thank everyone in Springfield for making our stay enjoyable.'

Jim Hickok had some advice, too.

'Hell, get her off the damned stage,' said my pard, 'and let's wipe out some Injuns.'

All Lulu could manage, though, was: 'Uhhh . . .'

Hugging her tightly, I said, more to the audience than to her: 'Now you can understand how hard your poor husband has to work to make a livin'.'

Folks liked that line, too. They stomped their feet as I walked Lulu off stage right,

218

where Major Burke waited with a snifter of brandy to steady Lulu's nerves. Not right sure what Lulu thought, I figured she'd let me know on the train ride to Pittsfield after the show. I had to hurry back on stage. Jim Hickok had started firing his Colts, and there were Indians to be killed.

Lulu wasn't as perturbed about the incident as I thought she'd be. I had her pegged to be madder than a hornet, accusing me of shaming her so, but, as the train rocked along, she even smiled at me.

Smiled, that is, till I suggested that we should make it a regular routine in the show, the way I had done with Jim Hickok and his 'cold tea don't count' outburst. Lulu wasn't about to let that happen.

'You'll do no such thing, Will Cody,' she snapped. She could turn that smile off like the spigot on a keg of beer, be sweet and warm one moment, and bitter and cold the next. I could predict her moods no more than I could Nebraska weather in the spring, although it was getting easier of late. Yes, sir, that woman was as disagreeable as fried rattlesnake, and as pitiless as Jack Omohundro's coffee.

'Oh, Mama,' I pleaded. 'You'll get used to it, the way I took to it. Takes time, is all. Why, you can even bring Arta, Kit, and Orra Maude with you. Folks would enjoy that just fine.'

'Newspapers would like it, too,' chimed in Major Burke, sitting behind us.

'I'd just look into the balcony, find you, and . . .'

'You'll have a hard time finding me, Will Cody,' Lulu said. 'I'll be hiding in the darkest, nethermost regions of the halls if and when I ever see another one of Elmo's asinine melodramas.'

Elmo would be Judson. I informed her that Judson had nothing to do with our Combination any more, although she already knowed that. She just put men like Judson, Maeder, and Robbins in the same tribe, a tribe lower than temperance screamers and mealy-mouthed Republicans.

'All right, Mama,' I said. 'Forget I brung it up.'

She forgot about it, too, for about a mile as the train lumbered along. Then she hauled off and whacked me a good one with her handbag, sending my hat flying to the aisle.

'What in tarnation . . . ?' I began.

'Is that what you think, Will Cody?'

'Think? Mama . . . ?'

'You think you can threaten me, drive me back to our home in West Chester with our children? Or maybe you'd prefer if I took the children back home to North Platte, to be as far from you as possible!' I looked around, hoping the children weren't near, wouldn't see their mama like this. I mouthed a silent prayer when I saw them three angels asleep away back in the coach. I thought up some choice

220

cuss words, too, when I noticed everybody in the coach staring at us. Although I didn't say anything, I sure wanted to.

'That's just like you, you rascally bastard,' Lulu went on. 'Threaten me with embarrassment so I'll take my leave? Well, I'm harder than that, mister. I'm not about to leave you with *that . . .!*'

I followed her big finger, pointing catty-corner from us.

'Jack Omohundro?' I said, all bewildered.

She smacked me again. 'You know damned well I don't mean Jack. It's her. That *actress!*'

'Louisa.' I fought down my own anger, and my cowardly desires to retreat to the smoking car and have a snort from Jim Hickok's flask. I fetched my hat, jammed it on my head, and told her: 'I don't want you to leave. I wasn't thinkin' of nobody but you when I suggested we bring you on stage for every show. All I've ever wanted . . . the only reason I even put up with these shenanigans . . . is for you and the little ones.'

She snorted, pawed the floor with her button-up boots like a mad bull, and just stared ahead at F.N. Watson's bald spot. She didn't say nothing, hardly even blinked, till we reached the station a little while later, although it felt a whole lot longer than a little while, with me sitting next to that frigid crone.

The night had turned bitterly cold, made even colder by the wet snow, blustery wind, and my wife's mood. From the Pittsfield depot, we hurried to our hotel—the Emler House, four stories tall but as rowdy and randy as that hostelry in Titusville, Pennsylvania. I'd have to speak to the major about his choice of accommodations, now that my family had joined me. The Emler House rested next door to the Opera Hall, but it also adjoined Ron's Saloon, and folks were having a fine time at Ron's that night when we checked in. How I longed to join them, but I had a family to care for. The clerk gave me a key to a room on the second floor, but upon a brief inspection I deemed it unsatisfactory, and hurried downstairs to confront the pockmarked innkeeper with the nasal whine.

'Is there something wrong, Mister Cody?' the gent asked.

I nodded. 'It's too noisy. It's on the wrong side of the hotel, too close to the grog shop next door.' I pointed my goatee at dear Orra Maude, asleep in her mama's arms, and then at poor Kit, asleep in mine, and finally at Arta, who could barely stand up, so tired was she. 'I desire a room with some peace and quiet.'

'It's the week-end, sir,' the clerk began.

'It's Thursday,' Lulu corrected him.

The fellow shrugged. 'Be that as it may, I can't control the noise at Ron's. I can scarcely keep our own customers quiet.'

'I'd like a new room,' I said, 'one where peace and quiet can be found.'

222

The fellow gave me a grin I didn't like. 'Mister Cody, ma'am, the only way you could have absolute peace would be to rent the whole fourth floor, and, of course, you don't want to do that.'

Sure as Satan, that fellow didn't know William F. Cody.

'Oh, don't I?' I said. 'How much is it?'

There appeared that grin again. 'Sir,' the innkeeper said, 'two hundred dollars would be a pretty stiff price to pay for peace and quiet.'

'Paid!' I pulled out the buffalo bull scrotum I had made into a money pouch, withdrew a handful of greenbacks that I tossed in the uppity gent's face. I must say I enjoyed the look on Lulu's face reflected in the mirror behind the front desk. 'Now, let's see how quick you can make things comfortable, my good man. I got a wife and babies, and we're all tuckered out.'

By grab, I thought that act of generosity would make my darling bride bring out the peace pipe, but she took to the warpath once we got the kids tucked into their beds in their fourth-story room. 'Two hundred dollars!' she screamed. 'Do you know how much two hundred dollars can buy, Will? You have not one inkling about finances. Two hundred dollars! For one night? My God, man, and I thought you were a skinflint when I first met you.'

So much for peace and quiet, I thought, and

223

then it struck me. By jingo, I didn't have to spend the night with the likes of her. I had a whole floor of rooms to pick from.

Chapter Nineteen

It is an *extraordinary* thing to have created in real life the character Buffalo Bill; it is a most difficult task to so impersonate that character upon the boards as to give an audience an adequate impression of its heroism and grandeur . . .
Daily Express, Easton, Pennsylvania,
December 16, 1873

February 23, 1874 started out just fine in North Adams, Massachusetts. My wife acted practically sociable as a citizens' group met us at the depot and gave us a fine parade to our hotel. Sight of those tiny streets lined with men, women, and children, all bundled up in scarves, hats, mittens, and greatcoats, peering over towering snowbanks and cheering our very arrival, left Lulu speechless, which don't happen often.

Hickok, Texas Jack, and I signed three score of autographs at the hotel, where the innkeeper finally wrestled us away from the cherishing public, and sat us down in his fancy restaurant, then started snapping fingers, and ordering the staff around till our goblets and plates had been filled with wine and turkey. Next came the reporters, followed by some pals I had met during my previous acting tour, along with a former officer I had scouted for with the 5th Cavalry.

I had just finished my piece of pumpkin pie and was spooning Kit's dessert into his mouth when we received our last visitor.

'Mister Cody, my name is Stokes O'Riley, and I wonder if you could assist me, sir. What a handsome daughter you have!'

'This is my son, Kit Carson Cody,' I told the cad.

'Ah, well . . . er . . . his curls, the hat . . .'

'It's all right, Stokes. I can't very well dress Kit in beaded buckskins yet. His mama frowns upon my wardrobe.'

Stokes O'Riley grinned. 'Sir, allow me to get to the point. I am running for mayor, and I am hoping for your endorsement. If you could just mention my name during your play tonight, why, I would do anything to return the favor.'

'I got elected once,' I told Stokes, after wiping Kit's mouth with my bandanna, then accepting Lulu's polite condemnation for not using a napkin. 'In Nebraska.'

'Yes, which is why you are called the Honorable Buffalo Bill. Er . . . not that you weren't an honorable man before that . . .'

'Never showed up to the Legislature, though.'

Lulu cleared her throat. 'There was a recount, Will, that showed you lost that election.'

I pretended not to hear. 'Mayor is a right powerful position, Stokes. I don't give my endorsin' to just anyone.'

'Unless whiskey's involved,' muttered Lulu.

'I'm a skinflint when it comes to things like endorsin',' I added.

'If only you didn't give away your money so freely,' mumbled Lulu, 'to any chawbacon with a story or a tear.'

I looked Stokes O'Riley up and down, sizing him up, then tugged on my goatee. 'Well, Stokes, like I said, politics is a delicate matter, not for everyone. Most politicians I knowed are crooked as an oxbow. Are you honest, sir?'

'Mister Cody,' Stokes said, 'I dare say that I am as true to my word as you are, sir.'

Lulu about choked.

I shook my head sadly. 'Ride on, Stokes,' I said. 'I'd hate to make a crook out of an honest man.'

We got some chuckles out of that one—wish the newspaper boys had been around to hear it—and soon retired to our rooms to rest up for the night's show, which turned out to be a romping good time. Our supes died gloriously, and I forgot about my marital struggles—leaving Lulu in the hotel with the children and a bottle of French brandy—and we spent twice the amount of powder and paraffin as we normally did, those New Englanders being eager to see us kill, maim, and scalp.

The crowd gave Jim Hickok an ovation when he shot dead the wicked Tom Doggett, played by W.S. MacEvey, after he ran off with Lettie Carter, played by little Eliza Hudson. They screamed for Wild Bill to kill Doggett again, so MacEvey rose, dusted himself off, and footed it toward the wings again, dragging Eliza by her arm. Hickok shook his head at the tomfoolery, cocked his Colt, and shot the coward again, who died real splendid. In fact, we were so caught up with all the slaughter that we forgot one important piece of our play. The curtain had closed, we had taken several bows, and folks had starting to leave the theater when a ragamuffin in the balcony stood up and hollered: 'Hold on there. You can't be finished. Why, Dutchy ain't dead yet!'

I looked around, thinking back, and realized that the lad was right. Somehow, we had forgotten to kill off Nick Blunder, the Irishman portrayed by Walter Fletcher. Blunder was not a villain, but a secondary hero murdered by the foul Jim Daws, but I drew my Smith & Wesson, and fired at Fletcher, who, always game, clapped his hand over his heart, staggered forward, and collapsed by the footlights. A couple of handsome women with bouquets began covering Fletcher's corpse with the prettiest flowers I had ever seen in February.

227

After a round of handshakes, the theater manager, a tall fellow named Lawrence Ash, suggested we retire to Jameson's Tavern to celebrate. He said he'd even stand me to as much whiskey as I could drink, the fool.

'Sir,' I said, 'you speak the language of my tribe.'

I grabbed my greatcoat and hat, wrapped my neck with a scarf, and peered over Major Burke's shoulder.

'How do we look?' I asked.

He set his pencil aside, and nodded at the cash box. 'I bet we clear two thousand or more. It was a tremendous night.'

'We're goin' to a waterin' hole named Jameson's,' I said. 'See you there.'

'What about Mizzus Cody?'

'She needs her rest.'

I made a beeline for the door, but a man I didn't recognize headed me off. He puffed and looked madder than Lulu.

'My name's Collins,' he said, 'and, if that bastard ever burns me like he did tonight, I'll kill him.'

I pushed back my hat, trying to recall. 'I don't recollect . . .'

'Lying dead I was, like I was supposed to do, and that fiend, Hickok, came over and put his muzzle not inches from my limb.' At first, I figured this man to be a fraud, but he lifted his trousers, revealing a powder burn and singed hair. Somehow I had missed Hickok's latest

228

assassination.

'You didn't jump up and scream,' I said.

'Of course not. I'm an actor. I take my work seriously, no matter how absurd the role, no matter how obtuse the play. But I'm telling you to warn that yellow bastard . . .'

That's as far as he got. Hearing the insults, Jim Hickok came over, and clubbed Collins good with the barrel of his Colt. The actor dropped to the floor without a word. I spun, afraid of what the major would do, but Burke had reburied his nose in the cash box and his ledger book, and had neither seen nor heard the incident. A couple more supes rushed over to drag Mr. Collins outside.

'We're headin' over to the saloon at our hotel,' I lied to Jim, suddenly not wanting to be with my cast and pards but to be alone with Mr. Ash and partake of his generosity. I took about seven more steps before Hiram Robbins begged his pardon.

'You shouldn't have shot Walter Fletcher,' Robbins told me. 'That's my job. That's the way I wrote it.'

'Well, why didn't you shoot him when you were supposed to?'

'How could I? Omohundro ruined the scene when he forgot his lines and started shooting Indians, and Walter wasn't on stage again after Omohundro roped him and drug him off. All I'm saying is this . . . if that happens again, if we somehow can't kill off Blunder during the

229

production, you just nod to me, and I'll shoot him.'

'With what? Your finger?'

'I'll say *bang.*'

'*Bang* don't mean nothin', Hiram. Those folks want to hear thunder, see smoke, and smell brimstone.'

Robbins didn't retreat. 'I won't be upstaged like that.'

I let out a sigh. 'Let's talk it over tonight,' I said, spotting Alfred Johnson, waiting behind my playwright. 'We're celebratin' at Coyne's Saloon.'

Robbins grumbled something before storming off, and I motioned Johnson over.

'You can't let Walter Fletcher die like that on stage,' he said. 'That's not right. He died during our bows, fell right in front of me, and those ladies with those flowers. They tossed them on Walter instead of throwing them to me.'

I figured those ladies meant their flowers for Hickok, Texas Jack, and me, but I let out a long breath and remained peaceable. 'I'll speak to Walter,' I said. 'Anything else?'

'Yes, sir. I don't like it that MacEvey got to die twice. He upstaged me, Cody. I only get to die once.'

'Let's talk it over in private,' I said. 'We're doin' a little celebratin'. I'm supposed to meet Mister Ash at Vaughan's Billiard Hall tonight. Head over there, grab a table, and we'll discuss it in fine detail when I join you.'

'I don't know how to play billiards,' the actor told me.

'I'll teach you,' I said, and made it outside.

The bitterly cold wind gave me a feeling of relief till I found little Eliza Hudson waiting for me at the bottom of the stairs.

'Would you mind tellin' that imbecile MacEvey not to pull my arm out of its damned socket? The fool liked to have broke it twice tonight, and came close to stovin' in my head with them enormous feet of his. God A'mighty, I don't get paid enough to get crippled permanent in this stinkin' show.'

I was out of saloons to name and considered Eliza too young to drink no how, although she held a cigarette between her fingers and had taught Jim Hickok how to roll a smoke. 'I'll mention it to W.S.,' I said, and rushed past her down the alley, turned a corner, and cursed my memory.

Was it Vaughan's? Coyne's? Jameson's? The hotel groggery? I had misguided so many members of the Combination, I had forgotten where I was supposed to meet Mr. Ash. Just then, a hansom cab stopped in front of me, and a pretty gal stuck her head out.

'Where you going, Buffalo Bill?' she asked. 'You want to ride with me?'

'Rescued again,' I said, and climbed in beside Jennie Fisher.

Major Burke and Fred G. Maeder had spent months trying to educate me about timing, how important it is in the stage business. 'You need to say your line quicker,' the major would say, or Maeder would inform me: 'You need to pause. You're contemplating what she just told you. Don't speak that line so fast. It sounds like you're in a hurry. Remember . . . timing!'

Well, I knowed I had botched my timing when Jennie Fisher and I strolled into the hotel at three in the morn. Lulu stood in the lobby to greet me, along with half the Combination, including Texas Jack and Jim Hickok.

'Get that vixen out of my sight!' Lulu punctuated her order by hurling an empty bottle of French brandy at me. I ducked, the glass shattered against a bronze statue, and Jennie Fisher ran into the darkness.

'Mama,' I pleaded, 'she was just givin' me a ride back to the hotel. We weren't doin' a thing.'

The innkeeper came out of his office and asked us please to be quiet.

Of course, nobody listened to him. Lulu just stood there, hands on her hips, her whole body shaking. A handful of actors accused me of lying to them. A supe with a knot on his head the size of a walnut threatened me with a lawsuit or imprisonment (even though I had

232

not laid a hand on the gent). Jim Hickok, after taking a sip from a stein of ale, gave me a let's-see-how-you-get-out-of-this-ambuscade look. Ever the true friend, Texas Jack Omohundro stepped in front of the mass of folks.

'Let's all settle down here,' Texas Jack pleaded. 'No need in wakin' half the customers in this place.' He shook his head, and started telling a story he said he was reminded of, about how Hickok, he, and me had been met by some hot Mexicans after we had relieved them of some beer they had been hauling, beer we had decided was better suited for the 5th Cavalry boys, or at least us scouts.

'For just once, Jack, can't you tell a story without wandering over half the countryside?' W.S. MacEvey said. 'Get to the point!'

'His stories have no point, W.S.,' Hiram Robbins said. 'He just likes to hear himself talk.'

Texas Jack shut up, looking hurt, or maybe it was what he called his dumb look.

'Can't this wait?' the innkeeper pleaded.

'Might as well get everything said now,' Major Burke said. 'Our next two stops are long engagements, two days in Troy and three in Albany, and I don't want any bad reports in those newspapers.'

Things turned quiet. I stared into a nest of sidewinders.

'All right,' I began, 'we've been travelin' the rails, playin' to audiences for quite some time

233

now.' This season felt like it had been going on for sixty years. I shuddered when I realized Hickok had been with us for not yet six months. 'I'm new to this actin' deal. I try hard, though, for my family, and you're all part of my family. But since y'all look to me as y'all's daddy, it's time for me to set some rules.' I searched out Hickok. 'Jim, this is it, your last warnin'. You can't shoot a supe any more with pistols at close range. I want you to shake hands with this gent here you burnt and walloped. Go on, now. Shake hands. That's a good fellow. Major, give Mister Collins an extra dollar for his headache and powder burn. He's a fine actor. Collins, you be smart, keep up your hard work, and I'll cast you in a prime part when we do *Macbeth.* Good night. God bless you.

'W.S., you need to be a little more gentler when you're abductin' Eliza. You're a great actor, W.S., but you came close to practically maimin' her in the show. I know. Where is Eliza? Asleep. That's good. Don't work yourself into a lather, W.S. Everything's all right now. We love your work.

'Walter, I want you to give Hiram a couple of them roses or whatever they was that you got tonight. Hiram, if we run into something like this again, you just come over to me, and you can borrow my pistol and kill the Dutchman. That sound fair? Good. Oh, and, Alfred, I promise to kill you twice in our next

234

show at Troy.'

'Could you do it in Oswego?' Johnson inquired. 'I have relations coming to our show in Oswego.'

'Oswego it shall be. Listen, even the best families have woes and wars. We made a good showin' tonight. Major Burke, I want you to give everyone in the Combination a twenty-dollar bonus. On the train this morn.'

I hadn't gotten shot or stabbed, but, of course, I hadn't addressed the person angriest at me. Reckon I was working up the courage when Lulu charged through the crowd, which I think I had won over.

'That's just like you, Will Cody!' she shouted. 'You think you can buy everyone off with money or whiskey.' She pivoted, pushed Alfred Johnson almost to the carpet, and screamed at him. 'Are you a whore, Johnson? That's what you all are acting like! Whores. Bought off by this . . . this . . . this damned faker.'

'Faker!' I had had enough. 'I'm not a faker, woman. What gumption! What storyin'! I'm a hard-workin' actor and father . . . and I work the hardest tryin' to please this hard rock I married. What do you think bought us that house in Pennsylvania? And most of our property in Nebraska? Or that new house we've been talkin' 'bout gettin' in Rochester? You think you'd be livin' like that if I was scoutin'? I ain't done nothin' apurpose to hurt

235

you, Lu. Jennie Fisher is just an actress, tryin'
to teach me how to act better so I can better
provide for you and the little ones. But I ain't
gonna stand here and let you insult me in front
of my friends and colleagues and this little
innkeeper. I ain't gonna let you call me no
faker!'

Lulu had spun around. Now she slowly
walked toward me. 'William Frederick Cody,
you are a low-down, whiskey-soaked, lying,
consorting, pig-headed faker. There's not a
damned thing about you that's true! You're the
biggest damned faker in this entire troupe.'

'Me? I'm a faker? What a shameless
falsehood, woman.' I looked for ammunition,
pointed at Texas Jack, hated using a friend for
a target, but it was either him or me. 'Texas
Jack Omohundro? *Texas?* By grab, he's from
Virginia. Arizona John Burke? He couldn't tell
you the difference between Arizona and
Oregon. Wild *Bill* Hickok? His name's *James.*
But you call me a faker? Thunderation, Lu,
I'm the only man in this tarnal Combination
usin' his rightful name.'

'You're a mule-headed inebriate, Will Cody.
I'm sick of seeing you.' She whirled again. 'I'm
sick of all you fools. I'm taking the kids to
Nebraska, Will. You can go to hell.'

As she walked up the stairs, Jim Hickok
broke the silence. He set his stein on the
innkeeper's desk and clapped his hands,
whistling as my wife walked out of my life.

236

'Bravo!' Hickok said. 'Bravo! Bravo, Mizzus Cody!'

When Jim looked back at me with that smirk of his, I broke my vow to my mama. I cussed him, cussed him the vilest cuss word I had ever heard, a cuss so wicked it caused Esther Rubens to gasp and the hotel clerk to flinch.

'Bravo!' Hickok told me, cackling like a giddy hen. 'Bravo, Buffalo Billy!'

Chapter Twenty

Mlle. Morlacchi, the celebrated danseuse, appears as an Indian maiden and with all the Indian fights and tragedies of the border which are depicted, there is a little of the frontier man's love making in the plot.
Daily Courant, Hartford, Connecticut, January 13, 1874

'Twas a miserable train ride to Troy, New York. Lulu had taken the children back home to West Chester, where she planned to pack up and light a shuck for North Platte. To my way of figuring, the next time I heard from my wife, it would be courtesy of her attorney. I felt sicker than a hollow-horned cow, and folks allowed me to despair in solitude. I sat alone in the smoking car till Texas Jack and Hickok joined me. Jim looked grieved, although he would never admit it or apologize, nor would I ask him to. It wasn't his fault. All right, it was partly his fault, but Jim Hickok couldn't help being Wild Bill.

Texas Jack filled three glasses with gin and bitters, then lifted his in a toast. 'Here's how,' he said.

'Boys,' I said, after downing my drink. 'I'd rather be tortured by the Cheyennes than never see my children again.'

'Ah, criminy, it won't come to that,' Texas Jack said. 'Louisa's just mad. She'll get over it.'

'She's a hard woman, Jack. I ain't so sure 'bout that.'

Hickok poured us another round. 'Who proposed anyway?'

'I did,' I said. 'And somebody should have punched me in the mouth.' I took a sip, and sighed. 'Nah,' I said. 'That ain't rightly true. She was . . . is . . . a fine woman. A great mother.' I shook my head. 'I never should have gotten into that hansom cab with Jennie Fisher. But the thing is . . .' I took another swallow. 'We didn't do a thing. Just rode around town to a vacant lot, drank some whiskey, and then she read some sonnets, and afterward we recited scenes from *Macbeth*. That fella drivin' us would say so, too, but Lu wouldn't have believed me, Jennie, or no eyewitness. That's the awfullest thing. I mean,

I know I can be a handful, but as God is my witness, boys, I ain't never been unfaithful to my wife.' I killed my drink, and thought to add: 'While she traveled with me.'

'We know that,' Texas Jack agreed.

'I ain't that low-down,' I said.

'Women.' Hickok snorted, then rolled a cigarette, stuck it in his mouth, and fired it up with a lucifer he struck on his thumbnail.

'How's Josephine?' I asked.

'Fine,' Texas Jack replied.

After pulling on his cigarette, Hickok blew smoke toward the ceiling, and shook his head. 'There's a fine how-do-you-do,' he said. 'The root of all of our problems is women. Louisa's left Cody. Josephine's troubling Jack.' He shook his head.

Texas Jack also shook his head. 'No, Guiseppina and I aren't having no problems. She's the love of my life. Wouldn't know what to do without her. She reminds me of that story about the Pawnee gal Luther North used to . . .' He stopped himself from rambling.

'Who's the woman bedevilin' you?' I asked Hickok.

He crushed out his smoke. 'Nobody.' Hickok stood up, pulled down his hat, and left the smoking car. That man was getting to be as hotheaded and ill-tempered as Lulu. I stared at Texas Jack, who stared back at me.

The root of my problem, I then determined, was not Louisa, not Jennie Fisher, not any of

239

those simpletons I had to associate with to put on our melodramas. The problem lay in James Butler Hickok, which was my fault, too. I had lured Wild Bill to the East. More than once, the major said I should fire Hickok, and deep down I knew the major was right. But I couldn't do that, not to a friend, no matter how many supes he tortured, no matter how many marriages he spoiled. Jim Hickok, my pard, had been a friend of my daddy's, had saved my hide from being nailed to a barn. We bordermen followed a code, a code city folks like John Burke didn't savvy, a code I was having a hard time trying to live up to myself of late.

'I got a peck of miseries, Jack,' I said.

'Yeah.' My scouting friend tugged on the ends of his mustache, scratched his chin, and looked off into the distance, trying to pick his next words right carefully. 'Cody,' he said at last, 'I ain't been hitched as long as you have, but, like I said, I couldn't see myself living without Guiseppina.'

Easy for him to say. Josephine Morlacchi was the most stunning woman I had ever ogled. She could dance, she could talk Italian, she could act. My Louisa could also dance, although she'd never do the can-can, could speak French, play the piano, and recite some poetry, and she had looked real pretty when I had first met her back in 1865, although years on the border had aged her considerably.

'If I was you,' Texas Jack went on, 'I'd send a telegram or write a note to Louisa. Beg for forgiveness, beg her to come back.'

'Beggin' ain't my fort, Jack.'

'Forté,' corrected Jack, ever the schoolteacher.

I blinked, looking as dumb as Texas Jack could.

'You might want to forget about your living hero image, Will, for just this once,' Texas Jack went on. 'If not for Louisa, then for Arta, Orra Maude, and Kit.'

'Yeah. Thanks, Jack. You got any other advice?'

'Well, yeah, you also might want to remember your living hero image, too. For the Combination. We'll be pulling into Troy pretty soon, and both the citizens of Troy as well as the members of our troupe, they want to see Buffalo Bill the leader, not a . . .' He shrugged.

'What else?' I asked.

'I hate to say it.'

'Spit it out.'

He fortified himself with the last of the liquor. 'Will, I love Wild Bill like a brother. Guiseppina and I have forgiven him for all his transgressions with her. We can even grin about it now. Hell's bells, I even laugh at the time when he had that numskull fill my revolver with candle grease. And burning supes once is funny, but that gets old in a hurry. But he's not funny any more, Will. He's

241

practically stampeded your wife and little ones from you, and he's got the whole Combination at each other's throat. You got to get rid of him, pard, if you want this show to survive.'

I wasn't sure I wanted it to survive. 'You want to be the one to fire Jim?' I matched Texas Jack's stare.

'It's not my place,' he said. 'You've known him longer than me, and, well, this is the Buffalo Bill Combination, not the Texas Jack Combination.'

I found myself alone again. Texas Jack left me to my miseries. Fire Jim Hickok? I just couldn't do that, no more than I could write to Lulu, for she'd just use my letter or telegram to start a fire without even reading my words. Women. I shook my head, and recollected Jim Hickok's talk. *The root of all of our problems is women.* When asked about it, he had gotten all huffy and left. Maybe a woman was bothering my friend, causing him to act so notional. Only what woman? Jennie Fisher? Not hardly. I ran the names of our other actresses through my mind. Esther Rubens—Lizzie Safford—Josephine Morlacchi—Rena Maeder—little Eliza Hudson. None fit. By my boots and socks, could he be in love with Lulu? Was that why he asked my wife to come join us? No, Hickok was cantankerous, not stupid. Perhaps some wanton woman he had dallied with had given him the clap. I'd ask him about it. No, that would be paramount to suicide.

I sighed. 'Maybe he'll just behave hisself,' I said aloud.

Of course, he didn't. He blasted every dead Indian he could find on our opening night in Troy. Why, you have never seen such gamboling. The supes hated it, but the crowd—mostly waifs, newsboys, and bootblacks—hooted and howled like they were hostile Pawnees. Not only that, but Hickok even gave Josephine Morlacchi an indelicate squeeze, which provoked Texas Jack so much that I thought I'd have to separate them before they came to fisticuffs. Luckily for us, one of the supes tackled Hickok, and knocked him silly with his toy tomahawk. Hickok jumped up, and gave the supe a right smart of a pounding. That riled all the other supes into retaliation, and we had us a regular Indian fight—fake Indians, real fight—on the stage that night.

It did us all some good, allowed us to expel our frustrations. I know what you're thinking: I should have let those extras whup Hickok, as he had it coming, but that wouldn't be right. Not on stage during *Scouts of the Plains.* Folks had paid good money to see us kill savages, not savages kill one of us. So I plowed into the fracas, and starting bending my pistol barrel over heads, and breaking noses. Texas Jack roped a handful with his lariat, waylaid several more by swinging his rifle like a club. W.A. Reid and Jas. Johnson joined the riot, and so did Rena Maeder. When Rena's dress got

243

torn, it really got the bootblacks and newsboys excited.

'Close the curtain! Close the damned curtain!' Major Burke shouted, and the curtain dropped like a ton of bricks.

We could hear the cheers, a commotion like one none of us had ever heard. My thoughts quickly turned to my business as Fred Maeder saw to his sister, and Josephine Morlacchi doctored her husband's bleeding nose. Once the newspapers wrote up how well our show had been received, how exciting and authentic it looked, why we'd have our biggest run yet. Maybe I could squeeze in a matinee tomorrow.

While I was surmising the possibilities, Wild Bill ran off all the remaining, conscious supes, who fled into the night still wearing what was left of all their costumes. That caused the major to take the Lord's name in vain, and he pointed a cane at Hickok. 'Now, you've done it, you damned yokel. I'll have to find more costumes, and that's coming out of your salary.'

'The hell it is,' Hickok said. 'You saved enough money to buy new outfits by never washing those. They stank to high heaven.'

'Not only that,' Major Burke charged ahead, 'but you just drove off all our Indians, and we have three more acts in this play. Good God, man, this is not a damned circus. You . . .'

'Circus!' Hickok snapped, and sent a right

powerful blow to the major's chin that rendered him unconscious.

Hickok was about to kick the major's head, when I pulled him off, and flung him aside.

'What's gotten into you, Jim?' I demanded.

'Circus!' He shook his head. 'What's gotten into me? I'll tell you. I'm fed up with this production. We're making fools of ourselves. We're making fools of what we done out West. For what . . . money?' He unfastened his suspenders, unbuttoned his britches, and dropped his pants, took his knife, and sliced open his long johns at the thigh. Esther Rubens gasped. That woman gasped more oftener than someone drowning.

The rest of us just gaped at that ugly scar in the center of Hickok's thigh. All but Jennie Fisher, who, I reckon, had seen it before.

'You want to laugh at this?' Hickok went on a-raging. 'A dog soldier gave me this with his lance. Had to cauterize it myself, then walk thirty miles to the nearest post surgeon, holding onto the horn because I couldn't pull myself into the saddle. Doctors had to peel it back to the bone to clean it. It wasn't funny then, and it still ain't funny. Why don't we just tell the truth about what it's like on the frontier? That's what I want to know.'

'Because,' I said, 'this is the East. Folks don't care 'bout the truth. They want to be entertained.'

'Well, I'm sick of it all.'

245

'Look at all the money we're makin', Jim.'

He snorted. 'I ain't no whore.'

'Well, I ain't never killed my own deputy!'

Never shouldn't have said that. I knew how much that bothered Jim. He never talked about it, but that incident in Abilene had cost him his marshaling job, had cost him a lot. He probably would never have joined the Combination if he could have gotten hired on as a lawman. Before I could take back those words, though, Hickok had tackled me, and began pounding my face.

I pounded him back, and we rolled over and over, got up, knocked each other down. We kicked, cursed, gouged, pulled hair. We bit, punched, ducked, sucked in wind. Above the screams and shouts and foot-pounding from behind the curtain, I somehow managed to hear Texas Jack take command of the situation.

'Criminy, boys,' he said, 'someone raise the curtain. Them folks paid to see some fighting. This is better than nothing.'

Chapter Twenty-One

The name and fame of Buffalo Bill and his two bowers added to the attraction of a drama struck out in a new and sensational style, draws larger houses everywhere than any of the 'legitimate' is able to.

Titusville, Pennsylvania *Morning Herald*
November 7, 1873

'No,' I told the lad hawking the *Press* the following day. 'Wild Bill is one of my staunchest allies. We weren't really fightin'. What we were doin', you see, was givin' you an exhibition on how we bordermen brawl, how different it is from what you might see in a bout between two of your Eastern pugilists.' Just talking made my busted lips ache, but I continued. 'You see, son, on the border, lawmen like Wild Bill and scouts like myself sometimes come across the roughest ruffians . . . men of low moral character . . . men who don't fight fair.'

'Like when Wild Bill planted his boot in your nuts?'

My stomach drew up at the mention of that dastardly act.

'Yeah, kid. You have to be always ready for foul acts like that from vermin.'

'You didn't look ready.'

I gave the waif a coin, and took my newspaper elsewhere, walking gingerly, careful not to slip on an ice patch or bruise my bruises, then ducked inside a smoke-filled tavern to brace myself for the day with a gin sling and coffee. It took a lot of bracing. I spent the rest of the day there, healing my wounds, before walking over to the Opera House to get ready for our evening show, having forsaken my idea of staging two shows in Troy after the previous evening's riot.

After Josephine Morlacchi powdered my face to hide the bruises and nicks, I found Major Burke examining a new batch of frocks and flannel made up to look like something Indians would wear on the plains.

'Have you seen Hickok?' I asked.

The major sagged. 'No.' He removed a cigar, and rubbed his scraped chin. I had forgotten how Hickok had knocked him out. 'I figured you'd run him off,' said Major Burke, talking like his heart had been broken worse than when Josephine began courting Texas Jack. 'I was planning to take the role myself tonight.' His eyes widened. Now he looked like he had been struck by a poleaxe swung by Hickok. 'Good God, Cody, I've seen men hit by a train that looked better than you. Perhaps I should play you, and we'll get Hickok's understudy . . .'

I shook my head. 'I'm fine. These people

248

want to see Buffalo Bill and Wild Bill, and they shall.'

Burke tossed aside the frocks. 'What happens if Hickok doesn't show up tonight?'

'He'll be here.'

When the major started shaking his head, getting that sick look on his face, I knew that he planned on assaulting Hickok's character, so I defended the friend who had loosened several of my teeth. 'Last night was as much my fault as Jim's, Major. I sent him a bottle of rye to his room this morn.'

'Along with a note of apology, I presume.'

'No, rye will suffice. We Western men are not much for notes. As far as I'm concerned, last night never happened. You'd do yourself a favor by forgettin' it, too.'

He rubbed his chin again.

'You cussed him,' I reminded our manager. 'A man like Hickok takes insults from no one. I've been tryin' to learn you that for goin' on six months now.'

The major changed the subject. 'Well, advance sales have been solid today. Everyone has been talking about the show. Somehow, I've even managed to replace our supes. And these clothes will do. I dare say we'll see the house filled from pit to dome tonight.'

'Good.'

'We'll need a good show. I'm not enthusiastic about Albany.'

'By the livin' hokey, why not?'

'I picked up an Albany newspaper someone had left behind at the hotel. There's a damned circus in town.'

'Barnum?' I could not control my excitement.

'No, the Hippo-Olympiad and Mammoth Circus.'

'Never heard of it, and we've outdrawn circuses, other plays, and even that Stowe lady before.'

'Hickok says this circus is the greatest show on earth. He saw it once when he was marshal of Austin.'

'Abilene.'

'Wherever. He's mentioned it a couple of times on the trains, when in good humor. That's been a while back, but I've heard of the lady running the show. Some high-wire daredevil named Lake . . . Agnes . . . Something . . . Lake. You sure you're all right to perform tonight.'

'Of course,' I said.

That's when Hickok barged into the theater, dressed in buckskins and sombrero, holding a half empty bottle of rye in his right hand. He spotted me first, looked away, then strolled over to Major Burke, and held out the rye.

'For last night,' he said.

Cautiously Major Burke took the bottle and stared at it. The cork was gone.

'I got thirsty on the way over,' Hickok said.

'It doesn't matter, Jim,' the major said,

picking his words real carefully. 'I'll pour you a glass.'

'Nah.' When Hickok offered me his hand, I shook it heartily. 'I won't shoot any supes tonight,' he told me. 'How do your nutmegs feel?'

'They're still there,' I said. 'How's your ear?'

'The lobe's not gone,' he said. 'Much to my surprise.'

We laughed, slapped each other's shoulder, and I sent him off to get his face cleaned up and powdered. Major Burke gave me a hard stare, but I elected not to notice him.

*   *   *

The plan conceived itself just before dawn in Albany. I leaped out of the hotel bed, pulled on my boots and a kimono, grabbed my hat, and hurried into the hallway. A few doors down, I banged on the pine till it opened, revealing a sleepy-eyed Jack Omohundro, Smith & Wesson in his right hand.

'Will, the roosters haven't crowed yet,' he said.

'I know.' I pushed myself inside, turned up the gaslight, and smiled at Josephine Morlacchi, who shook her head, fluffed a pillow, sat up in the bed, and opened her dictionary to read.

Texas Jack replaced his revolver with a bottle of whiskey, and poured us both a bracer.

'I've figured out how to settle down Jim,' I said.

Josephine muttered something in Italian, followed by: 'Not another . . . fight.'

We had arrived in Albany after our final show in Troy, which had gone off with nary a fist thrown or supe shot. I had slept well once we settled into our hotel, till the vision woke me up.

'You recollect how Jim said women was the bane of our existence, or something along those lines?'

Texas Jack shot a quick glance at his wife, but I don't think she had heard me, and shrugged. 'He said it. I didn't agree.'

'Yeah, well, I figured some petticoat has been pesterin' his heart.'

'J.B. has no heart.'

'Don't interrupt me. He does have a heart, and a soul. He loves children, loves dogs, loves the fiddle, and I think he loves a woman. A woman named Agnes Thatcher Lake.'

'The circus gal?'

'Indeed.'

Texas Jack let the whiskey roll around his tongue. 'Well, as little as he talks, he has talked a ton about her.'

I refilled our glasses. 'And her circus is in town, full of hippopotamuses and woolly mammoths, or so says the major.'

Texas Jack give me the dumb look, then polished off his whiskey. 'So, what's your plan?'

'It came to me in a vision. Our show's tonight, but the circus goes on all day. Starts 'bout noon. When Wild Bill wakes up, we take him out for breakfast, then drive over to the circus. We make him go see this Lake woman. He proposes to her. She accepts. He joins her troupe. We part pards. Nobody's fired. Nobody's beat up. Nobody's feelin's get hurt. Everybody lives happily ever after.'

'That was your dream?'

'Vision,' I corrected.

'*Tesoro,*' Josephine called out, 'I would not . . . take . . . such a . . . journey!'

'Why not?' Texas Jack asked his spouse.

'*Santo cielo,* your *amico* is not . . . how you say . . . Cupid?' She returned to her dictionary.

'Yeah,' Texas Jack said back to me. 'I'm not so sure about that. I mean . . . do you think Wild Bill will just up and propose to this lady?'

'If he's in his cups, and he will be after breakfast.'

'Well . . .'

'We're like musketeers, Jack, remember? All for one and . . .' I finished the whiskey. 'I'll see you for breakfast in a couple of hours.'

*   *   *

The Hippo-Olympiad and Mammoth Circus had set up underneath a big canvas tent just outside the city, but nobody was there at ten

253

that morning, except some circus workers and animal trainers. I paid the hack, and Texas Jack pulled Hickok out of the wagon.

Hickok stared at the big tent and posters, and spit. 'What the hell are we doing here?'

'You just behave yourself, Jim,' I said, 'and follow me.'

I asked a bald fellow with a chest the size of a Rocky Mountain boulder where we would find the Widow Lake, and he pointed to the ticket wagon, and we made a beeline to this petite woman with black hair standing in front of the vehicle, conversing with another gentleman with a shovel and long mustache. Agnes Thatcher Lake turned at the sound of Hickok's cursing, and lifted her fingers over a trembling mouth. The fellow with the mustache and shovel took off, and the circus lady straightened.

'Ma'am,' I said, 'I'm William F. Cody, better known as . . .'

'I know who you are.' When she smiled, I doffed my hat and bowed. I had thought her to be fairly old, with no meat on her bones hardly, and a face harder than my Louisa's. When I kissed her hand, I realized her fingers could crack walnuts. I reckon you had to be strong to hang from that trapeze or walk across ropes fifty feet in the air. I sure didn't see what Jim Hickok saw in the likes of her— couldn't be the money, as I had seen no wild animals anywhere, no Ringlings or Barnums—

until she gave another grin and said: 'Why, everybody in the world has heard of the legendary Buffalo Bill. And you must be Texas Jack Omohundro.'

Texas Jack muttered something, and swept off his hat.

Charming. That woman could charm the fangs off a rattler.

'I saw your performance at Cleveland last year,' she announced.

'You was there?' Wild Bill had finally spoken something other than swear words mumbled at Texas Jack and me.

'I was there, James,' she answered. 'Should have gone to see you backstage, but, well, I guess I showed yellow.'

'Richmond,' Hickok began, but we couldn't quite understand what else he said.

'You put on a splendid show, Mister Cody, Mister Omohundro. And that Morlacchi. Goodness gracious, how she can dance and sing. How have you been, James?'

'Fair to middling.'

'Let's get out of this cold wind.' She led us inside the tent, which smelled of sawdust and hippopotamus dung, although I saw only a couple of mules and a donkey. We took our seats, and she give Jim Hickok a squeeze of his hand. Their fingers interlocked, and I smiled at my vision. Then I frowned, thinking about Lulu.

'Maybe we should go take a look around,'

Texas Jack suggested. 'See how a circus compares to our theatrical group.'

'You go ahead,' I said.

'Well,' Texas Jack added, 'you know how you've always said it would be great to have horses in our plays? Real horses. Only we'd need a bigger arena. We could see . . .'

'Good idea, Jack. Why don't you take a look-see. I'll meet you here.' I wasn't about to leave Hickok alone with this widow. He might run away, although I doubted if he could have freed himself from that woman's grip. She might be tiny, but that lady had muscles in her limbs and extremities that I'd never seen on anybody—man, woman, or Missourian—before.

Texas Jack left, grumbling. Hickok stared at me, and it wasn't anything like an Omohundro dumb look.

'Don't mind me,' I said. 'Pretend I ain't even here.' I leaned back, pulled down my hat, and closed my eyes, although I'd take a peek every now and then.

'You look swell, Agnes,' Hickok finally said.

'How do you like acting?' she asked.

He snorted. 'It don't fit my pistols worth a damn.'

'You were quite fun, quite daring, when I saw you in Cleveland.'

'I was in my cups.'

'All those Indians you killed. All that noise. The music. The drama.'

'None of it's for real. Folks are laughing at us.'

'Laughing's good medicine, James. They're not laughing at you. They're laughing with you.'

'You saw us, Agnes. They're laughing at us. Billy and Jack don't give a hoot in hell about it, either. They'll play the fool as long as they can buy houses in Rochester and West Chester and diamond stickpins and silver-tipped whips.'

'You like to tell jokes,' Agnes said. 'You were always laughing in Abilene.'

'Well, that was different.'

'Dressing up at the depot.' Agnes shook her head. 'Oh, the stories you'd tell those tourists. They'd believe everything you said, no matter how outlandish. You made me laugh till I cried.'

'Well . . . that was out West.'

'I know.'

I opened my eyes in time to see the widow lift Jim Hickok's hand and kiss it.

'If it troubles you so, James, why not leave? I'm sure Mister Cody and Mister Omohundro would understand.'

My heart palpitated something ferocious. I felt invisible to Hickok and the widow. Things could not have been going any better.

'You want to see the show tonight?' Hickok asked.

'I can't,' she said. 'We open at noon, run all day through the week-end, then leave for

257

Pennsylvania, Ohio, then Michigan.'

'You wouldn't have need of an old pistol fighter, would you?'

I had to bite my tongue to keep from shouting.

'The famous Wild Bill Hickok would certainly be an attraction, but I'd fathom that traveling with a circus wouldn't fit your pistols, either.'

'That was not my meaning.'

'I know.' She leaned over and kissed his cheek. 'James, I have a daughter. You remember her. She's my concern now. Between her and this circus, that's all I can handle. I do care for you. I've been smitten with you since I first saw you in Kansas. But I need my daughter to grow up. Two years. That's all I'm asking. Maybe only eighteen months. Could you give a widow that long?'

'Two years?' I said that, but the widow and gunman did not hear me. I felt as if I'd been kicked in the groin again.

'Two years.' Hickok nodded.

'Or less,' the widow said.

'Two years,' I repeated.

Hickok rose, bowed, and kissed the widow's hand. 'Since I'm here, I'd like to look around, maybe see your act before I head back to the music hall, opera house, bucket of blood, or wherever we're performing tonight.'

'I'd be delighted. Have your companions join us. We'll introduce you all at the start of the show. Give you some business. We show people all have to stick together. I send some business your way, maybe you'll send some mine.'

'Two years,' I said.

They kissed—I didn't see them, as the news had blinded me, but I heard the smacking of lips, and then Agnes told Hickok: 'Be true to yourself, James. You've always been true to yourself. That's what I admired most in you. So be true to yourself now.'

Two years? Did she mean for Hickok to stay with the Buffalo Bill Combination for two years? Then they'd wed? No, Jim had told me he'd only act with me for a year. He wouldn't stay with us for another year, would he? How could my vision have turned out so wrong? I smelled whiskey, and opened my eyes—no wonder I had not seen them kiss—to find my pal offering me the bottle I had bought for breakfast while Agnes Thatcher Lake walked out of the big tent.

'I just remembered something,' Hickok told me as I gripped the bottle's neck and pulled long and hard. 'It's your birthday, pard. Happy birthday, Billy.'

Chapter Twenty-Two

The whole entertainment was amusing and entertaining, and no one will regret the time spent in its enjoyment. Lone Wolf, the Chief of the Kiowas, says he expects a ripping house tonight. We hope he will not be disappointed. Go and see the Scouts and Morlacchi by all means.

Daily Observer, Utica, New York
March 4, 1874

No supes got burned, and there were no donnybrooks, no damages. We packed the houses at Albany, Schenectady, and Utica, but I doubt if anyone in the Combination enjoyed themselves. Our two-bit actors seemed tauter than fishing line with a twenty-pound blue cat on the hook; they just knew Hickok would give them something to remember them by. Walter Fletcher even botched his lines, and Josephine Morlacchi twisted her ankle in Schenectady, and flopped on her fanny. It got to be like play acting just wasn't fun any more for anyone except our paying customers and New York ink slingers. They never noticed any difference. Why, even on stage, I, glum and downtrodden, sounded like Jim Hickok mumbling when I spoke my lines.

I should have felt happy. Hickok was

behaving again, and we were making money when few people in the East were. Yet all I could see when I shut my eyes was Agnes Thatcher Lake walking out of that circus tent, leaving James Butler Hickok, the love of her life—at least one of them, after her two late husbands. Only, it really wasn't the widow I saw disappearing, but Louisa Frederici Cody.

Without much interest, I dressed in my buckskins and wide belt in the quiet Utica hotel room, and joined Major Burke, Wild Bill, Texas Jack, and his wife downstairs. The major had agreed to a tour at the bequest of some city and state officials, although he refused to tell us where we were actually going, and we climbed into a hack, and took off down Whitesboro Street, followed by a wagonload of newspaper reporters.

Josephine Morlacchi leaned on her husband, and squeezed his hand, cooing something in Italian. I sighed, and stared at my boots.

'Well, this is fitting,' Hickok announced some time later, and I looked up to see the sign over the big iron gate surrounding the snow-covered grounds.

New York State
Lunatic Asylum

I punched the major's arm. 'You arranged for us to visit a madhouse?' Then I got scared, wondering if the major had hornswoggled us, was planning on imprisoning us here. He'd take off with all our money, and glory, and plays, and leave us with these crazy folks. Then I got scared again, wondering if I was irrational, maybe even muddled.

'Where's your curiosity, Will?' the major said. 'It'll be interesting. And, remember, when you talk to the newspaper reporters, this is a trip of benevolence.'

I felt safe. At least, the major wasn't waylaying us.

A couple of burly gents in greatcoats met us at the gate to guide us to a massive building— must have been 500 feet long, with columns straight out of Greece that looked fancier than any courthouse or government office I had seen in Washington, D.C., not counting the White House and Capitol. As soon as we had climbed out, a fellow in a white coat and fur hat rushed outside and started pumping our hands, excited to meet us.

I didn't know how to reply, didn't know if this fellow was deranged or a doc, even after he introduced himself as Dr. Wolfgang S. Reinwald.

The burly gents informed us that Doc Reinwald ran the place, had been an assistant to the late Dr. Amariah Brigham who had started up the lunatic farm in 1843—three years before I was even born. They had a commissary, root cellar, and a factory where the crazy folks made their own duds. 'We even have a slaughterhouse,' Doc Reinwald said. 'This place is entirely self-sufficient.'

'Slaughterhouse?' Josephine Morlacchi asked. She looked off her feed, and turned to her husband for support.

'He means they butcher pigs, not patients,' Texas Jack explained.

'Yes,' the doctor said with a chuckle. 'And do not be afraid. We have not held any criminally insane since before the war, when they were moved to Auburn. Also, for your protection, all of our more violent patients have been restrained in the Utica Crib.'

He didn't make the Utica Crib sound like a brass bed with a downy comforter.

'Where are the patients?' Hickok asked.

'Here, this way.' We followed him, listening to him give us the history of the place, the reporters taking notes but sticking real close together. We were touring New York's first state-operated asylum, and one of our nation's first. It housed some 600 patients. We'd walk through the women's wing first.

I expected the inside of the building to be colder than the Dismal River in the wickedest of winters, but it felt toasty inside. 'We have wood furnaces,' the doctor said, 'and running water . . . hot and cold . . . on every floor. The hot water is pumped by a steam engine. The cold water is from the snow melt off the roof.'

'Handy,' I said just to say something. A

263

couple of ladies stood in a doorway, pointing at us, giggling. I averted my eyes.

'Look at those men in wigs,' one of the gals said, and they laughed again.

I also expected to hear moaning and wailing, but the women in the lunatic house just giggled, if they made any sound.

The men's ward looked a little different, and I had never seen so many fellows sitting around in their robes at that time of day. Most of their eyes seemed vacant, and hardly anybody giggled or even made a noise. Hickok, being bold and daring in front of those newspapermen, shook a few hands and offered a few greetings, until a bald man dressed in plaid and stripes began twirling Hickok's locks in his fingers.

'You'd best stop that,' Hickok said, and one of the burly gents escorted the fellow into his room. After that, Hickok didn't act so bold or daring but held back and looked embarrassed, much like he did on the stage.

At the end of the hall, Doc Reinwald knocked on a door and said: 'Mister Cody, here is a man who has asked to shake your hand.'

So it was that I stepped forward and shook hands with Buffalo Bill Number Two. He didn't look at all like me, but he did have a handsome smile and firm grip, plus a cannonade of questions. What did I think of the Indian troubles? Would I go West with

Custer? Had I avenged my father's death? Had I considered running for Vice President for the Democrats? If I didn't, would I mind if he did so? I gave him my blessings.

Thus ended our tour. Doc Reinwald and the burly men escorted us back to our hack and the reporters to their wagon.

'Who was that fellow?' I asked.

'We only know him as Buffalo Bill Number Two.'

'How long has he been here?'

'He was sent from Binghamton last June.'

I paused. 'We were in Binghamton in June. When we was tourin' with Judson . . . uh . . . Ned Buntline.'

'Yes, I thought as much. You must have made quite an impression. He's a gentle soul, though. Simply delusional.'

'Ain't we all,' Hickok whispered. Texas Jack elbowed him in the ribs.

I looked back at the building, which no longer looked so prosperous but dark and forebidding. *There but for the grace of God . . .*

I shook off my thoughts as the doc announced: 'On behalf of my staff and patients, I appreciate men of such renown, and you, too, Miss Morlacchi, for taking time to visit us. Your kind hearts made a lasting impression, gave hope to such unfortunate men and women. Enjoy your stay in Utica. I hope you have another successful show.'

I pumped the doc's hand, and climbed out

of the cold. As we rode off, Hickok kicked my leg and grinned. 'You must be a better actor than you give yourself credit for,' he said. 'I mean, you drove a fellow to the madhouse.'

*   *   *

My spirits continued to spiral. 'I feel blacker than a flock of corkologians,' I told Texas Jack and Hickok during a late supper of spare ribs and fried potatoes after our performance at the Utica Opera House. 'I been doin' a mite of thinkin' that maybe I should just leave.'

Texas Jack ripped meat off the bone. It sounded like he was lifting a scalp. He chewed, staring at me, giving me his dumb look. Jim Hickok, sitting across from me, held a rib bone about shoulder high and, for some reason, stared out the plate-glass window. He had been doing that all night, lifting a gnawed bone, looking outside, smiling, and finally dropping the bone onto a pile on the floor. Nobody complained, not even the waiters, for all rigged out in our buckskins we looked rather ferocious. This time, Hickok froze, bone in fingers.

'Tell the newspaper boys that I'm needed out West,' I continued, 'that I've been called back to the border, to fight the Indians I know so well.'

After swallowing, Texas Jack tossed the bone on the pile beside our table. 'And then?'

266

he asked.

'Well, you, the major, and Jim could carry on.'

'I'm not talking about us, Will,' Texas Jack said. 'I'm thinking about you. Would you go see Lulu?'

'I could scout for the Fifth again, even if there isn't a war. Maybe guide some foreigners on another buffalo hunt.'

'What about Louisa?' Jack Omohundro could be one persistent cuss.

'The devil with her!' I snapped. 'I never want to see her rawhide face again. By thunder, I'd rather be livin' at the New York State Lunatic Asylum than with that woman. You saw how she was. Unreasonable. Demandin'. I can't have a snort of gin without her gettin' rowdy.'

'What about your children?' Texas Jack persisted.

With a heavy sigh, I shook my head. 'Listen, boys, we've been pards for a long time. We've had our differences. Even come to blows. But through it all, we've always remained tried and true. I got into the Thespian business for money, and I've made some money, though it don't even seem to slow up when it gets to me. I think I know both of you pretty good. Jack, you just wanted to become an actor, and you're better than Jim and me put together. Besides, you and Josephine make a handsome couple. You got a future on the boards. That's why you always nursed me, kept my confidence up, when we started out with Judson. It's just that I need a change, fellows. You know what I mean, Jim. You just wanted a change, to see the sights, to get as far from Abilene as you could. That's why you hitched up to this team. The Combination can go on without me. By jingo, folks watchin' our plays don't even think we're real heroes half the time, just actors. Jim was right 'bout that. Plus, Major Burke's been hankerin' to play Buffalo Bill for months now, so I say let's give him the chance.'

No one said a thing. Hickok finally released his bone, which fell to the floor, and he dropped his hands in his lap. He looked like a man shot in the belly.

'This is what you boys have wanted,' I said. 'It'll be for the best, for both of you. We can get Hiram and Fred to rework those plays. We can call it the Texas Jack Combination, and *Wild Bill! King of the Bordermen!* By grab, Maeder stole half of what's in that play from what Colonel Nichols wrote 'bout you, anyhow, Jim. That always got your goat. Now it'll be the real truth.'

Hickok shook his head. 'Nichols's truth is a bald-faced lie.'

'Well, then think of the Widow Lake, Jim. She wants you to wait two years, or less, till her daughter grows up. You just stay with Jack. Two years will go by in no time. By then, maybe I'll be ready to return to the boards.'

'Two years?' Hickok sounded as incredulous as I had back at the widow's tent.

'Two years. Boys, it's time we parted ways. You take over the Combination . . . but, Jim, this means you can't cause any more friction with the supes . . . and I go West. I was thinkin' 'bout what the Widow Lake told you, Jim. Be true to yourself. Well, as you well know, I haven't been true to myself for quite a spell. I've been a faker, just like Lu . . . just like she . . . well, I been a faker. To myself. To y'all. To the people who pay hard-earned money to watch us. What do I have to show for it? Some money, no family, and just one gent in the lunatic ward who thinks he's me.'

'Buffalo Bill Number Two,' Texas Jack corrected. 'You're still the original.'

'That's pretty much a falsehood, too. Billy Comstock was Buffalo Bill before me, and I don't know how many before him.' I lifted my glass in toast, to stop any further arguing, but mostly on account that my mouth was dry and I was parched. 'All for one . . . ,' I began.

Our glasses clinked.

'And one for all,' Texas Jack said without much enthusiasm.

'When do you plan on leaving?' Hickok asked.

'Rochester,' I answered. 'Had planned on buyin' some property there, big house, movin' from West Chester . . .' Another sigh. 'Well, I need to meet with this real estate fellow, tell

269

him to call off that deal. See some friends, say some farewells, telegraph General Sheridan. That'll also give us time to get everything settled for after I'm gone.'

I smiled, but I didn't mean it. Upon announcing my intentions, I thought for certain that anvil would have been lifted off my chest. The fact that I didn't feel any better troubled me, but maybe relief would come soon. We would perform the following night in Oswego—where I'd have to remember to keep my word and kill Alfred Johnson twice during the play—and the next two nights in Syracuse. After the last Syracuse show March 7th, we didn't play again until Rochester on the 10th and 11th. Plenty of time to get affairs in order.

'Best get to the depot,' Hickok said glumly.

After I tossed a few greenbacks on the table, we bundled up. When Texas Jack opened the door, a pack of dogs rushed in, and raced for the rib bones piled up on the floor. I hadn't seen such commotion in a coon's age, all those waiters and patrons screaming, dogs barking and growling, another one of Jim Hickok's jokes, I assumed. I'd miss that.

Of course, I didn't know it at the time, but Hickok had another joke planned. Fact of the matter is that Hickok himself didn't know it, either. He hadn't got to planning it yet.

Chapter Twenty-Three

Buffalo Bill, Texas Jack, Wild Bill, and troupe have departed. The "gallery gods' gave them another ovation last night. The agent of the troupe says that not a week has elapsed since the formation of the company in which the "living heroes' have not each received $500 as his share of the profits, and some weeks the dividend has been $800. At the lowest sum this would give each $25,000 a year. Perhaps the agent has exaggerated a little.

Daily Times, Troy, New York
February 26, 1874

By now, I warrant that you have read all about our March 11th show in Rochester, New York, and its aftermath, but I take pencil in hand to set the matter as straight as I can. Since stunning Hickok and Texas Jack with my announcement, I had told Major Burke of my desires, wired General Sheridan and Colonel Can of my resolve to return to the border, and let the Rochester real estate fellow know that I would not be purchasing that big home after all. I had informed everyone of my intentions, except cast members and newspaper boys. That I planned to do after taking our final bows at Wilson & Sturbin's Opera House.

When the big night arrived, such fear I had not felt since first stepping onto the boards with Judson and Texas Jack in Chicago back in 1872. Turkey vultures flapped in my stomach, but I clipped their wings by taking a pull from Hickok's flask. That's when I noticed a gleam in my pard's eye, and I suspicioned him.

'This is my last play, Jim,' I said, 'and I desire it to go smoothly. Don't cut up with none of your capers.'

'Me?' After screwing the flask shut, he dropped it inside his boot top. 'Not on your life, Billy. Do you know who's watching us tonight?'

'Who?'

'Lawrence Barnett.'

'Barnett!'

'Yeah, but not them Canucks that swindled me. I've had a belly full of them Canadian Barnetts.'

'I know who Barnett is.'

Shoot, everybody did around these parts. Barnett was one of America's greatest Thespians and had been performing in *The Black Crook* in New York City. I didn't believe Hickok at all for well I knew his ability at storying. Yet at that time, Major Burke announced to the crowded theater:

'Ladies and gentlemen, allow me to introduce a special guest, the one and only Lawrence Barnett, the greatest actor our

272

country has known.'

The major paused to allow some polite applause, and some heckler, no doubt a Secesh, hollered out: 'What about John Wilkes Booth?'

Ignoring the fiend, Major Burke continued: 'Mister Barnett traveled by rail from Manhattan. He could have gone to the Booth Theater to see Edwin Booth in *Julius Caesar*. He could have taken in a myriad of shows at Niblo's, the Bowery, Hooley's, or The Olympic, but he came here to see what all the fuss is about.' Laughter, more applause.

'Mister Barnett, you sha'n't be disappointed, for you and the rest of you great folks will be witnessing history as we present Hiram Robbins's acclaimed drama, *The Scouts of the Plains,* a true story of the violent border of our frontier of the not so distant past, featuring . . .'—I took a deep breath, trying to steel myself one final time as Major Burke's voice rose to a crescendo—'as himself, the patriot of incorruptible integrity, the soldier of approved valor, the statesman of consummate wisdom . . . *William F. . . . Buffalo . . . Bill . . . Cody!'*

Thus, my final performance as an actor began, and went along trouble-free until the end of the first act when Hickok burned the bitter Hades out of a dead Indian with a pistol blast. Then, for spite, he shot another. Both actors jumped up, cursed, hopped, and

273

stormed around the stage to the hoots and howls of hundreds of Rochesterians and Lawrence Barnett, Esquire.

The curtain closed, and we stormed off stage. Furious, I wagged a gloved finger in Hickok's face. 'I should have known I couldn't trust you, Jim Hickok! On my daddy's grave, you are the lyingest, meanest, most vexin' son-of-a-cur that I have ever laid eyes on. Were it not for the show, I would punch you in the nose again, and this time it would be me who kicked you so you couldn't fork a saddle, not the other way around.'

Hickok just stared at me.

'The hell with the show!' I thundered, removed my beaded gauntlet, and slapped his face, practically challenging the deadliest pistol fighter the West had ever known to a duel.

Hickok, who typically took such abuse from no one, stood there like a knot on a log while the major and Texas Jack pulled me away. The curtain rose, and I got pushed out onto the stage even though the opening of Act II required Esther Rubens to do a soliloquy, so I just stood off to her side like a prop. Finally she walked off, and I started my line: 'I would face . . .' I stared into the audience.

'Mister Barnett's over here!' a rowdy hollered from the front row, but my vision remained focused at the far corner of the balcony. It couldn't be. My eyes screwed shut, and I shook my head, yet when I looked again, the apparition remained seated. 'I would face a thousand Modocs . . . er . . . Mandans . . . uh . . . Sioux, no, Comanches! By grab, I'd face every Indian on the border for that girl!' I said to my wife.

Well, I knew then that my mind had played a trick on me, because the woman up there just smiled, and I hadn't seen Louisa Frederici Cody smile in ages. Besides, she was in Nebraska by now, with my little angels.

Texas Jack Omohundro wandered onto the stage, and we began some sort of dialogue. I had just begun telling Jack a long windy when I detected a gentleman in a tailored suit and silk hat pushing his way down the front row, and head to the center aisle.

At first, I thought this to be Lawrence Barnett, figured he had grown sick of the melodrama and, rather than waiting for intermission, had decided to head back to New York City. Then I recognized those long auburn locks and determined gait. Jim Hickok walked out of Wilson & Sturbin's Opera House.

Texas Jack saw him, too, and muttered a little oath. We hurriedly finished our scene, and rushed to the wings as soon as our supes ran out and got killed.

'Where's Hickok gone to?' I demanded.

The major looked ashen. Folks searched this way and that, but the only things we found

275

resembling Wild Bill were his buckskins and an empty bottle. A short while later, the theater's carpenter approached me.

'Mister Cody?' he said.

'Yes.'

'That long-haired fellow, the one who went out the front door a few minutes ago . . .'

'Go on.'

'Well, sir, he told me to tell you that you could go to hell with your damned show.'

What a pickle! The major, realizing the gravity of this situation, rushed to me.

'You can't quit the show now, Will!' he shouted. 'We'd be ruined!'

I looked around, hoping no one had heard the panic in the major's voice, hoping I could salvage things. Too late. My *compadres* fired out questions quicker than Jim Hickok could empty a Navy .36 or a shot of Taos lightning.

'What do you mean, Burke?' Walter Fletcher said. 'Is Cody leaving the Combination?'

'Hellfire!' Jennie Fisher said. 'Say it's not true, Willie!'

The curtain saved me, and I raced onstage to say I would avenge my pa's blood. We did the rest of the show without Hickok. Nobody in the crowd even hollered where had he gone.

Backstage became a tumult after the ovations and curtain calls. I had not given my fare-thee-well address because Major Burke was right. I couldn't leave Texas Jack and my colleagues in such a fix, with Hickok vanished.

'We have to find him,' I whispered to Texas Jack. 'But where should we start?'

Texas Jack shrugged. 'Rochester has scores of dram shops. It could take weeks to fish him out.'

A daunting task, I agreed, but it had to be done. I quickly pulled off my buckskins, and dressed in Sunday-go-to-meetings, pumping the hand of the distinguished Lawrence Barnett as he congratulated me on an outstanding show, saying that he had never imagined how a hollow-headed melodrama like ours could practically bankrupt *The Black Crook* and Edwin Booth's theater.

'Why, had I known that, sir, I would have jumped at the chance to play Buffalo Bill in *King of the Bordermen* rather than *King Lear* or *The Black Crook*.'

'Yes, yes, thank you.' I stuck a pocket pistol in my waistband, and rose. 'If you'll excuse me, sir, I have important business to attend.'

Texas Jack and I bolted for the exit, but the most joyous words I had ever heard stopped me in my boots.

'Daddy!'

Footing it to me were my darlings, Arta and Kit, and behind them stood Lulu, holding little Orra Maude in her arms. I dropped to my knees, and got showered with kisses and almost crippled with hugs. After scooping my two eldest into my arms, I approached Lulu with a mite of trepidation, the way I would ride out to parley with a dog soldier or a Methodist.

'Great show,' Lulu said.

I snorted. 'I was horrible, Mama. You know that. I . . .'

Orra Maude reached for me, so I lowered Kit and Arta to the floor, and took the littlest one in my arms, cooing and pressing my big nose against her little button of one. At last, I looked up to face my wife again.

'I thought you'd be in Nebraska by now,' I said, bracing myself for an assault from her tongue or fingernails.

'I . . .?' She shrugged. 'They missed you, Will. So did . . . well, I got Wild Bill's letter.'

Texas Jack picked that moment to tap me on the shoulder. 'Pardon me, Will, but speaking of Wild Bill, we ought to go find him.'

My legs wouldn't move, though, and I heard myself saying the strangest thing: 'You go ahead, Jack. Take Mister Barnett or the major with you. I need to stay with my family.'

*   *   *

The little ones lay sleeping while Lulu and I sipped coffee in bed and read the newspapers the bellboy had brought us early the next morn. I found the notice of our play at Wilson & Sturbin's Opera House, satisfied my

278

curiosity, nodded in approval, then heard myself say another danged thing. 'I'm glad you didn't go, Lu.'

She set her china cup on the nightstand. 'I had my tickets, and was heading out the door for the depot,' she said, 'when Wild Bill's letter was placed in my hands, special delivery. It was an apology.'

Jim Hickok, I thought, *apologize? Strange.* Lulu also did something strange. She leaned over and kissed my cheek. 'You stoke the embers of my wrath, Will Cody,' she said. 'I know you can't help it, and I can't control my temper. We're a pair of misfits, but we do make beautiful babies.' She nodded at the three angels. 'I get upset when you give money away like it grows on trees, but you're the most generous man I've ever met, and Father O'Rourke says that is a blessing. You drink too much, but I've been known to pull a cork. You're hardly ever around, always gallivanting across the countryside, risking your life or fortune. And those actresses!'

I braced myself for the slap, but Lulu just fluffed her pillow.

'Well, Wild Bill said in his second letter that he was jealous. That's why he lied in his first letter to me. He envied the attention that Jennie Whatever-Her-Name-Is kept showing you, and not him. That's why he said you had . . . well . . . been . . . well . . . he apologized to you and me, said all Jennie Fisher ever wanted from you was to make you a better actor, that when you said you had never done anything unfaithful, you hadn't. After all, I should know that Buffalo Bill Cody's a man of his word.'

I needed some fortification, but the bottle on the dresser looked a thousand rods away. 'Jim Hickok,' I mouthed, barely audible, 'said that?' Hickok had lied—had lied for me. I could hardly comprehend that any more than all those cues the major kept demanding I learn for our melodramas.

'He did,' Lulu said softly. 'I'm sorry, Will. We'll never be Romeo and Juliet. I'll lose my temper. You'll get intoxicated. But . . .' She nodded again at the children. 'But I'm thinking maybe we should call a truce, for their sakes.'

'Truce?'

'Yes. I was hoping you'd show me the house in Rochester. Instead of North Platte, I'd like to stay here till we go West after the theatrical season.'

I shrugged. 'Well, the thing is, Lu . . . the thing is I figured I had no need of the house. I was plannin' on quittin' the Combination, joinin' the Fifth Cavalry to scout.'

'You'll do no such thing, Will Cody! Your future is here, not on that god-forsaken border.'

Arta rolled over and mumbled something, but the three children didn't wake up.

'I'm horrible on the stage, Mama,' I softly explained. 'But I'm a fine scout.'

'You're not horrible, and I'm not letting you get yourself killed by some savage, leaving me a widow and those babies of ours fatherless. You selfish bastard.' I wasn't ready for that blow, but at least she used a pillow and not her fist. 'Didn't you see how many people came to see you last night? They adore you, Will. So we're moving to Rochester! You can go West to hunt and fish when the season's over in the fall, scout if you must, drink your fill of that rotgut, kill as many buffalo and antelope as you and those silly friends of yours want to. But, damn it, I'm not giving up this lifestyle, and I'm not dressing Kit, Orra Maude, and Arta in scratchy woolens, and sending them to some subscription school with a deficient teacher. You . . .'

I braced again for another blow, but she sighed, and apologized.

'I'm sorry, Will. It's a truce, remember?'

'Yeah.'

She turned my head, and kissed me on the lips.

'Mama!' My face flushed. 'The children might see.'

'Hush.' Lulu giggled that girlish laugh I hadn't heard since before we got hitched. 'And to think, we owe this all to that man-killing friend of yours. Where is Wild Bill, by the way?'

Chapter Twenty-Four

We would advise our readers to go and
see the play if they would get a good idea
of life on the plains. Those who witness
the performance of this play will not care
to take Greeley's advice to go West.
Gazette, Terre Haute, Indiana
October 10, 1873

Where Hickok was, we hadn't the foggiest
notion till an account of him appeared in the
Democrat and Chronicle. Wild Bill, the
newspaperman wrote, had left the Buffalo Bill
Combination. His duty was to his country, and
with the Sioux wearing war paint and trouble
brewing at the agencies he had been called
away to the West, to 'the free, wild life he loves
so well.' That 'noble fellow,' so 'true-hearted,'
spoke kind words of Texas Jack and Buffalo
Bill, who understood that duty and destiny
awaited him on the border.

'By my boots and socks,' I said upon reading
the article Texas Jack had just showed me, 'he
stole my idea. I was goin' West.'

Suddenly I laughed. That old dog had done
another caper, had tricked me. Now I
understood what Fletcher, Johnson, and
MacEvey had meant all this time with their
bickering after performances. Hickok had

upstaged me. I couldn't leave the Combination now, couldn't say my services were needed on the frontier, not after Hickok had said so first. Besides, I was stuck with the show. I had purchased a house in Rochester, which Lulu loved, had been given another chance at being a better husband and daddy, and had even told Jennie Fisher that we no longer could consort like we had done, that everyone knew Buffalo Bill Cody was a man of his word, and, by thunder, I was a married man with three little angels.

'It says here that Wild Bill isn't going West just yet,' Texas Jack pointed out. 'He left Rochester for New York City.'

'For business,' I added.

'What business would he have in New York?'

I pondered Texas Jack's question, but didn't answer. The Buffalo Bill Combination was scheduled to board a westbound train for performances in Lockport, Buffalo, and Dunkirk before entering Pennsylvania and traveling on to the Midwest and Canada. We wouldn't return to New York until the end of the season in June.

'Well,' I said.

'Well,' said Texas Jack.

We stared at the tavern across from the depot, stood, headed that way for a drink, went inside, ordered a shot each, and leaned against the bar next to a walking whiskey vat whose head was buried atop the spilled suds and cherry wood.

'Wild Bill can look after himself,' Texas Jack commented after our whiskies arrived.

'Yes, he can.'

We downed the shots, and ordered another.

'He quit us,' Texas Jack said. 'We didn't quit him.'

'Yes, I know.'

We downed the whiskey, and told the barkeep to leave the bottle.

'We don't owe him a thing,' Texas Jack said.

Instead of agreeing, I refilled our glasses. The locomotive's whistle screamed. Major Burke would be in a panic now, trying to find us before the train pulled out of the station.

'Fiddlesticks.' Texas Jack leaned against the bar with a heavy sigh. 'Wild Bill helped get me my first job,' he said. 'Saved my hide a time or two, as well.'

I nodded. 'He stopped some bullwhacker from stovin' in my head when I was just a boy. We never had no harsh words till . . .'

'I don't fancy leaving him in New York City,' Texas Jack said.

'Nor do I, and I sure don't want to leave with bad feelin's betwixt us.'

'Wild Bill,' Texas Jack said.

'Jim Hickok,' I said.

The walking whiskey vat lifted his head, and slurred out a string of profanity and slurs about the Buffalo Bill Combination and

284

something called the Daniel Boone Company. I couldn't catch all of those words, but I did make out 'Wild Bill . . . damned fools . . . Buffalo Bill . . . sons-of-bitches . . . Texas Jack . . . shit.'

I swung around, almost spilling my whiskey when I reached out to catch the drunkard before he fell to the floor.

'Criminy,' Texas Jack said, 'that's Lawrence Barnett.'

Sure enough, it was. Texas Jack tossed some coins on the bar, and helped me carry the world's greatest Thespian outside to feel the morning sun. We almost knocked over Major Burke, on his way inside to find us.

'The train's about to leave!' the major shouted, then gaped. 'Great Scot, is that . . . ?'

Barnett vomited all over Major Burke's boots. Texas Jack and I released the actor and jumped back, as if the man was spitting out fire. Barnett fell to the boardwalk, groaned, and rolled over.

'Ruined,' Barnett said. 'I'm ruined.'

'What do you mean?' Texas Jack asked.

'My show's failed . . . all because of . . . the Buffalo Bill Combination . . . and Hickok's new show.'

New show? I dropped beside the actor. 'What do you mean? What new show?'

'Hickok's in New York . . . *The Black Crook* is finished. I . . .' His eyes rolled back into his head.

'Damnation!' Texas Jack yelled. 'Wild Bill has betrayed us!'

The whistle shrieked again, and the conductor begged us to hurry. The major cleaned his boots, and cussed Lawrence Barnett. I waved the conductor over, my mind working rapidly.

'Sir,' I said, 'help Major Burke get this man aboard the train. Burke, you listen, and listen good. You're takin' Mister Barnett. He said he always wanted to play me, and he shall.'

'But I wanted . . .'

'All right, you can play me. Get Barnett to play Wild Bill.'

'But he doesn't know the lines!'

'It don't matter, Burke. Hickok never knowed his lines, neither! Now, shut up and listen. Get J.P. Winter to play Jack.'

'But you said you weren't quitting the show, Will!'

'I'm not. We'll be back. We'll meet you in Erie, I hope. Maybe before. All you have to do is get through the plays in Lockport, Buffalo, and Dunkirk. Jack and I are headed back to New York to fetch Hickok.'

'But . . .'

We didn't give the major any more time to argue. We hurried back to the tavern to formulate a plan and finish our whiskey.

*   *   *

286

Lawrence Barnett, Esq., had not been mistaken for newspaper advertisements and placards throughout the theater district proclaimed that 'The True Hero of the Border, Wild Bill Hickok,' would be performing with Colonel Kenneth R. Stevens's Daniel Boone Company for two weeks at Dewitt Davidson's Globe Hall in Manhattan.

Texas Jack and I arrived at Globe Hall shortly before the ticket office opened. Recognizing us as living heroes ourselves, since we had performed at the hall before, Mr. Davidson himself escorted Texas Jack and me backstage to meet Wild Bill and Colonel Stevens. A short, pale man with a big mustache, plaid sack suit, and an old Army dress hat, Colonel Stevens looked more like a drummer than a theatrical manager, and his hand felt all sweaty when I shook it. The 'Wild Bill' beside him didn't stand much taller than the colonel and wore a blond wig and buckskins, and carried a brace of Remingtons when everyone knew that Hickok preferred Navy Colts and Williamson Derringers.

'We're looking for Wild Bill,' Texas Jack said, and the fake Wild Bill smirked, sniggered, and said that we were addressing the same.

'Mister.' I stepped forward. 'My name's William F. Cody, and I know Wild Bill Hickok. Wild Bill is a friend of mine. You, sir, are no Wild Bill Hickok.'

Colonel Stevens quickly slipped between us, telling his Wild Bill, who he called Claude, to excuse us for a few minutes. The fraudulent Wild Bill sulked off into a corner, while the colonel guided us, along with Mr. Davidson, to his office, and offered us a whiskey, but we declined, not wanting to drink with the fobbing little weasel.

'I met Wild Bill in Rochester,' the colonel explained. 'The real Wild Bill, your friend. Offered him fifty dollars a week to play himself, and he agreed to do so. I had my advance man place notices in all the New York City papers, but Wild Bill performed only once, then quit.'

'He'll do that,' Texas Jack commented.

'Gentlemen,' Colonel Stevens went on, 'I had no choice. The advertisements were already printed, and people have been busting down the doors to see him. So I hired Claude Cooper to take over.'

'Where's Hickok?' I asked.

'I haven't seen him since day before yesterday. That's the honest truth, I swear.'

Well, believing the man, I nodded at Texas Jack, and we took our leave, followed by an apologetic Mr. Davidson. The colonel hollered out: 'Please, you won't tell . . .'

'Don't worry,' I said.

As he escorted us down the aisle, Mr. Davidson inquired if we'd care to take in tonight's show, and I started to decline, figuring to begin searching the saloons in the area, but I abruptly reined in and accepted the gent's generosity.

'I'll introduce you . . . ,' Mr. Davidson began, but I asked him to do no such thing.

'We'll be incoherent,' I explained, tucking my hair underneath my hat.

'Uh . . . incognito,' Texas Jack added.

'I understand,' Mr. Davidson said, and left us as we made ourselves comfortable on the back row.

We ate nuts and sipped whiskey from my flask while the theater filled up with patrons.

'I don't understand why Wild Bill would do such a thing,' Texas Jack said. 'Quit our show, only to join this skipjack colonel?'

'Jim's notional,' I offered.

'So, why are we here since Wild Bill quit the show?'

I gave him a dumb look better than Texas Jack could ever give. My pard blinked, smiled, and grabbed a handful of nuts.

'Oh,' he said.

We didn't have to wait too long. The play began, and Claude 'Wild Bill Hickok' Cooper stepped out on stage, speaking a bunch of flapdoodle and began relating how he had wiped out the McKandlass Gang to avenge the death of his pa. Seconds later, a commotion began in the wings to his left, then a body flew across the stage, then another, and at last Jim Hickok rushed onto the stage, and Claude Cooper soiled his buckskins.

'Nobody's Wild Bill Hickok,' Hickok shouted, 'but me!'

He broke Cooper's nose with one punch, pulled off the wig, and tossed it to an urchin in the front row, hit Cooper in the stomach, lifted him over his head, and tossed the actor into the orchestra pit. Colonel Stevens, cussing louder than my Lulu ever done, sent his supes, actors, and stagehands to corral Hickok, and a few burly men in the front row leaped onto the stage. Although I had him pegged for a coward, Colonel Stevens proved me wrong. He charged right in there with his boys. You've never seen such a plug muss.

'Shall we?' I asked Texas Jack.

'All for one, and one for all,' Texas Jack said, and we leaped from our seats, raced down the aisle, jumped onto the stage, and partook of the ruction.

Hickok cut loose with a Comanche yell when he spotted us, and flung Colonel Stevens into the Netherlands. I tackled the two burly men, and Texas Jack grabbed a lariat—don't ask me where he found it and roped a couple of members of the Daniel Boone Company, dragged them to him, and knocked them out with the barrel of his Smith & Wesson. After dispatching the burly men, I rolled over, kicked at one gent, got tackled by two more, crawled from underneath them, and smashed their faces when they kept on coming.

'Hip-hip-hurrah!' I shouted, and the crowd at Globe Hall echoed back: *'Hip-hip-hurrah! Hurrah for Buffalo Bill. Hurrah for Texas Jack! Hurrah for Wild Bill!'*

You see, our hats had been knocked off by then, so everyone recognized us as the true, living heroes. The sound of gunfire made me gasp, but I recognized those screams, and realized that Hickok must have grabbed Cooper's pistols and had started singeing and tormenting the colonel's supes. I dare say the people at Dewitt Davidson's Globe Hall got their money's worth that night. We had run just about everyone on stage to either unconsciousness or parts unknown when the first cop arrived, blowing his whistle.

'You men are under arrest,' he said.

Hickok wiped his bloody lip, and tossed Cooper's pistols on the floor. 'Just you?' he asked.

'Yes.' The cop had grit.

'I don't think so,' Hickok said. 'Wild Bill, Texas Jack, and Buffalo Bill don't go along peaceably with just one peace officer.'

The crowd cheered.

'Very well,' the cop said. He walked to the rear door, and tooted that whistle again. Two more policemen arrived shortly thereafter.

'How about now, scouts?' the first cop said. 'Will you come along peacefully?'

I started to answer, but Hickok spoke first: 'You best get some more men, lad.'

291

The crowd cheered. Even the cops grinned.

So we waited till about ten more police officers arrived, signing a few autographs for some of them who had seen our performances and knew us to be heroes, but still Hickok wasn't satisfied.

'You got a sergeant in that bunch?' he asked.

'No, sir,' the first policeman said, 'but I'll get one.'

Sure enough, he not only fetched a sergeant, but a captain, too.

'Well,' Hickok said, 'I guess we can surrender to more than a dozen policemen, as long as one of them's a captain.'

The crowd, even Mr. Dewitt Davidson himself, gave us a standing ovation as the cops escorted us to the calaboose. That was the last time Wild Bill, Texas Jack, and Buffalo Bill ever appeared on stage together. I reckon it was our best performance.

*   *   *

'Why did you join that grafter's outfit after quittin' us?' I asked Jim Hickok as we waited in a Manhattan precinct's dark jail later that evening.

'Was broke,' he admitted. 'Needed some cash to get back to Kansas.'

'But all the money we've made . . . ,' Texas Jack began, but Jim Hickok silenced him with a wave of his hand.

'Give it to kids,' he admitted, 'spent it on whiskey.'

I crossed the cramped dungeon in mighty fine spirits, slapped my old pard Wild Bill on his back, and howled: 'Pard, you are a demon! But don't worry. When we leave here, I'll have the major keep part of your salary so you won't spend it. I mean . . .'

'I'm not going back, Billy.' The announcement, the resolution in my friend's voice, silenced me and soured my stomach. 'Not with you. Not with Dan'l Boone. I meant what I said about heading West.'

'But . . . ,' I started. Hickok didn't seem angry, yet I knew this time he was bound and determined to leave the Combination.

'Remember what Agnes told me, Billy?' he began. ' "Be true to myself"? Well, it's time I started living my life again. *My* life, boys. Not yours. How's Louisa, by the way?'

'She was in wonderful bliss, thanks to you, Jim,' I answered. 'Course, she might not be so joyful when she arrives here in a couple of hours . . . I hope . . . to go our bail. But we've buried the hatchet.'

'I'm glad,' he said, and, by jingo, he meant it. 'Hell, it was my fault anyway. I tormented you more than I should. And you, too, Jack. You'll be better off without me. And I'll be better off on the border.'

'I wish you'd reconsider,' Texas Jack chimed

293

in.

'I appreciate that, boys,' Hickok said. 'I surely do. But I've made up my mind. It's like this, pards. All the world's a stage. There are exits and entrances, and a man, in his life, plays many parts. Well, we've played some parts these past six months or so, but it's time for Wild Bill to make his exit.' He held out his right fist, which Texas Jack and I clasped. 'All for one,' he started.

'And one for all!' we finished, and broke out laughing.

'That Dickens was a great writer,' I said with delight. 'Almost as good as Judson, Hiram Robbins, and Fred G. Maeder.'

CLOSE CURTAIN

Author's Note

Part of this story is true. Some of it is bogus. And much of it, since Buffalo Bill, Wild Bill, and Texas Jack often blended fact with fiction, is bogus truth. William F. 'Buffalo Bill' Cody, John B. 'Texas Jack' Omohundro, and James Butler 'Wild Bill' Hickok did star on stage together during the 1873-74 season, and appeared in the cities mentioned in the preceding pages. The newspaper quotations heading each chapter are actual accounts, although I doctored up typographical errors. Some of the stories I traced to various newspapers or memoirs, and I moved a couple of events from the Cody-Omohundro-Buntline season to the Cody-Omohundro-Hickok tour. I made up a few tall tales, but several others can be attributed to Cody, Omohundro, Hickok, and/or their contemporaries. I reworked one story heard over breakfast with two friends, and stole a handful from my father, who borrowed at least two from his father. Anyway, I'll let you guess what's real, or allegedly real, and what I invented.

I found myself hooked on the theatrical careers of Cody, Hickok, and Omohundro after reading Sandra K. Sagala's account of the 1873-74 season in the June 1993 issue of *True West* magazine. That prompted me on a research endeavor—I even wrote my own article covering the acting careers of the threesome for *The Elks Magazine*. Sagala kept up with her research, culminating in *Buffalo Bill, Actor: A Chronicle of Cody's Theatrical Career* (Heritage Books, 2002), and I would have been hard-pressed to write this novel if she hadn't blazed that trail. She was also gracious enough to share some of her research with me.

In addition to Sagala's book, I relied heavily on three biographies in writing this novel. *They Called Him Wild Bill: The Life and Adventures of James Butler Hickok* by Joseph G. Rosa (University of Oklahoma Press, 1974) is the best Hickok biography, while *The Lives and Legend of Buffalo Bill* (University of Oklahoma Press, 1964) by Don Russell is the most definitive biography of this extraordinary showman to date. Sadly only one full-length book has been dedicated to John B. Omohundro's life and career, and Texas Jack deserves better treatment than Herschel C. Logan's *Buckskin and Satin* (The Stackpole Company, 1954).

Other primary sources included *Buffalo Bill and His Wild West: A Pictorial Biography* by Joseph G. Rosa and Robin May (University Press of Kansas, 1989); *The West of Wild Bill Hickok* by Joseph G. Rosa (University of Oklahoma Press, 1982); *Memories of Buffalo Bill by His Wife* by Louisa Frederici Cody in collaboration with Courtney Ryley Cooper (D. Appleton and Company, 1919); *Buffalo Bill Cody: The Man Behind the Legend* by Robert A. Carter (John Wiley & Sons, 2000); *Buffalo Bill: Last of the Great Scouts* by Helen Cody Wetmore (a 1994 Longmeadow Press reprint of the 1899 original); *Wild Bill Hickok* by Richard O'Connor (Konecky & Konecky, 1959); *Buffalo Bill: His Family, Friends, Fame, Failures and Fortune* by Nellie Snyder Yost (Swallow Press, 1979); two books by J.W. Buel—*The Life and Adventures of Wild Bill Hickok* (a 1976 Leisure Books reprint of the 1882 original) and *Heroes of the Plains* (Historical Publishing Co., 1891); *The Noblest Whiteskin* by John Burke, not 'Arizona John' Burke (G.P. Putnam's Sons, 1973); and the anonymous *Buffalo Bill and His Wild West Companions* (M.A. Donohue & Company, no date, but probably circa 1893). Another source was Craig Francis Nieuwenhuyse's doctoral dissertation, *Six-Guns on the Stage: Buffalo Bill Cody's First Celebration of the Conquest of the American Frontier* (University of California, 1981), courtesy of the McCracken Research Library at the Buffalo Bill Historical Center in Cody, Wyoming.

Naturally I also frequently turned to Cody's various autobiographies: *The Life of Buffalo Bill* (a 1991 Indian Head Books reprint of the 1879 original); *Story of the West and Camp-Fire Chats* (Thompson & Thomas, 1902); *The*

Adventures of Buffalo Bill (Harper & Brothers, 1904); and *Buffalo Bill's Life Story* (an undated Dover Publications reprint of the 1920 original).

Special thanks to historian Louis Warren of the University of California-Davis and documentary film director-writer-producer Dan Gagliasso for letting me pick their brains about Cody lore during the 2003 Western History Association conference in Fort Worth, Texas.

I am equally indebted to the staffs at the aforementioned Buffalo Bill Historical Center as well as Buffalo Bill Museum & Grave in Golden, Colorado; and the public libraries of Akron, Ohio; Bangor, Maine; Easton, Pennsylvania; Erie, Pennsylvania; Fort Wayne, Indiana; Hartford, Connecticut; Indianapolis, Indiana; Lexington, Kentucky; Louisville, Kentucky; Philadelphia, Pennsylvania; Pittsburgh, Pennsylvania; Providence, Rhode Island; Richmond, Virginia; Sandusky, Ohio; Terre Haute, Indiana; Titusville, Pennsylvania; Troy, New York; Utica, New York; and Williamsport, Pennsylvania.

No copies of *Buffalo Bill! King of the Border Men!* or *Scouts of the Plains* have survived, so much of the plots (if you can call them *plots*) of the two plays were pulled from Sagala's research and contemporary newspaper accounts.

The theatrical career of Buffalo Bill Cody

has been overshadowed by his Wild West exhibition, yet I doubt if there would even have been a Buffalo Bill's Wild West if he had not dabbled in acting with Ned Buntline in 1872 and formed his own combination the following year.

Cody and Omohundro finished the 1873-74 season without Hickok. Hickok met his destiny in Deadwood two years later, shot dead by assassin Jack McCall, and the often-forgotten Texas Jack Omohundro eventually formed his own combination with his wife and John Burke. While in Leadville, Colorado, however, Omohundro contracted pneumonia and died on June 28, 1880, at age thirty-three. His widow, Guiseppina Morlacchi, never returned to the stage, succumbing to stomach cancer (or a broken heart, if you're a romantic) at her summer home in East Billerica, Massachusetts, in 1886. She was only thirty-nine.

The Buffalo Bill Combination continued, staging plays including *The Red Right Hand, or Buffalo Bill's First Scalp for Custer* and *Knight of the Plains, or Buffalo Bill's Best Trail,* both written by dime novelist Prentiss Ingraham, and *May Cody, or Lost and Won,* written by Andrew S. Burt, through 1886, with the exception of 1884 when Cody was extensively involved in his Wild West. The Wild West, of course, overtook the plays, and Cody left the theater for good after the 1886 season ended in Denver. Cody and the Wild West went on to secure permanent places—rightfully so—in the history of the frontier, not to mention show business.